Praise for Elaine Viets

Dying

"Viets writes laugh-out-loud ... twists and turns to make it to the top of the mystery best-seller charts."
—*Florida Today*

"Stars one of the most lively, audacious, and entertaining heroines to grace an amateur sleuth tale."
—*Harriet Klausner*

"A fun read with a top-notch heroine."
—*Mystery News*

Murder Between the Covers

"Wry sense of humor, appealing, realistic characters, and a briskly moving plot." —*South Florida Sun-Sentinel*

Shop Till You Drop

"Elaine Viets has come up with all the ingredients for an irresistible mystery . . . I'm looking forward to the next installment in her new Dead-End Job series."
—Jane Heller, national bestselling author of *Best Enemies*

"Elaine Viets's debut is a live wire. It's Janet Evanovich meets *The Fugitive* as Helen Hawthorne takes Florida by storm. Shop no further—this is the one."
—Tim Dorsey, author of *Torpedo Juice*

"I loved this book. Six-toed cats, expensive clothes, sexy guys on motorcycles—this book has it all."
—Charlaine Harris, author of *Dead as a Doornail* and *Shakespeare's Counselor*

"Fresh, funny, and fiendishly constructed. . . . Attractive newcomer Helen Hawthorne takes on the first of her deliciously awful dead-end jobs and finds herself enmeshed in drugs, embezzlement, and murder. A bright start to an exciting new series. This one is hard to beat."
—Parnell Hall, author of The Puzzle Lady crossword puzzle mysteries

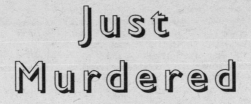

Just Murdered

A DEAD-END JOB MYSTERY

Elaine Viets

A SIGNET BOOK

SIGNET
Published by New American Library, a division of
Penguin Group (USA) Inc., 375 Hudson Street,
New York, New York 10014, USA
Penguin Group (Canada), 10 Alcorn Avenue, Toronto,
Ontario M4V 3B2, Canada (a division of Pearson Penguin Canada Inc.)
Penguin Books Ltd., 80 Strand, London WC2R 0RL, England
Penguin Ireland, 25 St. Stephen's Green, Dublin 2,
Ireland (a division of Penguin Books Ltd.)
Penguin Group (Australia), 250 Camberwell Road, Camberwell, Victoria 3124,
Australia (a division of Pearson Australia Group Pty. Ltd.)
Penguin Books India Pvt. Ltd., 11 Community Centre, Panchsheel Park,
New Delhi-110 017, India
Penguin Group (NZ), cnr Airborne and Rosedale Roads, Albany,
Auckland 1310, New Zealand (a division of Pearson New Zealand Ltd.)
Penguin Books (South Africa) (Pty.) Ltd., 24 Sturdee Avenue,
Rosebank, Johannesburg 2196, South Africa

Penguin Books Ltd., Registered Offices:
80 Strand, London WC2R 0RL, England

First published by Signet, an imprint of New American Library,
a division of Penguin Group (USA) Inc.

First Printing, May 2005
10 9 8 7 6 5 4 3 2 1

Copyright © Elaine Viets, 2005
All rights reserved

Ⓟ   REGISTERED TRADEMARK—MARCA REGISTRADA

Printed in the United States of America

Without limiting the rights under copyright reserved above, no part of this
publication may be reproduced, stored in or introduced into a retrieval system, or transmitted, in any form, or by any means (electronic, mechanical,
photocopying, recording, or otherwise), without the prior written permission of both the copyright owner and the above publisher of this book.

PUBLISHER'S NOTE
This is a work of fiction. Names, characters, places, and incidents either
are the product of the author's imagination or are used fictitiously, and
any resemblance to actual persons, living or dead, business establish-
ments, events, or locales is entirely coincidental.

If you purchased this book without a cover you should be aware that this
book is stolen property. It was reported as "unsold and destroyed" to the
publisher and neither the author nor the publisher has received any payment for this "stripped book."

The scanning, uploading, and distribution of this book via the Internet or
via any other means without the permission of the publisher is illegal
and punishable by law. Please purchase only authorized electronic edi-
tions, and do not participate in or encourage electronic piracy of copy-
righted materials. Your support of the author's rights is appreciated.

For Zola Keller, who knows the bridal business from A to Z

Acknowledgments

Special thanks to Zola Keller and her staff at Zola Keller, 818 East Las Olas Boulevard, Fort Lauderdale. Millicent's Bridal Salon in my book resembles Zola Keller's shop in no way except one—Zola and Millicent know and love the bridal business. Oh, yes, they also get customers in Rolls Royces. Thanks also to Zola's veteran saleswoman, Sandy Blagman, who should write her own book.

Thanks to Scott Jueckstock, Bravissimo Event Orchestration, 2212 S.E. 17th Street Causeway, Fort Lauderdale.

Once again, I want to thank my husband, Don Crinklaw, who believes for better or worse includes proofreading and three a.m. questions.

Thanks to my agent, David Hendin, who always takes my calls.

Special thanks to Kara Cesare, one of the last of the real editors, to her assistant, Rose Hilliard, and to the Signet copy editing and production staff.

Many people helped with this book. I hope I didn't leave anyone out.

Particular thanks to Detective RC White, Fort Lauderdale Police Department (retired), who patiently answered my questions on weapons, police interrogations, and emergency procedures. Thanks also to Rick McMahan, ATF Special Agent, and to Anthony-award winning author and former police detective Robin Burcell. Any mistakes are mine, not theirs.

Thanks to Joanne Sinchuk and John Spera at South Florida's largest mystery bookstore, Murder on the Beach in Delray Beach, Florida.

Thanks also to Susan Carlson, Valerie Cannata, Colby Cox, Jinny Gender, Karen Grace, Kay Gordy, and Janet Smith.

Rita Scott does indeed make cat toys packed with the most powerful catnip in kittendom. They have sent my cats into frenzies of ecstasy. Read all about them at www.catshigh.us.

Thanks to the librarians at the Broward County Library and the St. Louis Public Library who researched my questions, no matter how strange, and always answered with a straight face.

Thanks also to public relations expert Jack Klobnak, and to my bookseller friend, Carole Wantz, who can sell sand in the Mojave Desert.

Special thanks to librarian Anne Watts, who let me borrow her six-toed cat, Thumbs, for this series. Check out his picture on my Web site at www.elaineviets.com.

Chapter 1

"Uh-oh, here comes trouble," Millicent said.

If this was trouble, Helen Hawthorne wished she had it. A Rolls-Royce Silver Cloud pulled up in front of Millicent's Bridal Salon on Las Olas Boulevard.

This was a vintage Rolls, the car of new movie stars and old money. Its long, sculpted curves were the color of well-polished family silver. The shiny new Porsches, Beemers, and Ferraris on the fashionable Fort Lauderdale street looked like cheap toys next to it.

The driver's door opened with an expensive *thunk!* Out stepped a chauffeur in a uniform tailored to show off his broad shoulders and long legs. His pants hugged the best buns beyond the Gran Forno bakery. His hint of a beard would feel deliciously rough on bare skin.

The chauffeur jogged to the rear passenger door with an athlete's grace.

"Baby, you can drive my car," Helen said.

"Sorry, sweetie, Rod's taken," Millicent said, "and it's battle stations. They have an appointment here."

The chauffeur opened the door, and Helen saw a candy-pink spike heel like something from Barbie's dream closet pop out. Was the woman wearing a size-four shoe? Did they make shoes in a size four? Helen was six feet tall and didn't know much about petite people wear.

The woman barely reached five feet. She had on a sleeveless pink dress with a flirty pleated skirt.

"Oh, my God," Helen said as the woman slid out of the car. "She's not wearing any panties."

"Typical," Millicent said. "How can Kiki spend so much money and look so cheap? That dress cost two thousand dollars and it's suitable for a child of fourteen."

"On a woman of forty," Helen said.

"Forty!" Millicent said. "Kiki Shenrad is fifty if she's a day—and tucked so tight she has hospital corners."

Kiki threw her arms around the hunky chauffeur and pulled him toward her. She soul kissed him and ran a slender leg along his muscular one.

"She'd better pick out a dress quick," Helen said. "I think they're going to consummate the marriage right on the sidewalk."

Millicent didn't hear her. She was pulling wedding gowns from the racks. Helen knew she should help her boss, but she couldn't tear herself from the show outside the shop window.

A small figure emerged from the huge Rolls like a mouse from a hole and crept around the nearly copulating couple. Miss Mouse was about twenty with no-color hair scraped into a messy ponytail. Her gray sweats were baggy, but Helen guessed a slender figure was buried underneath that lumpy cloth.

"You'd think Kiki would give her maid a decent castoff dress," Helen said.

Millicent looked up from the snowstorm of white

chiffon and satin on the silver display stand. "Maid? That's the bride—Desiree Shenrad."

"Uh-oh," Helen said. "We've got trouble."

Kiki finally pried herself off the chauffeur, slapped his perky posterior, and sent him back to stand by the car. She flung open the salon door and said, "Millie!"

Millicent winced. Only big spenders called her that. She hated it.

Miss Mouse scurried in her mother's magnificent wake. The shop's pink paint was designed to flatter most complexions. The mirrors made double chins vanish. But they couldn't transform dreary little Desiree.

Kiki started to air kiss Millicent, then swiveled her head so abruptly, Helen thought she'd get whiplash. Kiki had seen the rose dress.

"I want that," she said. Helen had never heard a soft voice sound so hard.

Every woman who came into Millicent's wanted the rose dress. There was nothing quite like it. The strapless gown had a beautifully beaded bodice. But the skirt was the show stopper. Made of dark red taffeta that shaded to black, the skirt was swirled to look like an enormous bouquet of velvety roses. If Helen ever won an Oscar, she'd wear that dress onstage.

"I'd like to wear it to my daughter's wedding," Kiki said.

"That's not a mother-of-the-bride dress," Millicent said.

"I am not going to wear some pathetic little powder-blue dress," Kiki said.

"I don't sell pathetic little dresses," Millicent said. "But my customers leave here properly dressed for special occasions."

"I'll decide what's proper. You!" Kiki pointed at Helen. "Take the rose dress to fitting room A."

The largest room, naturally. Helen looked at Millicent, who gave her a slight nod.

"Oh, yes," Kiki said. "We should get something for my daughter, too." The bride was an afterthought at her own wedding.

"And when is the wedding?" Millicent said.

"Saturday," Kiki said.

"June, July, or August?"

"This coming Saturday, December fourth," Kiki said.

Millicent looked stunned. "Impossible. Three months is a rush job. We can't order the dresses in time."

"Then we'll buy something in stock. And you'll have to alter it in the store. Money is no object."

Millicent's eyes narrowed. "You'd better tell me what happened. I can't help you if I don't know the whole story."

"It's that bitch at Haute Bridal. I saw what she got in for the wedding and canceled everything. The fabrics looked cheap. The colors were horrible. Nothing was as she promised."

"But bridal sales are final," Helen said.

Kiki laughed. "My ex-husband is a lawyer. Nothing is final."

"It is at this store," Millicent said. "Do what I say, and I'll make you look like every one of your thirty million dollars."

Millicent was pointing a red talon at Kiki, punching each word for emphasis. Helen thought the bloodred nails were the mark of Millicent's success. She'd clawed her way up to the chicest shop on Las Olas with only a small divorce settlement and one major talent: She had a gift for making women look good.

Millicent knew how to emphasize their good points and downplay their figure flaws. She was her own best example. Her hair had turned snowy white years ago. Millicent had the courage to leave it that dramatic color. It made her look younger than most of the highlighted salon jobs in her shop. An unface-lifted fifty, Millicent looked forty. Colorful tops drew attention to her remarkable chest, held high by a cantilevered bra. Dark pants minimized generous hips. But she couldn't hide her clever, appraising eyes.

Kiki shrugged like a spoiled child. "Millie, darling, help me into the rose gown."

Kiki stepped out of her pink dress and revealed an even pinker body. Her blond pubic hair was sculpted into a dollar sign.

Helen gaped.

"Any man who gets me hits the jackpot," Kiki said and winked.

It took Helen and Millicent both to wrestle her into the rose dress. The skirt had four layers, including the only hoop Helen had seen since *Gone With the Wind*. Helen had to admit the outrageous gown suited Kiki. She had the carriage and the attitude to wear a skirt the size of an SUV.

"I have to have it," Kiki said.

"So buy it," Millicent said. "But don't upstage your daughter at her own wedding."

"No one can upstage the bride," Kiki said. "I'll take the dress."

"Only if you promise to buy another dress for the church service," Millicent said. "You cannot wear a ball gown to a daytime wedding, Kiki. You'll look like a joke."

Those words got through to Kiki. She settled on a

sleek black knit for the church and a gauzy gold gown suitable for a minor goddess for the rehearsal dinner. Then she put the rose gown back on "to get used to wearing it." Helen thought she just liked parading around in it.

Finally Kiki remembered her daughter. Desiree stood silently in the corner like Cinderella. Helen didn't know whether to offer her a chair or some ashes by the fireplace.

"I want a wedding dress with a full skirt and a cathedral-length train," Kiki said.

"That's a ten-foot train," Millicent said. "A petite bride like Desiree will be swallowed by all that fabric."

"Not if she stands up straight." Kiki's French-manicured nail poked her daughter between her slumping shoulder blades.

"I want something expensive," Kiki said. "I want snow white, not that off-white color. It looks like dirty teeth."

Desiree stood there, mute.

"What do you want, Desiree?" Millicent asked. "It's your wedding."

"It makes no difference. I won't get it." Desiree's little voice was drowned in disappointment.

What was Millicent doing? Helen wondered. She was too smart to get between warring mothers and daughters. Did she forget Kiki had the money?

Desiree tried on a simple white strapless gown. Her mother said, "Oh, Desiree. You're only twenty years old and I can see you as a nun."

"And I see you as an old tart." That soft voice. Those hunched shoulders. That meek expression. Yet she'd insulted her mother with acid-stinging accuracy.

For five hours, Desiree tried on dresses while her

mother stabbed her with stiletto slashes. Desiree seemed sad and beaten. Only later did Helen realize the young mouse had fought back with feline ferocity.

Helen did know one thing: She was worn out from being in the same room with that rage. Hauling the heavy wedding dresses didn't help. They were encrusted with scratchy crystal beading and itchy lace. Many of the dresses weighed twenty pounds or more. Helen had to hold the hangers over her head to keep the long skirts off the floor. Her arms ached. Her neck and shoulders screamed for relief.

When she ran for yet another dress, she saw the chauffeur, Rod, sweating in the shimmering sun. It wasn't fair to keep him standing by the car in the brutal Florida heat. Helen pulled a cold bottle of water from the fridge.

"You look like you could use this." She handed the frosty bottle to Rod. A little sweat improved the man. The chauffeur's black curls were tousled by the Florida breeze—or an expensive stylist.

Rod turned pale under his tan and backed away. "Don't let her see you," he said. "You could ruin everything." He sounded really frightened.

"I'm sorry," Helen said. "I don't want you to lose your job. It's a hot day and—"

"Job? You could cost me a lot more than any job. Get away from me with that."

Why would a water bottle frighten a big, strong man? Helen didn't have time to think about it. She heard Millicent calling, "Helen, where's that dress I sent you for?"

Helen ran inside, grabbed it off the rack, and hurried back with a pearl-and-crystal concoction. Desiree put it on like a hair shirt.

"It's regal," Kiki said, after Helen fought the dress's one hundred white satin buttons.

"I look like a homely Hapsburg princess," the despairing Desiree said.

She was right, Helen thought. She did look like a sad, chinless royal bride. Desiree was one of those women who looked her worst in white.

The desperate Millicent went into the odd closet, where she kept her mistakes. She brought out the spider dress. The bride had broken her engagement and defaulted on the seven-thousand-dollar gown. The spider dress had been impossible to resell. It looked bad on a hanger and worse on most women. The color was peculiar: Its pale pink undertone looked dingy next to the true white gowns. The style was odder still, a cobwebby lace that floated on the air like cat hair. Helen itched every time she saw it.

Desiree tried it on, and for the first time that day, smiled.

Helen quit shoving a beaded gown back on the rack and stared at the little bride. She had never seen a dress make such a dramatic transformation.

Mousy little Desiree lived up to her name for the first time in her life. She was beguiling in that dress, a fey fairy princess. The lace was a gossamer web. The crystal beads gleamed like enchanted dewdrops. The subtle pink color turned Desiree's flour-white complexion creamy and put highlights in her dull hair.

On this bride, the spider dress looked elegant and extraordinary.

"It's perfect," Millicent said.

"I love it," Helen said.

"I want it," the bride said.

"You can't have it," her mother snapped. Kiki was

still wearing the rose dress. But she was no longer a showstopper. Now she looked overblown in the extravagant gown. "That wedding dress will never do."

Of course not, Helen thought. You can't have your daughter outshine you.

"Then I'll buy it myself," Desiree said softly.

"Using what for money?" her mother said. "It's seven thousand dollars. You won't come into your grandmother's trust fund until you're thirty."

"Daddy will buy it for me," Desiree said.

"Daddy is fighting off bankruptcy," Kiki said. "Daddy the hotshot lawyer spent millions on that computer-stock class-action suit and lost. Daddy can barely pay his half of the wedding."

"Why do you keep running up the costs for Daddy?" Desiree cried. "I wanted a simple beach wedding, not a sit-down dinner for four hundred."

"What you want is beside the point," Kiki said. Helen thought those were the truest words ever spoken in that store.

"A beach wedding is fine when a secretary marries a mechanic," Kiki said. "But for our sort, weddings are for the parents. We're paying the bills. Your father will invite his important clients. I will invite patrons of the arts. They will expect to see a traditional bride walk down the aisle, not some hippie. I will buy that one."

Kiki indicated the Hapsburg princess dress. Its wide, stiff skirt looked like a satin pop-up tent. Its ten-foot train was loaded with crystal beads. Helen wondered how the tiny bride could drag all that fabric down the aisle.

Desiree hated the dress. So did Helen and Millicent.

"Mother, I can't dance in that at the reception. Not with that huge train."

"We'll bustle up the train," her mother said.

"Can't," Millicent said. "It's too bulky. It will look like a bale of fabric on her back."

"Is the train detachable?" Helen said.

Millicent raised an eyebrow at Helen's faux pas.

Kiki's smile dripped malice. "Let me guess. You had your reception at the VFW hall next to the turkey-shoot posters."

"Knights of Columbus Hall," Helen said. "And it was the Holy Redeemer rummage sale."

Millicent frowned. Helen shut up. She'd let a detail from her old life slip out in her anger. Her fingers itched for the crowbar she'd used to end her marriage. She was on the run, but she never regretted the satisfying crunch she'd heard when she first started swinging and connected with her target. The cries and crunches felt good. Kiki was a candidate for just such a shattering experience.

The silence stretched on. Then Kiki said, "We shall buy two wedding dresses. One for the church ceremony and one for the reception. If Desiree will wear the dress with the train for the wedding ceremony, I will buy her the hippie dress to dance in."

The bride said yes, happy for even a half victory.

Helen was surprised that Kiki would compromise. Thank goodness for the trend among rich brides for two dresses—and Kiki's eagerness to run up bills for her cash-strapped ex.

"We'll take these and come back tomorrow to pick out the veil and bridesmaid dresses," Kiki said.

Another welcome surprise. Helen didn't think she could survive another five-hour fight. She did some quick calculations. Kiki would be spending maybe sixty thousand dollars on dresses, accessories, and alterations at Millicent's. Helen would have to work more than four years to make that much at this dead-end job.

Kiki left in a tornado of promises and air kisses, invigorated by the afternoon battle. Desiree trailed listlessly behind her. Rod, the delectably sweaty chauffeur, opened Kiki's door. She slid inside decorously.

When the Rolls pulled away from the curb, Helen and Millicent collapsed into the pink chairs. They were soft, but not too yielding. A tired woman could get out of them with dignity. No woman ever sat on the gray "husband couch." She knew her eyes would glaze with boredom if she went there.

Helen sighed and kicked off her shoes. Millicent fanned herself with a bridal consultant's brochure.

"The things I do for money," Millicent groaned.

"Rod the chauffeur is doing something strange for his bucks," Helen said. "You won't believe this, Millicent. He was afraid to take a bottle of water from me. I mean, really scared. He said, 'Don't let her see you. You could ruin everything.' He acted like I was handing him a bomb. Why is he so afraid?"

"Because Kiki is a jealous bitch. She doesn't want her chauffeur talking to a younger, better-looking woman."

"I wasn't coming on to him. I'm happy with Phil." Boy, am I happy, Helen thought.

"Then don't interfere," Millicent said sharply. "Kiki's name should be kinky. She likes watching her chauffeur stand by that car and sweat. She probably does him that way. Don't feel sorry for Rod. That's his job. Don't cater to him like he's married to a client. He's not a husband, although God knows he has some of the same duties."

"At least Rod is well paid," Helen said.

"He thinks he is, the fool," Millicent said. "Kiki's had many chauffeurs. She pays them minimum wage and puts them in her will for a million bucks. When she bounces them, she writes them out. Gets herself cheap help and first-class service that way. It must be a shock for those young men to go from millionaire dreams to minimum-wage reality. I can't imagine what it's like."

I can, Helen thought. I used to make major money and live in a mansion before I caught my ex-husband with my next-door neighbor. I'd kill Kiki if she pulled that on me.

"How do you know these things?" Helen said.

"It's the talk of the town," Millicent said.

Which town? Helen wondered. No one discussed it where she lived.

"This chauffeur will get his walking papers soon," Millicent said. "Kiki didn't grope him when she got back into the car."

Millicent talked so easily about the outré world of the overrich. Helen felt like a stranger in a parallel universe. "Well, they're gone," she said. "I'm glad it's over."

"Over?" Millicent said. "It's just begun."

Chapter 2

The Coronado Tropic Apartments were the most romantic place Helen had ever lived. At nightfall, the sweeping white curve of the Art Deco building was softened by mauve shadows. Waterfalls of purple bougainvillea surrounded the pool. Palms whispered subtropical secrets. Little lizards with throbbing red throats scampered through the leaves.

Helen's house in suburban St. Louis had been more impressive. Its six bay windows had overlooked a backyard forest. Her St. Louis home was bigger, too. Helen could have put her whole Coronado apartment in its great room.

She would have put her Coronado furniture out for a Goodwill pickup. In her old life, it would have been tacky. Here, it seemed witty. Helen loved the curvy 1950s boomerang table, the lamps like nuclear reactors, and the turquoise Barcalounger. She was a different person now. Living on the run had changed her.

Who was she trying to impress with her tract mansion in the burbs? Helen had worked long hours as director of pensions and benefits. While she was staying late at work, her husband, Rob, was stepping out with another woman.

Helen's fingers twitched when she thought of Rob and Sandy naked on the back deck. Strange thoughts crossed her mind when she saw her husband in another woman. Sandy's bare legs were waving in the air. Helen thought, Sandy has waxed her legs. I couldn't do that without anesthesia.

Then Helen had picked up the crowbar and changed her life. She didn't regret it. She was happier in Florida. Freer, too. If she wasn't so worried about money, her life would be perfect. Helen went from making six figures a year to six-seventy an hour, plus a two-percent commission.

Helen could imagine what her old ambitious crowd would make of the Coronado residents. "Weird" would be their kindest term. But she tried to remember one St. Louis party where she'd laughed with her friends. She was always networking, making deals, advancing her career.

Here in South Florida, the Coronado residents sat out by the pool and toasted the end of each day. Helen loved her seventy-six-year-old landlady, Margery Flax, with her purple shorts, wild shoes, and red nail polish. The relentless Florida sun turned her face to brown corduroy, but Margery had slender legs and loved to show them off.

Her landlady made a mean screwdriver. After the day she'd had, Helen could use one. She was ready for the evening party by the pool. In the summer, they saluted the sunset. Now, in December, they warmed the winter nights with their laughter.

Helen hated coming out of work when it was dark. She felt like someone had stolen her day while she was trapped inside the store. It was pitch-black by the time she got to the Coronado. The lights were on by the pool. Helen was surprised to see a couple moving silently in the darkness at the edge of the light.

She went closer to the pool. A man and a woman were dancing gracefully to music only they could hear. Helen stood by the pool gate, watching them. The couple twirled, dipped, and danced to their ghost orchestra.

The man seemed in his mid-seventies. He had broad shoulders and a tall, straight figure. His suit did not hang on him, the way old men's clothes often did. He had the most beautiful silver hair, like moonlight on water.

The woman wore a violet dress with a full skirt that flowed with their imaginary music. Her daring spike heels had silver tips. Her gray hair was done in an elegant French twist. Helen stared. It was Margery. But tonight, her raucous hard-drinking landlady was a romantic vision. Helen had never seen this side of Margery. The woman had style. Even her wrinkles were interesting.

Helen would have said they danced like a much younger couple, but she was thirty years younger than Margery and she couldn't dance like that. Helen had learned to dance in the seventies, which meant she bounced up and down and shook various body parts. Next to these waltzing wonders, she'd look like she'd stepped in a fire-ant nest.

The man spun Margery in a final pirouette and they bowed.

"Bravo!" Helen applauded.

Margery and the man looked up, surprised. They'd been in a dancing trance, unaware of their audience.

Margery recovered first. "This is Warren Webley. He

has a new dance studio off Las Olas. He's renting apartment 2C until his River House condo is ready."

Those condos started at six hundred thousand bucks, Helen thought. This guy must have money.

Warren dabbed at his forehead with a white pocket square, then bowed slightly. Helen noticed his tie had a hip geometric pattern. Old men's ties were often out of style, too fat or too thin.

"A dance studio," Helen said. "You're obviously qualified, Mr. Webley. It should be a terrific success."

"Call me Warren," he said. "And thank you for the compliment. But I won't spoil your evening with shop talk."

Good, Helen thought. He's not one of those sleazy operators who tries to sign you up for lifetime lessons.

"It was lovely to meet you," he said to Helen. Then he turned to Margery. "I must unpack, my dear." Warren kissed his landlady's hand and left.

Was Margery blushing? It was too dark to tell. She definitely had a sparkle in her eyes.

"Do I see dance lessons in your future?" Helen asked.

"I already know how to dance," Margery said. "But he is good-looking."

"You may have beaten the curse of apartment 2C," Helen said.

"I hope so." Margery's lighter flared in the darkness as she set fire to a Marlboro. "Seems like I rented that place to every shyster in South Florida. The last two tenants tried to steal me blind."

"Don't forget the one who became a nine-hundred-number psychic," Helen said. "I see her ads on late-night TV. And I guess the con artist is still in jail."

Margery nodded. "He'll be there for a while. What a bum. They all looked so promising. It's weird. My renters in the other apartments are wonderful. Somebody put a double whammy on 2C."

"It looks like the jinx is dead now," Helen said. "Let's have a drink to celebrate."

"Did someone say drink?" Peggy said.

"Awwk," Pete said.

Pete was a Quaker parrot, bright green with sober gray trim, who spent most of his time on Peggy's shoulder. Peggy looked rather like an exotic bird herself, with her crest of dark red hair and elegant beak of a nose.

The Coronado had a no-pets policy, which meant when Margery was around, everyone pretended Pete wasn't there. Pete sat on Peggy's shoulder, munching an asparagus spear. Margery sat in a deck chair, smoking her Marlboro. Both held their addictions at the same angle.

"Where's Cal the Canadian?" Helen asked after another Coronado resident. "I haven't seen him for a while."

"He's visiting his grandchild in Toronto," Peggy said.

Margery snorted a dragon spurt of white smoke. "Ha. He's up in that icebox because he's afraid he'll lose his Canadian health insurance. He needs to spend a certain number of weeks in his country to qualify."

"I can't blame him," Helen said. "Who can afford American health insurance?"

"Why do you defend that cheapskate after he stiffed you?" Margery blew another furious stream of smoke. Helen hoped it was from her cigarette. "Canadians are cheap," Margery said.

"Not all of them," Helen said.

"Oh, yeah?" Margery said. "Did you see what's spray painted on the supermarket wall? 'Canadians— Give us your money or go home!'"

"That's all? You should see what the gangs sprayed on the walls in—" Helen almost said St. Louis. "Miami," she finished.

"Awwk!" Pete moved restlessly along Peggy's shoulder. Disagreements made the little parrot uneasy. Peggy petted him with a finger until he settled down.

"Have a homemade screwdriver," Margery said. "You need your vitamin C to think straight. I made the juice myself. That electric juicer was the only good thing to ever come out of 2C."

Her landlady had helped herself to the contraption when she cornered a deadbeat renter with a .38. Now Helen heard the juicer's buzz-saw whine daily, as Margery mangled oranges for screwdrivers. She poured the powerful brew into three glasses, then topped each one with a Key lime slice.

Helen took the tall, cool screwdriver and stretched her long frame on a chaise longue. It was a good idea to sit down if you had one of Margery's drinks. By the time Helen finished it, she could be flat on her back.

"So what's happening at that soap opera you call a job?" Margery said. "Any more tears, tantrums, or fist-fights?"

"Today was a five-star drama." Helen filled them in on the undesirable Desiree. "Kiki, the mother of the bride, is a real piece of work. She has a chauffeur who has 'other duties.' "

"You mean sex?" Peggy said.

"Awwk," Pete said.

"Yep," Helen said. "They practically did it on the sidewalk."

"You sound like you disapprove," Margery said.

"I do," Helen said.

"I admire the woman," Margery said. "She's got life

figured out. If I had the money, I'd have some young stud drive my car."

"Margery!" Helen said.

"Oh, don't look so shocked. It's a drag having to please a man. I'd like to have one around for sex without having to worry about his feelings."

"Sex when I wanted it," Peggy said. "Instead of in the morning when he likes it."

Helen wondered how Peggy's romance with her policeman was going.

"A chauffeur is a man with no complications," Margery said. "I'd never have to hear about his jealous kids or crazy ex-wife."

"When I got tired of listening to him, I could say, 'Shut up, Jeeves,' and raise the glass window," Peggy said.

Hmm. Not a good sign for the policeman, Helen decided.

"I could send him home when I got tired of him," Margery said. " 'I'll see you tomorrow, Jeeves. And wash the car.' All that, and he'd drive in the tourist traffic, too."

"Now that's a dream lover," Peggy said.

"You guys are awful," Helen said. But she was thinking of her own dream lover, Phil. Who ever thought the perfect man would live right next door?

Helen finished her screwdriver and looked at her watch. It was eight thirty. "I'd better go. I have work in the morning."

"Are you seeing Phil tonight?" Margery said.

"Probably not. He's tied up with that court case. The lawyers are keeping him late every night, going over his testimony."

"That man did you a favor keeping you out of that mess, Helen," Margery said. "I hope you're grateful."

"Oh, I am," Helen said. "And I know how to show my gratitude."

The cigarette cloud Margery snorted could have escaped from a smoke stack. "Spare me," she said.

Helen stood up and felt woozy. Must be a vitamin C overdose from the screwdriver. She needed dinner and so did her cat, Thumbs.

When Helen unlocked her door, the big cat threw himself at her feet and tripped her. Helen pitched forward and grabbed the kitchen counter. "If I break my neck, you'll starve," Helen told him.

Thumbs was a gray-and-white tom with the biggest paws on any cat this side of a zoo. He was a polydactyl and had six toes on his front paws. He also had golden eyes and a rumbling purr when he was pleased. Right now, he wanted dinner.

She poured Thumbs a bowl of chow. She was fixing herself a hash-house dinner of fried eggs, potatoes, and onions when there was a knock on the door.

Helen opened it and smiled. It was Phil.

She was always a little startled by his striking good looks. With his white hair and lean body, Phil looked like a pirate—or a rock star. His crooked nose only made his face more interesting. Helen liked her men a little flawed.

He kissed her and sniffed the oniony air. "Grease! My favorite food group."

"And the only thing I can make. Let me fry you a heart-stopping dinner."

"Fine with me," Phil said. "I sure don't want to live forever. Not after the day I've had in court. Damn lawyers."

Phil was a private investigator. A case he'd been working undercover got him mixed up with a federal agency, two murders, and Helen.

"Tell me about it," she said and popped bread in the toaster.

"I'd rather forget about it until after dinner. Tell me about your day."

"I saw Margery dancing by the pool with the handsomest older man. They looked so romantic, Phil. I hope I have a lover when I'm seventy-six and can dance with him by the pool."

"I hope it will be me," Phil said. He took her in his arms and kissed her until the fried eggs were two rubber coasters.

Helen felt his scratchy, end-of-the-day beard against her cheek and kissed the tender spot at the base of his throat. His shirt smelled of starch. He smelled of coffee and something spicy.

Phil kissed her again, and the onions and potatoes turned to cinders.

They didn't notice.

"I will dance with you now, Helen," he said, waltzing her around the living room. "But I will love you forever."

Helen kissed him again and tried to forget the other man who'd made that promise. Suddenly the smoke alarm blared and the moment was lost.

34366000054259

Chapter 3

"I love this black strapless dress," Kiki said. "But will it fit all eight bridesmaids? I mean, will it stay up on them?"

"Are their breasts real or man-made?" Millicent said. Helen blinked.

"Man-made," Kiki said. "All eight of them. Or should I say sixteen?"

"Good," Millicent said. "Real breasts shift and sag. Fake ones are hard. You can hang anything on them."

Eight college-age women, all with implants, Helen thought. Welcome to Florida, where the biggest boobs weren't always in bras. Instead of Beemers, doting Sunshine State daddies bought their babies boob jobs on their sixteenth birthday.

At first, Helen was surprised that Kiki had picked a plain black bridesmaid dress. Outrageously expensive, it didn't look like much on a hanger. But put that dress on, and it was magical. It transformed awkward young women into slim princesses. Desiree's blond bridesmaids would seem regal when they walked down the aisle.

The bride would look like a frump, dragging a fortune in pearls and crystal.

Why could Kiki make everyone look beautiful but herself and her daughter?

In her too-young outfits, Kiki looked scrawny and hard, like a hooker dressed as a schoolgirl. Her daughter was a ragbag. Today, Desiree wore wrinkled sweatpants the color of cold oatmeal. Her baggy gray T-shirt made her firm young chest seem saggy.

"Chop-chop," Kiki said. "We need to keep moving."

Millicent was giddy from the green gush of money. Rush orders! Overnighted dresses! Overtime alterations!

"I can get all eight bridesmaid dresses in the right sizes," Millicent said. "But there will be an additional rush charge."

"Splendid," Kiki said.

Helen was not sure if Kiki was delighted over the availability or the extra cost. Millicent disappeared into her office, her bloodred nails itching to dance on the calculator keys.

"Now where's the goddamn wedding dress?" Kiki asked.

Helen ran upstairs to the seamstress's room. Desiree's heavy Hapsburg princess dress hung on a rack, bristling with colored dressmaker's pins and encrusted with crystal. Helen carried it carefully as an irritated porcupine.

The walk to the fitting room was cheerful as a funeral procession. The room had a triple mirror, a gilt chair, and a spindly table with a box of Kleenex. There was a lot of crying connected with the so-called happiest day of a woman's life, and it wasn't all tears of joy.

Kiki refused to sit. She prowled the room restlessly,

nearly tipping over the gilt chair. Desiree flinched whenever her mother came near her. Helen was relieved when Kiki's cell phone played an annoying tune. Kiki snapped it open, then announced, "My ex, Brendan. I have to take this."

She stepped out of the fitting room, but Helen could hear Kiki as clearly as if she were shouting in her ear. Her first words declared war. "Let me guess. You're calling to bitch about money."

Desiree looked stricken. Helen didn't want to listen to Kiki's call, but she was afraid to leave the bride alone. She might hang herself with a rope of Aleçon lace.

"Listen, bigshot, that's what things cost," Kiki snarled. "You can't do decent flowers for less than forty thousand dollars. Yeah, well, you should have thought of that before you ran off with Miss Fake Tits."

The bride stood on the alteration platform, a statue of despair. She clutched a tulle veil so hard Helen thought she'd tear it in two. Helen gently pried the veil from her cold fingers. Desiree didn't notice. Helen started working on the gown's slippery satin buttons.

"I don't care where you get the money, Brendan," Kiki shouted. "But you better get it. Or the whole town will know you're a deadbeat who can't pay for your daughter's wedding."

Eighty buttons to go, Helen thought desperately. She tried to distract Desiree with small talk. "Eight bridesmaids," she chirped. "You're lucky to have so many friends."

"They aren't friends," the bride said in a flat voice. "They're in my sorority. Mother's sorority, really. She made me join.

"Mother picked the bridesmaids from their photos in the sorority house. They're all blond. They're all beautiful. Mother is buying their dresses and shoes. She's made their hair and makeup appointments. She's picked their escorts, too. She chose the handsomest actors at Luke's theater. She made sure the men were straight."

Helen was afraid to ask how Kiki did that. Sixty-five buttons to go.

"My real friend isn't good enough to be in the wedding because she's fat," Desiree said.

Her mother entered the room briskly, shutting her cell phone. "That's not true, darling. I thought Emily would be more comfortable handling the guest book."

"Mother bought Emily the plum Vera Wang," Desiree said. "She wouldn't let her pick out her own dress."

"Emily has an unfortunate penchant for flappy fabrics," Kiki said. "She looks like a clothesline in a hurricane."

Forty-eight buttons. Kiki was spoiling for a fight. Helen tried to steer the conversation to a safer subject. "What kind of flowers do you want for your wedding, Desiree?"

"I want red roses," the bride said.

"So romantic," Helen said.

"So ordinary," her mother said. "I can give her any flower that she wants, and she asks for roses like a shopgirl."

Helen froze at the insult.

"No offense intended," Kiki said.

"Of course not," Helen said.

"But I couldn't let her embarrass me. We're having chartreuse lady's slipper and cymbidium orchids."

"Science-fiction flowers," the bride said. "I wanted roses, but I won't get them."

"You'll have plenty of roses at your wedding, sweetheart. The flower girls are throwing rose petals. So are the guests."

"Instead of rice or bubbles?" Helen said.

"No one has thrown rice in decades," Kiki said. "And bubbles are so eighties. The bride and groom will be showered with rose petals when they leave the church. At the reception, the attendants are sprinkling rose petals in the commodes."

Helen thought she'd heard wrong. "You're putting roses in the toilets?"

"I'm not," Kiki said. "The attendants are. After each flushing. It's such an elegant touch."

"That's what my mother thinks of my choice," the bride said. "My roses will be walked on—and peed on!" Angry tears cascaded down her small face and slid into the accordion wrinkles where her chin should have been.

"Prewedding jitters," Kiki said. She watched her daughter weep as if it were a third-rate performance. She made no move to comfort her. Helen handed Desiree a fistful of Kleenex. She blew loudly. The little bride had a trombone for a beezer.

Twenty-seven buttons to go. Helen had reached Desiree's upper back, and the buttons kept escaping from their loops. The bride was annoyingly limp, like a protestor who'd collapsed on police lines.

"Straighten your shoulders," her mother commanded. "And smile. You're a bride, not a corpse."

The bride did look more dead than alive. Helen finished the last button. Desiree failed to smile, but she dutifully tried on veils. Some went to her fingertips. Others fell to the floor. Desiree could have been in a coma for all the reaction she showed.

"Which do you like?" Helen asked, hoping for some response.

Desiree shrugged.

Of course, Kiki had an opinion. "That long veil has the same beading as the dress. I like it."

"It's a bit heavy, don't you think?" Helen tried to be tactful. In that long veil, Desiree looked like a ghost haunting her wedding.

"It needs something to brighten it up," Kiki said.

Two rooms away, Millicent heard another chance to make money. She said, "Helen, go get that crystal crown off the display."

The crown was five hundred bucks, more than Helen made in a week. Helen came back and crowned the chinless little heiress. Desiree looked like she had a headache.

"Do you like it?" Helen asked.

Desiree shrugged. Helen wanted to shake her. Why didn't she stand up for herself? Helen was grateful when Millicent stuck her head in the dressing room and said, "The groom's here. Should I send him back?"

"Isn't it bad luck for the groom to see the dress?" Helen said.

"Join the twenty-first century," Kiki said. "These days, the groom may pick out the dress."

"Luke might as well see it," Desiree said, as if he were viewing a fatal accident. "I'll be out in a minute. Leave me alone, please."

Helen tiptoed up front for a quick look at the groom. Luke was definitely scenic. He wasn't tall, probably about the same size as Millicent. But he was perfectly made from his cleft chin to his well-shod feet. His deep-brown hair was so thick, Helen wanted to run her fingers through it. Luke's lightweight blue sweater and gray pants were nothing special. Yet Helen noticed them, because they seemed so absolutely right.

Luke was with a skinny man about sixty dressed in black. His clothes and goatee screamed, "I am an artiste."

"I'm Luke Praine," the groom said to Helen and Millicent. "This is my director, the owner of the Sunnysea Shakespeare Playhouse, Chauncey Burnham."

"Kiki, darling, so glad to see you." Chauncey had a sycophant's smile. His lips were unpleasantly red and flexible. Helen wondered if that was from smooching patrons' posteriors.

"Really, Chauncey, can't I have any peace?" Kiki said.

"I saw your car and I had to come over and say hello." Chauncey's smile slipped slightly.

"You've said it. Now go." Kiki started to turn away.

"Er, could we have a moment alone?"

"Anything you have to say, Chauncey, you can say right here." Kiki was daring him.

The director took a deep breath, rubbed his goatee, and pursed his rubbery red lips. "All right, I will. Kiki, you promised my company five thousand dollars so we could get through December. Now you say you can't give us any money until January first."

"I can't, Chauncey. The wedding has been expensive."

"The landlord says he'll close us down next week in the middle of the run. We haven't been reviewed yet, Kiki. The critic for the *Herald* can't come until next Thursday. I know we'll get a big crowd when we get a favorable review." Chauncey was pleading now, like a mother begging for the life of her child.

"*If* you get a favorable review. He called your last

production 'uninspired and derivative.'" Kiki's face was a frozen mask of meanness.

Chauncey showed a brief flash of anger. Then he puckered properly. "Kiki, please. You know Luke is marvelous in this production. I beg of you, help us. We won't make it to January without your support. We'll die."

Kiki's smile was cruel. "Don't beg, Chauncey. It's weak."

Chauncey hung his head. Millicent moved away. Humiliation might be catching.

Desiree appeared in her frumpy wedding dress and veil, an expensive specter. "Poor Chauncey," she said softly. "You're much too nice. If you were only more like your Shakespeare characters, you could save your theater. The bard knew what to do with inconvenient women." Her smile was honeyed malice.

Chauncey looked stricken. "Please, dear lady, that's not funny."

"Screw your courage to the sticking point," Desiree said, a demure Lady Macbeth.

Sweat broke out on his forehead. "Please, it's bad luck to quote the Scottish play."

"Perhaps." She shrugged. "But my mother's death would be good luck for you."

There was a shocked silence. Chauncey turned white, down to those mobile lips. "I'd better go," he said. "You look lovely, Desiree." He backed out of the shop.

"Money is so important in the theater," Desiree said. "Everyone thinks Luke is marrying me for mine, but that's not true. I won't have any money until I'm thirty and Luke is thirty-five. That's old for a leading man, you know. He's getting a little thin on top now, but I think balding men are attractive, don't you?"

She patted the groom on his head. Helen thought she saw his hair eroding like a Florida beach.

"Luke is giving up his big break for me, aren't you? He has a chance to be in a Michael Mann movie—you know, the *Miami Vice* producer. It's a big part for an unknown.

"Mother hates the part. Hates it. That's why she said no. She doesn't want Luke to be this drooling, brain-damaged coke addict. She says her friends and her committees may not understand that he's acting.

"Luke can do Shakespeare, though. Everyone understands Shakespeare, even at Chauncey's little theater. Luke can do that forever. Oh, and he has that dog food commercial. It's still running on cable. Do your dog bark, sweetheart. You're so clever."

Helen was dazed by this display. Desiree had gutted her husband-to-be with knife-edged praise. How could he stand her?

But Luke took Desiree in his arms and gave her a smoldering kiss. "Darling, don't do this to yourself," he said. "Take off that dress. Let's go out for an early dinner before the show."

Luke's performance of a man in love was flawless, but that's what it seemed, a performance. It convinced Desiree, though. She wrapped her arms around Luke's neck and kissed him as if he were going off to war.

"You're right, Luke," she said, becoming a heroine in her own romance. "Let's leave here. I'll get ready."

"I'll help you." Millicent wanted this emotion-charged scene out of her salon. She herded the bride and her mother back to the fitting room. "Helen, stay with Luke, will you?"

"You're in the current production?" Helen said, trying to break the uncomfortable silence.

"I have the lead in *Richard the Third*. But I'm leaving the production after next Thursday. I've got a part in a movie."

"I thought your mother-in-law wouldn't allow it," Helen said.

"I'll bring her around," he said. Luke's long lashes had to be natural. They didn't have eyelash transplants, did they? Helen thought his eyes were brown, but now they looked green. She couldn't stop staring. Maybe they would turn blue, or gray, or start spinning stars.

"I bet you will," Helen said. Had she really said that out loud?

Luke didn't seem offended. He hesitated, then said, "Look, Desiree has the bridal version of stage fright. She didn't mean what she said. Here are two tickets to next Thursday's show. A critic from the *Herald* is coming. Will you help us pack the house? You'd be doing me a huge favor."

How could a muscular man look so winsome? "Why, thanks." Helen hadn't been to a theater since she had money in St. Louis. She smiled back.

Desiree came out of the fitting room, saw Helen's smile, and frowned. She almost ran across the room to grab Luke's arm.

The couple was gone before Kiki tip tapped out in her spike heels, talking on her cell phone. "Friday night then," she cooed. "After the rehearsal dinner." Kiki looked sly as a cream-fed cat. Helen wondered if she was arranging a horizontal interview with a new chauffeur.

"I'll take that crown and the long veil," Kiki said. "You'll be at the rehearsal tomorrow night. I'll also need you at the church Saturday morning."

"Helen will be there," Millicent said.

"I will?" This was the first Helen had heard of it. She didn't want to spend her weekend with the wedding horror show. "I don't have a car."

"Take the shop van," Millicent said. "I'll pay you overtime."

Overtime? Kiki would pay through the nose for this personal service. Well, Helen could use the money.

"Good," Kiki said. "We'll see her at six."

"My name is Helen."

Kiki didn't acknowledge her. "Oops. I forgot my checkbook. I'll give your check to what's-her-name at the rehearsal."

"My name is Helen." Kiki still ignored her.

"Can't you send your chauffeur with it this afternoon?" Millicent said.

"He'll be busy with me."

Busy how? Helen wondered. But Kiki was heading for the door. Helen could see Rod the chauffeur standing next to the car, mopping sweat off his brow with a handkerchief.

Helen and Millicent simultaneously plopped into the pink chairs.

"How long do you think that marriage will last?" Helen asked.

"Here's the Millicent Marriage Rule: The length of the marriage is in inverse proportion to the amount spent on the wedding. The more you spend, the sooner it's over. I give this marriage a year, tops."

"A year? The bride is worth millions."

"Not for another ten years. Luke will have to spend a decade with the mother-in-law from hell to see that money."

Millicent studied the bloodred nails that had clawed their way to the top of the bridal business. "Luke has big plans for that handsome face. It will take lots of money to get it on movie posters. There's been no mention of a prenup for the groom. Desiree's parents are too busy fighting with each other to worry about their daughter.

"If Luke's smart—and he is—he'll stay with the bride a year or so, then file for divorce. He'll ask for big bucks, settle for a million, and spend it on his career. Desiree's father will still be paying off the wedding when the groom calls it quits."

"I guess a year is a long time with those two," Helen said. "How you can stand Bridezilla and her mother?"

"I'm not marrying them, dear. I'm just taking their money. I rather admire Kiki. She's smart, she's tough, and if she'd been born ten years later, she'd be running the family business. But her Neanderthal father refused to train her for business and her silly mother pushed her into society. I admit she's vulgar. But if she were a man, would you even notice her outrageous behavior?

"Besides, Kiki may not seem like it, but she's a godsend. I need this order to survive. Business has been too slow for too long."

"Was it 9/11?" Helen said.

Millicent leaned forward to confide. "You won't believe this, but for a month after the disaster, my sales shot up. I sold dresses like there was no tomorrow. You know why? Because the brides believed there was no tomorrow.

"One bride came back here six times," Millicent said. "She wanted a twenty-six-hundred-dollar dress, but she was budgeted for two thousand. She couldn't justify that price—and women are great justifiers. Come September twelfth, she bought the dress. She said, 'What's six hundred dollars when I could be ashes tomorrow?'

"Around November, reality returned and my sales slumped with everyone else's. They've never quite come back.

"The eighties were the great days of retailing in Florida. That's when the cocaine cowboys were riding high. The drug dealers would come into the shop with a suitcase full of cash. I'd lock the door and they'd pick out twenty dresses for their girlfriends. I'd have a forty-thousand-dollar sale in one afternoon. Those days are gone for good. Now I have to work to sell a two-thousand-dollar dress.

"So I can take all the dirt Kiki hands out, because it looks green to me."

Chapter 4

It was bad luck. It was also unnatural.

There were no mistakes during the rehearsal. Not one.

In Helen's experience, if the wedding party stumbled around during a rehearsal, missed their cues, and laughed a lot, then the ceremony would be perfect. But everything went right at Luke and Desiree's rehearsal. Something bad was going to happen tomorrow at the wedding. Helen knew it. She also knew that was superstitious nonsense.

Kiki had chosen Coco Isle Cathedral, the most fashionable church in South Florida, for the wedding. She did not belong to the congregation, but a big donation made her devoutly welcome.

Jeff, the wedding planner for Your Precious Day, was directing the extravaganza. Jeff was high-camp wholesome. He looked like a cute kid brother, right down to his freckled nose, but he fluttered, fussed, and talked in italics.

"Kiki, this cathedral is just *divine*," he said.

Helen stifled a laugh. Jeff didn't realize he'd been punning. The cathedral wasn't a sacred place for him. It was a theater. The altar was a stage.

"Wait till you see how those stained-glass windows look in the *photos*," Jeff said. "The altar is up *four steps*. That's *so* important."

"Why?" Helen said.

"So the bride is *displayed* properly. The way that cathedral train *drapes* on those marble steps. *Oh!*"

Jeff was practically palpitating. Helen wondered if she should get the smelling salts from her emergency kit. Millicent had packed her a suitcase with everything from sewing materials to spot cleaner.

Jeff had recovered from his surge of ecstasy and was now only wildly enthused. "Wait till you see the *orchids*. Absolutely *faboo*."

Helen felt sad that no one in the wedding was as excited as Jeff. Some wedding party. Helen had never seen a grimmer gathering.

The blond bridesmaids had the bland young features that passed for beauty and the slightly superior expressions of private-school graduates. Their skin seemed steam cleaned. They stood a little apart from the others. Helen knew their names were Lisa, Allison, Amy, Jessica, Jocelyn, Julia, Meredith, and Beth, but she couldn't have said which was which if you put a gun to her head.

The groomsmen looked like actors hired for the occasion. Most were. Kiki had chosen the best-looking men from the Shakespeare company. Jason was the studliest, but Helen thought his arrogance spoiled his good looks. Jason had the overconfident manner of someone who'd always been handsome—and knew it.

Still, his blond hair, bold green eyes, and beefcake body were eye-catching. Jason had leading-man looks, until he stood next to the groom. Luke glowed with energy. People turned toward Luke like flowers toward the sun.

Next to Luke's star power, Jason wilted. He moved to the far side of the church. Helen wondered if Jason was jealous. He outshone Luke only one way: Jason was the best-dressed man at the rehearsal. His Hugo Boss outfit could have paid Helen's rent.

Jason was paired with the blond Lisa. They exchanged smoldering looks and hot smiles for almost an hour at the rehearsal. Then Kiki homed in on Jason. She'd flirted with all the groomsmen, but her behavior with Jason was outrageous. She enjoyed taking the young man from Lisa, who turned sulky and snippy.

Kiki practically propositioned Jason in front of Lisa. She looked like a has-been movie queen in her gold gown.

The creamy blond Lisa sniped back with carefully disguised insults. In between bouts of marching down the aisle, one bridesmaid said, "Have you seen Pamela? She's so skinny. How did she lose that weight?"

"It's the South Beach Diet—Ecstasy and Corona," Lisa said. "Right, Jason?"

Jason shot her a murderous look. The others giggled.

Helen was relieved when Kiki and Jason disappeared, until Jeff sent out a search party for them so they could do another run-through. This wedding had more rehearsals than a Broadway musical.

The church's elevator was out of order. Helen had to lug the dresses up the steep back stairs. That's where she stumbled over the missing Jason and Kiki. Kiki's breasts were nearly popped out of her low-cut gold gown, and Jason had popped out as well. Was he auditioning for the role of chauffeur?

"God, you're making me so hot," Kiki said. "Let's come back here after the rehearsal."

"I've got a bed," Jason said, grinding his pelvis into hers. "We don't have to do it on the back steps."

"I want to do it in the church," Kiki said.

Oh, Lord, Helen thought. She wished she hadn't heard that. The couple was so intensely wrapped up in—and around—each other, they didn't notice her. Helen stepped around them and said nothing. Let someone else find them *in flagrante.*

Rod the chauffeur sat in the car like an abandoned pet. Helen wondered if Rod knew his days were numbered.

The only man in the wedding party who hadn't been personally selected by Kiki was Chauncey. The groom insisted on the theater director as his best man. Helen liked Luke for that. There was a decided coolness between Chauncey and Kiki.

But it was nothing compared to the frost between Kiki and her ex-husband, Brendan. Under their ice was real fire. Helen heard them exchange hot words when no one was around.

Helen gave Jason and Kiki enough time to put their body parts back in their clothes, then hauled more dresses up the steps. Now Jason was gone. Kiki and her ex were fighting on the landing. The little lawyer looked like his daughter, except he had more vitality and more chin.

"You're making a spectacle of yourself." Brendan was dangerously red in the face.

"It's none of your business. I'm not married to you." Kiki's face-lift was stretched at the seams. Helen could see white scars under her anger-reddened skin.

"You should think of our daughter," Brendan shouted.

"You're a fine one to talk, questioning every penny I spend on her wedding."

"Penny!" Brendan sputtered like an overflowing radiator. "You're bankrupting me with this goddamn wedding."

Helen couldn't stand there, listening to them fight. She shook the bagged dresses until they rustled like sacks of autumn leaves. Brendan broke off abruptly and left.

Kiki said, "Oh, girl."

"My name is Helen."

"Whatever your name is, I won't have you sneaking around, listening at doors."

"There isn't any door," Helen said. "This is a public stairwell."

Kiki's eyes narrowed. "Listen here, you little c—"

Helen put up with a lot, but there were limits. "Don't you dare use that word."

"Don't you dare talk back to me," Kiki said. "I'll buy that store, just to have you fired."

Helen shrugged. "If you want to spend a million bucks to get rid of a salesclerk, be my guest."

Kiki pointed a long gold fingernail dangerously close to Helen's eye. "And then I'll make sure you never work in South Florida again." She whirled off in a flurry of gauzy gold skirts, like a brilliant dragon.

"I hate rich people," Helen muttered when Kiki was gone. "Worthless, useless bloodsuckers."

Helen heard a soft cough and realized she wasn't alone. Jeff the wedding planner was on the steps. Four frightened bridesmaids peered over his shoulder. Helen wondered how much they'd heard.

"Can I help you carry those dresses upstairs?" Jeff said.

"No, thanks. I'm fine," Helen said.

"Okay, *people,* let's get back to the *rehearsal,*" Jeff said. Everyone carefully stepped past Helen. No one said a word.

Helen delivered the dresses upstairs, then paused to

watch the rehearsal. As her mother's behavior grew more flamboyant, Desiree seemed to wall herself away in a stricken silence. Desiree sleepwalked down the aisle wearing Jeff's "training train"—yards of white muslin tied around her waist to give her the feel of a cathedral-length train. Her movements were perfect, but lifeless.

The only person Desiree talked to was the large young woman whose yellow outfit flapped like a bedsheet on a clothesline. Helen guessed she was Emily, the bride's only friend. The bridesmaids snickered and talked behind their French-manicured fingers whenever Emily appeared.

The handpicked blond bridesmaids and professionally handsome groomsmen moved as smoothly as if they were on rollers. Even the ring bearer and flower girls were model children. Jeff scampered about, saying, "All right, *people*, that was perfect. Let's do it one more *time*."

Helen went back to the van and piled the last two bridesmaid dresses on top of the Hapsburg princess gown. Halfway up the steps, she felt a seismic shift in the slippery fabric. The princess gown started sliding out of the plastic cover. She should have put it in a zippered bag.

"Shit!" Helen said as the dress skittered out of the bag. She made an awkward grab and scratched her arm on the gown's crystal beading. Blood droplets welled up on her skin. Oh, no. She couldn't afford to bleed on this dress.

"Are you okay?" Desiree stood in the stairwell.

"I'm trying not to bleed on your dress," Helen said.

"I hate it. I'll give you fifty dollars to ruin it."

"Sorry," Helen said, "but I'd lose my job." Unless I've already lost it.

Desiree sighed.

"Why aren't you at the rehearsal?" Helen said.

"Jeff's working out the bridesmaids' processional. I'm

not needed. I don't think I'm needed for this whole ceremony."

Helen felt a stab of pity for the forlorn little woman.

"There you are. Where have you been?" It was Luke, looking fetchingly worried. Was he afraid his meal ticket was having second thoughts?

"My awful dress scratched her arm," Desiree said. "I'm trying to get her to bleed on it. I hate that dress. It makes me look dumpy."

"Desiree, you're beautiful no matter what you wear. Come." Luke was such a good actor, Helen almost believed him. He smiled and held out his hand. After a slight pause, Desiree took it.

The pair left Helen to struggle up the stairs alone with the three dresses. She was puffing by the time she made it to the top. She shoved the bridesmaid dresses into a closet, then examined the heavy Hapsburg princess gown. It was an ugly, unlucky dress, covered in crystal beads by wage slaves for the captive daughter of the rich.

Helen saw a tiny discoloration on the skirt that could have been blood. She put a little spot cleaner on a Q-tip, and dabbed at it until the mark disappeared.

Helen was not sure if this church answered the brides' spiritual needs, but it understood their worldly ones. The bride's room had long, lighted dressing tables, bales of Kleenex for wedding tears, comfortable couches, and acres of closets. There was enough moisturizer, nail polish, cotton balls, and Band-Aids to stock a drugstore. A cup held every kind of scissors, from nail cutters to pinking shears.

Helen hung the wedding gown next to the bridesmaid dresses. She had one more dress to carry upstairs. She wearily wrestled the rose gown up the narrow stairs, cursing the springy hoop all the way. At least she didn't meet anyone on the steps.

The scratch on her arm had opened again, and blood dripped on the hall tile. Helen hoped she didn't get anything on the rose dress. She searched the skirt for blood spots. She didn't see anything, but it was hard to tell with the dark red taffeta.

To hell with it. Helen pushed the rose gown into the closet with the cobweb dress. Jeff, the wedding planner, ran into the room, looking anxious. "Helen, Kiki wants to go. She says you're holding her up."

"Believe me, I want out of here, too." Helen ran down the stairs. Kiki stood at the door like a jailer, jangling the keys to the church. As soon as Helen was outside Kiki locked the huge doors.

"Uh, Kiki, I need the check for Millicent," Helen said.

Kiki held up her tiny gold evening purse and walked over to her car. "No room for a checkbook in here." She slid into the waiting Rolls. The door shut with an insolent clunk.

Helen didn't look forward to calling her boss with this news. She walked slowly to a pay phone.

Millicent's fury nearly melted the phone. "Helen, go back, get those dresses, and put them in the shop van."

"Kiki locked up the church, Millicent. I can't get back in."

"Then go home, Helen. I have her cell phone number. We're going to have a little talk. If I don't get a satisfactory answer, I'll go to the rehearsal dinner. She'd better pay me, or I'll rip those dresses right off her bridesmaids' backs. That chinless wonder of a daughter will be walking down the aisle stark naked. Kiki's not pulling her tricks on me. I need that money."

* * *

It was after ten when Helen parked the shop van in the Coronado lot. She would have to leave again at six a.m.—unless Kiki called Millicent and had her fired. Helen didn't much care.

Thumbs met her at the door with his starving cat routine.

"You're a lying feline," Helen said, scratching his ears. "I left you plenty to eat."

But she put out a scoop of canned food, a rich cat pâté. Thumbs ate it greedily. Helen wished she could like anything in a can that much.

There was a knock on her door. She peeked out the peephole and saw Phil with a rose in one hand and a paper bag in the other. Her heart melted.

"Presents for you and Mr. Thumbs," he said.

"I love roses," she said, but Kiki's nasty remark about shopgirls stuck in her mind like a thorn. How could Desiree live with those petty insults year after year?

"The present for Thumbs is from Margery, but she didn't want to give it to you directly because of the no-pets policy. I'm the delivery boy."

The sedentary house cat leaped on the bag like a starving lion on an antelope.

"What's in that?" Helen said.

"Organic catnip toys. Margery's friend Rita Scott makes them. This is her most powerful batch yet."

Thumbs was pushing the bag around with his nose.

"It must be," Helen said. "He doesn't usually behave like that." She dumped out the bag on the kitchen counter. There were six cloth packets the size of mailing labels, stuffed with catnip.

Thumbs skidded across the counter, taking a pile of papers with him, and fell off. He stuck his head under the couch and wiggled his tail. He did backflips. He ran through the house and knocked over a footstool.

Helen and Phil watched, laughing.

"Where'd he go?" she said.

They found Thumbs lying in his pet caddy. "He hates pet caddies. They mean trips to the vet," Helen said. "What's he doing in there, staring at the ceiling? Look at his eyes. He's zonked."

"Thumbs, have you ever looked at your paw? I mean really looked at your paw?" Phil said. "He's having fun. We should, too. Let's go out for mojito martinis on Las Olas. You need some romance."

"I don't have time for romance, Phil. I'm working on a wedding."

"Weddings are romantic."

"Most weddings are as romantic as a root canal," Helen said. "Especially for young brides. I feel sorry for them. They're told, 'This is your day.' But the wedding isn't about the bride. It's the last chance for her mother to have the wedding she wanted."

"Come to think of it, the romance went out of my marriage with the wedding," Phil said. "My ex got caught up in making sure the bridesmaids' ribbons matched the groomsmen's cummerbunds. I felt like an afterthought. I never lost that feeling."

"I've got an idea," Helen said. "Let's skip the wedding and have the honeymoon."

"Right now?" Phil said.

"Yes."

Phil picked her up and carried her over the threshold to the bedroom.

Chapter 5

The stark white cathedral shone like an iceberg in the morning sun.

Inside, the deep-blue stained-glass windows made Helen feel like she was in a drowned ocean liner. The *Titanic*, perhaps. She still couldn't shake the feeling of disaster.

Yet the wedding preparations continued in seamless perfection. Even the iffy winter weather cooperated. The temperature was ideal for the bridesmaids' strapless dresses. The playful breeze promised to waft the rose petals prettily as the bride and groom ran down the church steps.

When Helen got to the cathedral at six thirty, Jeff, the wedding planner, was already supervising the flower placement.

"No, people, that's too close to the *pillar*."

He waved, but Helen wasn't sure if he was greeting her or in a flap over the flowers.

She ran upstairs to the bride's dressing room. Everything was in order. She checked the Hapsburg princess gown again for bloodstains. In the morning sun, the dress glittered like frost. Just looking at it made her arm throb. But she couldn't see any trace of blood.

Helen felt sick with relief. If she'd ruined a seven-thousand-dollar dress, she'd lose half a year's salary. Kiki would make her pay, too—after she had her fired.

Helen didn't have the nerve to check out the rose gown. Besides, she was not wrestling that monster hoop skirt this early in the morning. It might reopen the scratch on her arm. She hoped her luck held and there were no blood spots on the rose dress, either.

Jeff, bless him, had set out an exquisite breakfast buffet of pastries, bagels, and fruit. The room was fragrant with hot coffee. Helen poured herself a cup, enjoying the last peaceful moments of what she knew would be a long day.

What kind of life would Desiree and Luke have together? They were starting with advantages many young couples never knew: the bride's money, the groom's good looks and talent—things couples dream about, yet Helen felt sorry for them.

She wasn't sure either one was in love. Desiree clung to Luke, but that seemed more desperation than passion. And Luke was an actor, so it was tough to know his true feelings.

Besides, what chance did any marriage have with Kiki for a mother-in-law? The bride's father didn't seem to care about his daughter. Brendan had never hugged or kissed Desiree at the rehearsal last night. He'd hardly spoken to her. But he'd certainly had words with her mother.

Poor little rich girl.

She hoped the bride would have as much fun on her honeymoon as Helen had last night after Phil carried her over the threshold. They'd spent the whole night in bed, but they didn't sleep much. That man was one hot lover. Helen stretched luxuriantly, her body pleasantly tired and sore.

She looked out the dressing room window. Four cars pulled into the parking lot. She downed the last of her coffee and rinsed the cup. It was bridal battle stations.

Four makeup artists and three hairstylists began setting up in the dressing room. They would paint and prep all the women in the wedding party except Kiki. The mother of the bride was having her own makeup artist and stylist come to her home. Kiki planned to breeze in about forty-five minutes before the ceremony.

Why she didn't arrange the same service for her daughter, Helen didn't know. But she was grateful for Kiki's absence. It was more pleasant without her. Kiki left havoc and hurt feelings in her wake.

The first three bridesmaids straggled in at seven, looking hungover. Helen hoped the makeup artists had packed plenty of concealer. Those young blondes had enough bags to stock a Coach outlet.

Desiree and her friend Emily arrived at seven thirty. Emily was wearing what looked like an orange tablecloth. Desiree was a walking corpse. Her skin even had a slightly livid tinge.

The stylists went to work. Desiree's droopy hair was twisted into a stylish knot. Then the makeup artist started smearing goo on the bride's face. Helen had painted entire rooms in less time. But the woman was an artist. When she finally put down her brush, Helen thought she'd created a minor masterpiece. Desiree wasn't exactly radiant, but she no longer looked like she should wear a toe tag. She even had a chin.

Soon the room was abuzz with activity. The blond bridesmaids giggled and gossiped while their hair was done in identical twists. Hair dryers screamed. Cans of hair spray spritzed. One makeup artist brandished a mascara wand and said, "Now look up at the ceiling while I get those bottom lashes." Another held up a sponge and said, "Let me cover that nasty scrape on your arm."

At nine o'clock, Desiree was ready to be helped into the Hapsburg princess dress. Helen held it carefully, so Desiree wouldn't get scratched. The bride already had a long, thin scab on her arm.

"Did the dress do that when you tried it on at the store?" Helen said.

"No, the cook's cat got me," Desiree said.

Helen started on the one hundred slippery satin buttons, each the size of an aspirin.

Desiree, who'd been inert most of the morning, began fidgeting.

"Hold still or I'll never finish by ten o'clock," Helen said.

"I hate this dress," Desiree said.

"You don't have to wear it. You have a beautiful wedding dress in the closet. Let's put it on." Helen was in a rebellious mood. She headed for the closet to get out the cobweb dress. She was prepared to battle the dreaded rose dress to get Desiree what she wanted.

"No!" the bride shouted over the shrieking hair dryers. Heads turned. Eight bridesmaids stared like startled gazelles. Desiree had turned pale under her makeup. Was she that afraid of her mother?

"I only have to put up with this dress for an hour or two, and then I can wear what I want. I don't want to have to deal with Mother."

Helen understood, but said nothing. She still had

eighty-one buttons to go. Where was Mommy Dearest? She should be here by now.

The room resumed its dull roar. It was nine thirty when the last button was done and the ten-foot cathedral train was arranged. Helen's fingers ached and she'd torn a nail.

"There. That's it. Now I can pin on the veil," Helen said.

"Hold it! The mother should be here for that," the videographer said. He'd been buzzing around all morning like an irritating gnat.

"I don't want my mother putting on my veil," Desiree said. "She wouldn't anyway. It would mess up her manicure."

"The pictures won't look right without your mother," the still photographer added.

"I don't care." Desiree stamped her foot. Tears trembled at the edge of her eyes. The makeup artist hovered with powder and a foam wedge. Bridal tears could undo her work.

"Honey, you don't have to do anything you don't want to," her friend Emily soothed. At least, Helen thought it was Emily. Her hair was done up in a fashionable twist and she was wearing an elegant plum-colored Vera Wang. "But Kiki's late. I'll go look for her."

When the young woman ran from the room to begin her search, Helen knew for sure it was Emily. She made her Vera Wang flap. Helen liked that.

"Put my veil on," the bride commanded Helen.

"We can always stage it with the mother later," the still photographer said.

"It won't look the same," the videographer said. He was an auteur.

Helen pinned on the trailing veil.

"Ouch," the bride said.

"Sorry. I have to anchor it in your hair. There. You look beautiful." Helen patted Desiree on her shoulder. This was such a sad moment. Those words should have been said by the bride's mother, pronounced with love, pride, and teary eyes. Helen wanted to hug the forlorn little creature, but she didn't dare. With that dress, it would be like clutching glass shards to her bosom.

The bride studied herself in the full-length mirror. "I don't look as bad as I expected."

"You look lovely," Helen said.

Desiree smiled and almost seemed to believe her.

This is so sad, Helen thought. I'm bought and paid for—or maybe not. Helen wondered if Millicent had collected her money last night, but didn't have the nerve to ask.

"I'm glad it's you and not that awful Millicent," Desiree said. "She called my mother last night and said the most shocking things. She wanted her money right then, at the rehearsal dinner."

Imagine that, Helen thought. A merchant who wanted to be paid.

"Did she get it?" Helen said.

"Of course not. Mother said she'd give it to you today. I'll make sure she writes the check as soon as she shows up," the bride said.

Helen decided debt collection was Millicent's problem. She had enough to worry about. Helen checked the bridesmaids, making sure everyone was properly zipped and hooked, and no tags or straps showed. Then she unwrapped the bridal bouquet from the florist's tissue paper. The greenish white flowers looked like they'd been grown in a test tube.

Emily came flapping back, face flushed, makeup

smeared, hair hanging. The hairstylist and makeup artist hovered nearby for emergency repairs, but they couldn't do anything about the sweat stains on the plum Vera Wang.

"I've looked everywhere for your mother," Emily said. "No one's seen her. The organist wants to know when to start the procession. She's playing the same songs over and over."

"Better get my father in here," Desiree said.

Emily broke free of the flurry of combs and makeup and ran out again. She returned shortly with the bride's father. Brendan looked splendid in his pearl-gray morning coat. Helen wondered if his silver hair had been touched up. Helen expected Brendan to turn teary-eyed when he saw his daughter in her wedding dress, but he ignored her bridal beauty.

"What's she done this time?" he demanded. He couldn't even say Kiki's name.

"She hasn't shown up yet," Desiree said. "We're supposed to start at ten, and it's ten fifteen."

Brendan whipped out his cell phone and began punching in numbers. He had long, thin scratches on both hands. The cook's cat must have been busy.

"She's not answering her home or cell phone," Brendan said.

The blond bridesmaids looked bored. Their foreheads were shiny. The makeup artists kept patting them with powder, which speckled their black dresses. Hairstylists poked their coiffeurs with pins.

"People, what's the *problem?*" Jeff, the wedding planner, looked like a worried little boy. "If we don't start soon, the *flowers* will wilt and the *dinner* will be delayed, the *chocolate soufflés* will fall, and the *band* will . . ."

The dominoing disasters were cut short by the appearance of the groom, against all protocol.

"Desiree, darling," Luke said, "is there a problem?"

Chauncey, his best man, was right behind him, mobile red lips in their perpetual pucker. The bride's father strutted back and forth, looking at his watch and dialing his phone.

The room grew smaller and hotter. Desiree seemed overwhelmed by the heavy dress and the crushing crowd. She stood like a melting snow queen in her crystal-frosted gown. "It's ten thirty," she said. "The wedding should have started at ten. What should I do? Should we postpone the ceremony or go ahead?"

"Marry him," her father said. Helen could see the man's panic. His wife could delay this wedding, then run up even bigger bills for a second ceremony.

"Marry him," Chauncey the best man said. His voice quavered theatrically.

"Marry me." Luke kissed her passionately, but the bride remained rigid and unyielding.

The bridesmaids said nothing. Emily patted Desiree's back as if she were a colicky infant.

"Is that your mother's Rolls in the parking lot?"

Helen wasn't sure who said that.

The bride broke from Luke's embrace and looked out the window. When she turned back, Desiree's face was a mask of hate and shame. "That's her car. She's with her chauffeur. She's disgusting. I'm not holding up my wedding so that old tart can screw her chauffeur."

The bride took her father's arm defiantly. "Let's go."

The bridesmaids were shooed down the aisle like a flock of chickens.

The makeup artist gave Desiree a final dusting of powder. The organist launched into the bride's music. It was supposed to be a wedding march. But Helen thought the bride and her father looked like two invaders crossing enemy borders. They stomped down the aisle, Desiree's cathedral train raising small flurries of rose petals in their wake.

Just before they reached the altar, Desiree turned around and scanned the church for her mother. For one instant, Helen saw a vulnerable young bride who wanted her mother—even a mother like Kiki.

But there was no sign of the woman. Desiree squared her shoulders and faced the altar.

Her father presented her to Luke. Brendan did not kiss his daughter good-bye.

Chapter 6

"I now pronounce you man and wife," the minister said.

He could have pronounced them dead.

The bride glittered in the cold blue light of the stained-glass windows. The groom looked cyanotic.

"You may now kiss the bride."

Luke wrapped his arms around Desiree for a soap-opera smooch, then jumped back as if he'd been stung. That sent her staggering backward. The maid of honor caught the rejected bride. Desiree burst into tears.

There were titters and disapproving murmurs from the congregation. Only Helen guessed what had happened: The groom had cut his hand on the crystal dress. It was a vicious cut. Helen could see blood drops on the white carpet.

A quick-thinking bridesmaid swung the cathedral train away from the dark red spatters. The best man whipped off his cummerbund and gave it to Luke for a bandage.

Muddy brown tears ran down the bride's face and splotched her dress. So much for waterproof mascara.

Desiree dabbed at the tears with her veil, leaving nasty brown smudges on the delicate fabric.

Another couple might have laughed off the mishap. But Luke didn't laugh, nor did he comfort his new wife. Desiree did not care about his bloody hand. They stood at the altar, separate and self-absorbed. They'd failed as a couple from the first moment of their marriage.

The whole sorry incident was caught by two video cameras and a still photographer. Helen wondered if it would be edited out of the wedding photos or saved for the divorce proceedings.

This marriage was doomed, she decided. The perfect rehearsal led to a wedding-day disaster. All the practice and planning couldn't prevent these problems. Who knew a randy Kiki would skip her daughter's wedding for hot sex with her chauffeur? The bride didn't wear her crystal dress at the rehearsal, so the groom had no idea it was like embracing broken glass.

Luke never did kiss the bride. When the confusion died down the minister said, "Let me present the new Mr. and Mrs. Praine."

The traditional applause was tentative. Luke frowned. He was used to thundering ovations. He grabbed his wife's hand and held it up triumphantly, like a victorious boxer. Now the applause was louder and mixed with laughter.

Helen wasn't sure what Luke's gesture meant, but she didn't like it. Was he saying his wife was a prize? The little bride with her tear-blotched face looked confused.

That look pierced Helen's heart. She felt tears in her eyes. Helen never cried at weddings, but she felt sorry for poor unloved Desiree. She was a showpiece for her parents' ambitions and a bankroll for her husband's career.

The organist had the presence of mind to start the recessional music. Desiree walked down the aisle with her new husband. Helen could see the ugly brown stains on her veil. The groom's hand was wrapped in a bloody cummerbund. He smiled sheepishly. The bride seemed dazed.

Jeff, the wedding planner, was waiting in the cathedral vestibule with his emergency kit. While the receiving line formed, Jeff expertly bandaged the groom's hand. Then he and Helen worked on the bridal veil. They were hidden behind the bride's wide skirt, but they could hear the wedding guests.

Some stumbled through the reception line like bomb-blast survivors, too stunned to say anything. They just wanted out of there. Others made spiteful comments in what they thought were whispers. The cavernous cathedral magnified their voices. Jeff winced at every catty remark. He seemed to suffer for the bride.

Two black-clad women with bird legs, like crows in gold jewelry, were typical. Helen could hear snippets of their soft-voiced malice: "Her mother never showed up."

"She was screwing a chauffeur twenty years younger."

"Only twenty?"

"Personally, I'd go for the groom."

"Maybe she already has."

"Have you seen the bride's dress? She looks like Michael Jackson marrying Elvis."

When they got to the bride, the two crows cawed, "Darling, you look divine," and smothered her with perfume and Judas kisses.

Desiree turned to stone. The groom smiled through clenched capped teeth.

At last, the receiving line ended. The guests who hadn't fled picked up beribboned baskets of rose petals and straggled out to the cathedral steps. They threw the petals at the bride and groom like they were flinging trash, then rushed away. Helen couldn't bring herself to touch the mangled flowers. The petals looked like blood spots on the marble steps.

Jeff seemed near tears at his ruined wedding plans, but he pulled himself together and herded the wedding party inside for the pictures. Kiki still hadn't shown up.

Helen was furious. It felt good. It burned away her sadness for the bride. How could that selfish woman destroy her daughter's wedding for a backseat quickie? Except Kiki's quickie was turning into a sexual marathon. The Rolls sat in the parking lot, engine running, windows up. Helen wanted to knock on the black-tinted windows and drag Kiki out by her dyed hair, but it was not her place.

No one from the family approached the car. Helen wondered why.

Emily stayed with her friend, Desiree. The blond bridesmaid Lisa pulled Helen aside and said, "Do you know where the mother of the bride is?"

Her eyes strayed to the Rolls. Lisa already knew the answer.

"No," Helen lied.

"Do you know when she'll be coming?" Lisa's face turned bright red. "I mean, when she'll be here?"

"I have no idea," Helen said.

Helen knew exactly when Kiki would appear. She'd wait until Desiree was changing for the reception. Then Kiki would put on that blasted rose gown and make her grand entrance at the reception, glowing from her sexual athletics. She'd revel in the scandal.

Helen also knew why Kiki had pulled this stunt. Her daughter was marrying a handsome young man, but she'd show them she was still one hot mama.

Her absence had an impact on the pictures. The photographer and the videographer had to work around the lopsided wedding party. The bride refused to smile. The groom looked like a department-store dummy. The rest of the wedding party fidgeted like four-year-olds. The photos took two hours, including time out for powdering and hair pinning. Helen thought she would go mad if she had to drape Desiree's cathedral train on the altar steps one more time.

Finally, every photo opportunity was exhausted, along with every member of the wedding party.

"The photos are finished," the videographer pronounced.

Desiree brightened. She managed a smile, although it resembled a corpse's grin. "Now I can wear my real wedding dress."

Desiree ripped off her heavy veil and crown and dropped them on the floor. Then she ran upstairs to the dressing room.

That's right, girl, Helen thought. Get rid of what's dragging you down. She picked up the crown and veil and followed Desiree at a slower pace. She was drained by the wedding's raw emotions. Helen's magical night with Phil seemed years away. Today she could not believe any romance had a happy ending.

Memories of her own wedding haunted Helen. She'd been so in love with Rob. At the reception, she'd given him a bite of wedding cake. He'd mashed his piece into her face, to the delight of his cronies. Her maid of honor had applauded. Helen had laughed.

Her wedding photographer caught the scene. Helen thought it was the symbol of her marriage. She had seventeen years of sly humiliation, while she smiled and took it. Later, she learned Rob had had an affair with her maid of honor. She'd learned a lot she didn't want to know, after she picked up the crowbar and smashed her marriage.

Run, Desiree, she thought. Run away before it's too late. Luke doesn't love you. Don't waste your best years with a man who'll use you. Don't make the same mistake I did. You've only been married two hours. You can get an annulment.

Could she say that? Helen took on a mother's duties when she put on the bride's veil. A good mother would tell her daughter to get out of this mess.

Helen was greeted at the dressing-room door by the bracing smell of hot coffee. The breakfast buffet had been cleared. Jeff had set out plates of chicken and cucumber sandwiches, and dainty cookies.

What tempted Helen was the fresh coffee warming on the burner. Coffee would give her courage. After a cup of caffeine, she could drop some hints to Desiree. If the bride seemed receptive, she'd mention an annulment. Helen draped the dropped veil over a chair and reached for the coffeepot.

"You don't have time for that," Desiree said. "I want this thing off. Now."

So much for Helen's maternal fantasies. She was a servant and she'd better not forget it.

Helen approached Desiree as though the bride were a rabid animal. She carefully swung the heavy cathedral train out of the way and began unbuttoning the wretched dress for the last time. Desiree wriggled impatiently. A button slipped from Helen's grasp.

This poor bride has had a terrible day, Helen thought, then rebelled at her sudden attack of saintliness. She was not going to play Victorian maid to Lady Desiree.

"The more you move, the longer this will take," Helen said.

She stopped unbuttoning until Desiree stood still. Emily the peacemaker came over with coffee and cookies for the bride. That seemed to calm her.

Helen finished the last button and said, "There, you're free. Step out of this carefully so you don't get scratched."

"Are you going to preserve your wedding dress?" said Amy, one of the dumber blond bridesmaids.

"So I can always remember this day?" The bride tore the dress from Helen's hands, but that didn't satisfy her fury. With one swift movement, Desiree grabbed the coffeepot and hurled it at the dress. Coffee splashed and shattered glass flew across the floor. A bridesmaid screamed.

"What are you doing?" Amy was shocked. "You could at least give that dress to charity."

"So another woman can be as miserable as I am?" Desiree said. "Throw it in the trash."

Emily bundled the ruined gown into a trash bag and hauled it out of sight. Jeff mopped up the spilled coffee and swept away the broken glass. The bridesmaids were afraid to say anything.

Desiree stood in her pure white La Perla underwear, showing off her slender body in a way that reminded Helen of Kiki. Desiree stretched like a cat, then started talking as if her seven-thousand-dollar tantrum never happened. "That dress hurt my back and shoulders. What do you think it weighed?"

"About twenty-five pounds, plus the train," Helen said. "Why don't you rest a moment or have a sandwich?"

"No, I want to put on my real wedding dress," Desiree said. "The beautiful one. That ceremony was my mother's idea. The reception is for my father's business. But the afternoon cocktail party is mine. I'm going to have fun."

I'm happy to help, Helen thought. Once the bride was buttoned into her fabulous cobweb dress, Helen could leave. She forgave Desiree her strange, sudden flash of temper. Maybe in her case, rage was a healthy response. Helen didn't much care. She wanted to sit by the Coronado pool with a book and some wine. She could feel the cold glass in her hand and the warm sun on her hair.

"Terrific," Helen said. "I'll get your dress out of the closet."

The door was stuck, a common phenomenon in the Florida humidity. Helen pulled on the handle and felt a weight behind it. The door was jammed.

It was that blasted hoop skirt. Helen knew she shouldn't have shoved the rose dress into that closet with Desiree's precious cobweb wedding dress. Now the door was caught. If she ripped that dress, Kiki would tear her heart out.

Helen's arms were strong from hauling heavy wedding dresses. She pulled harder on the door. It wouldn't budge.

"What's keeping you?" Desiree tapped her foot impatiently.

"The door's stuck."

"Let's get Jeff," the bride said.

Helen didn't want Jeff to see the rose dress squashed in the closet. He might report her to Kiki.

"Just needs a little old-fashioned female force." Helen tugged harder. Nothing happened.

She would not be defeated by a lousy door. Not when a cold glass of wine was calling. Helen gave the door a mighty yank.

It opened.

Out tumbled a waterfall of red-black taffeta, yards and yards of it, tucked and folded into a giant bouquet. The rose dress must have fallen off the hanger—and fallen into something. It sure didn't smell like roses.

The slippery dark fabric was wrapped around logs. Then Helen saw the logs were legs, shapely legs ending in size-four heels. She heard screams and realized they were coming from her.

She'd found Kiki.

The missing mother of the bride slid out of the closet in the rose dress. Helen couldn't see her face. It was covered with a white cobweb. Helen pushed it aside.

Kiki stared blindly at Helen. Her mouth was open and angry, her eyes were wide and cold. She was dead, smothered with her daughter's marvelous wedding dress.

"Oh, no," the bride wailed. "Oh, no, no. I loved that dress."

That's when Rod the chauffeur burst into the room.

"Has anyone seen Kiki?" he said.

Chapter 7

"Ewww," Amy said. "What's wrong with her nails?"

Nails? What nails? Kiki looked like a big, stiff doll. Helen didn't even notice her fingers.

She felt strangely warm and disconnected, as if she were wrapped in cotton.

Shock, said one side of her mind.

Shit, said the other. I'm never going to get that cold wine.

There were shrieks and screams as a dozen cell phones simultaneously called 911.

Only Amy, the airhead bridesmaid, noticed the dead woman's manicure. "Her nails are too short." Amy's gray eyes were wide with horror. For her, a broken nail was a tragedy. Murder was unthinkable.

Kiki's small curled fingers seemed pathetically childlike. The gold daggerlike nails were gone. They'd been cut to the quick. Why would she mutilate her manicure?

She didn't, Helen realized. Kiki would never do her own nails. She'd have a manicurist come to her house the morning of the wedding.

This morning. A thousand years ago.

The curled fingers no longer looked sad. They looked creepy. Anyone who watched TV knew about DNA. If Kiki had scratched her killer, she'd have traces of the DNA under her nails. Her killer had cut them before she—or he—shoved the body in the closet.

Then I opened the door, Helen thought, and left my prints all over it. She felt sick.

Run! she told herself. The police will be here any minute. Everyone heard me fight with Kiki last night. With my past, I haven't a chance.

Helen looked around frantically for her purse. She could slip out the side door before the police arrived.

Stay! said her rational side. You're a servant who opened the wrong closet. Nobody noticed you. Nobody cares about you. Sit tight. Of course your prints are on that door. You're supposed to help the wedding party.

"Somebody help me turn her over," Brendan said. "I want to look for wounds."

The father of the bride—and a lawyer—was tampering with a crime scene, but nobody said anything. The groom and the best man rushed over to help. Helen thought she saw Chauncey's too-red lips form a fleeting smile before he assumed a properly solemn expression. He had reason to smile. His theater was saved. Kiki's untimely death brought him a hundred thousand dollars.

Chauncey, Brendan, and Luke had trouble lifting the unwieldy body in the outrageous belled skirt. Helen saw the skirt had a huge rip on the side. The stitching had given way in spots, and the roses bulged like tumors.

"Give us a hand here," Brendan called. Another groomsman, Jason, pushed forward to lift Kiki. The men looked like high-class undertakers in their formal black tuxes.

Terrific, Helen thought. The crime scene was contaminated by the four chief suspects. Make that five. Rod the chauffeur was holding the cobweb dress.

No, six. Desiree grabbed the dress out of his hands. "What are you doing with your filthy paws on my wedding dress?" she said.

"I had to get it out of the way or someone would step on it." Rod did not sound quite so deferential now that he was a millionaire.

"Don't touch anything of mine." Desiree, now wrapped in an oversized white robe, looked shrunken and older than her mother.

As the four men turned over the body, the hoop skirt flipped up, exposing Kiki's bare bottom.

"No gunshot or stab wounds on the backside," Brendan said coldly.

Jason seemed to be suppressing a smirk. Luke looked poleaxed by this new view of his mother-in-law. Good thing he didn't see the golden dollar sign on the other side, Helen thought.

"OK, let's put her back the way we found her," Brendan said.

Fat chance, Helen thought. She surveyed the chaos in the room. The staff was standing against the walls, trying to make themselves invisible. The hairstylists held silent dryers. The makeup artists put down their brushes. Even Jeff looked lost. He had no plan for this wedding emergency.

In the center of the room, the bride shed bitter tears into the magical cobweb dress she would never wear. "It's ruined. It's all ruined," she cried, and wiped her eyes on the gossamer skirt.

Whether Desiree was weeping over her wedding, her marriage, or her dress, Helen didn't know. She certainly wasn't crying for her mother.

"She didn't have the decency to die in her underwear," Desiree said. "She mooned everyone."

Amy started giggling wildly. Bridesmaid Beth gave her a sharp elbow in the ribs, and she shut up.

The bride shook with shame and fury. The groom patted her back with the same hand that had held her dead mother. His touch was tentative, as if he expected his bride to sprout leathery wings and scales. Luke had the devil's own luck on his wedding day. His vicious mother-in-law was dead—and her fortune went to his new wife.

The father of the bride barked into his cell phone, "I don't care! Get his ass off the golf course and get him over here right now." Brendan strutted back and forth, a short, energetic general calling in reinforcements.

The blond bridesmaids cried and clung to one another. Their black dresses were no longer symbols of sophistication. They were mourning clothes.

"I'll never wear this dress again," Beth said sadly, "and it's a Vera Wang."

"I've never seen a real dead person before," Amy said. "She looks gross."

No one went near Kiki. That made her death even lonelier. Helen thought she looked oddly pretty with her gray-green skin, blond hair, and dark rose dress. As long as you didn't look too closely at the popped eyes speckled with red pinpoint petechiae.

Poor Kiki. She seemed so small in death. Helen remembered what Millicent had said. "If she were a man, would you notice her outrageous behavior?" The heart of a Hollywood mogul had been trapped in that little body.

All eight groomsmen crowded into the room. Helen felt as if the air had been sucked out of the place. She leaned against the wall next to a silent hairstylist, and hoped everyone would keep quiet until the police arrived. But the drama wasn't over.

Lisa, looking like Nemesis in her black bridesmaid dress, marched straight up to Jason. Her brown eyes were electric with malice. "Since you were the last one to see Kiki alive last night," she said, "maybe you can tell the police who killed her."

Jason's handsome face took on a feral look. "You're crazy," he said. "I left the restaurant with everyone else."

"And waited for her in your car," Lisa said.

Everyone in the room stared at her. Last night Jason, her sometime escort, had humiliated her. Today she was getting her revenge. "I heard Kiki tell the chauffeur to go on without her after the rehearsal dinner because you would take her home."

Jason's voice was a knife. "Here's what I heard: You went home alone. Nobody wants a bitch like you."

"Quiet! Both of you," the father of the bride said. "Nobody talks to the police without a lawyer. I've called in some favors. Friends of mine in the legal community are on their way."

Now Helen understood Brendan's frantic cell phone calls.

Lisa was outraged. "You're getting lawyers for the wedding party? Do you want your wife's killer to get away?"

"Ex-wife," he corrected. "And our kind are not killers."

Helen suddenly realized the offer of attorneys did not extend to the help. The staff was being set up to take the rap. One makeup artist turned so pale her foundation looked like a beige mask.

Helen began edging toward the door. She would run if she was going to be a scapegoat.

"Where are you going?" Brendan snapped his cell phone shut.

"I need some air," Helen said. "I feel faint."

"Open a window, somebody," Brendan commanded. "You! Sit down and put your head between your knees."

And kiss my rear end good-bye, Helen thought. They're going to pin this on me for sure. She felt trapped. There was no way she could make it to the door.

"I know you. You had the fight with my wife last night," Brendan said.

"Ex-wife," Helen said. "Everybody had a fight with her last night, including you."

"But your fight was special," Brendan said. "She threatened to fire you. You killed her to keep your job."

Helen laughed, although she was so frightened it sounded wobbly. "You think I killed her for six-seventy an hour? I'd make more money stamping license plates in prison. At least there my living expenses would be covered."

She thought it was a good bluff. Now she attacked. "I can always get another low-paying job. But what about you? Kiki was after your last nickel. The cops will check your bank records and see you're headed for bankruptcy and Kiki was demanding more money each day. I heard her."

Brendan's eyebrows shot up. Helen knew she'd

scored. She tried another thrust. "And your daughter had a few fights with her mother." As soon as she said that, Helen knew she'd made a mistake.

"You leave my daughter out of this." Brendan's voice was low and dangerous. His face was a weird wine red. Brendan didn't love Desiree, but he wouldn't let an inferior attack anything that was his.

"Shut up," Desiree shouted. "Everyone shut up."

Helen could hear the sirens now, howling like lost souls outside the church.

"The Sunnysea police are here." Amy was never afraid to state the obvious. "And a bunch of gray guys are getting out of Beemers. Are those the lawyers?"

Brendan looked out the window. "Yes," he said. "Now remember, everyone. No talking unless the lawyers say it's okay."

But it was much too late for that.

Chapter 8

"Listen here, Detective, I know Bob Cambridge. Do you know who he is?"

Brendan, the father of the bride, was swollen with self-importance. He looked like a lovesick frog.

Detective Janet Smith neatly deflated him. "The person you really need to know is me. I'm the detective in charge of this investigation. Senator Bob Cambridge trusts me to get the job done right."

Detective Smith whipped out her cell phone. "But if you'd like to talk with him, I can call his private number right now."

Brendan did not take her phone. He backed away slightly and ran his hands through his hair. Helen saw he had a small bald spot.

"No, no, that's not necessary."

"Good. Then take off your shoes. We need them for comparison to the shoe prints we'll find at the crime scene. We'll be using an electrostatic dust print lifter."

Helen bit her lip to hide a smile. She wondered if Detective Smith had the senator's number—or just Brendan's. She'd pulled a few bluffs like that herself. Smith was all business, but Helen thought the detective enjoyed ordering around the pompous Brendan.

"I don't see—" Brendan started to say.

"I know you don't see," she said. "You also didn't see anything wrong with moving the body and disturbing the crime scene, although you are an attorney and an officer of the court. You do realize that has complicated the case, sir? It's going to take longer now to find the killer. It makes you look suspect."

Smith sounded sad rather than angry, as if Brendan was one more burden she had to bear.

Brendan started blustering. "Young woman, are you accusing me of murder? I demand to see my attorney."

"I'm stating a fact. We cannot have any more people contaminating this crime scene."

"What crime scene?" Brendan said. "The room is roped off and we're standing in the hall."

"This whole building is a crime scene and you will be removed from it as soon as possible. Now take off your shoes and you can see your attorney."

Brendan leaned against the wall and reluctantly removed his perfectly polished shoes. He had a small hole in his black sock. Maybe that's why he'd fought so hard to keep his shoes on, Helen thought.

At first the bridesmaids were happy to take off their high heels. They wiggled their red, tortured toes. Then airhead Amy said, "When do we get our shoes back?"

"When we don't need them anymore," said a tech crawling around on the floor near the bride's room door.

"When's that?" Amy said.

"Depends," he said. "Could be hours. Could be years."

"Those shoes are Jimmy Choos!" Amy cried. "Do you know what they cost?"

"I know my wife can't afford them," the tech said.

Even Amy had enough sense to shut up. Helen wondered if any of the men were renting the shoes with their formal wear. They could run up a colossal bill if this was a long investigation. Her own shoes were so old, she didn't care if she ever got them back.

Helen had been frightened when the police first arrived. When she saw Detective Smith take on the bully Brendan, her fear turned to respect. She didn't think Smith would railroad her just to make an arrest.

Now Helen was fascinated. She loved crime shows like *CSI*, and here she was in the middle of a real investigation. She could see the police preparing the roped-off room for the electrostatic dust print lifter, or ESDL. Pieces of plastic film about a foot square were laid on the floor in and around the closet where Kiki was found. On one side, the film was shiny, like chrome. On the other, it was black. The black side was down on the hardwood floor.

The ESDL was about the size of a shoe box. The techs explained that the film would be electrostatically charged. Dust particles would be attracted to the film. They would pick up shoe prints and other evidence in the dust.

Helen wondered if the ESDL would pick up anything useful. The floor had been trampled like the Kansas prairie in a cattle drive.

The wedding party surrendered their shoes. Each pair was marked, tagged, and bagged. Then Detective Smith said, "Now, if you will accompany Officer Fernandez to the church school building."

"Is that absolutely necessary?" Brendan said. "Can't you take our statements here?"

"As I said before, this is a crime scene," Detective Smith said. "It's been contaminated enough already."

Brendan heard the rebuke.

But it was a good question, Helen thought. That high-priced herd of lawyers wasn't going to let anyone say anything. Maybe the cops enjoyed running up a big legal bill for the rich jerk Brendan.

The wedding party walked in a barefoot procession across the parking lot. In their formal dress, Helen thought they looked like that old Beatles album, *Abbey Road.* They were an eerie sight: eight perfectly matched bridesmaids and groomsmen, all in black, all silent, their heads down. Only the bride wore white. She was wrapped like a mummy in her terry robe.

Helen followed in their wake, the only servant. The police had taken the phone numbers and addresses of the wedding planner, hairstylists, and makeup artists, then let them go home. They would be interviewed later. But Helen had discovered the body. She was a major witness.

The wedding party and Helen were put into the honeycomb of church classrooms and offices, one person to a room. A uniformed police officer patrolled the hall like a school monitor.

She heard weeping but couldn't tell who it was.

Helen wound up in a Sunday school classroom with tiny chairs. Even the teacher seemed to be a midget. Helen tried to sit in a pint-sized chair, but her knees were under her chin. She felt huge and misshapen.

She stretched, stood up, and walked around the room. The blackboard was surrounded by children's drawings of Noah's ark. Two by two. That was what started the trouble—all those mismatched couples: Brendan and Kiki. Kiki and Rod. Kiki and Jason. Desiree and Luke.

The blackboard's emptiness was tempting. Helen wrote the suspects' names on it. There were a lot of them. Enough, she hoped, to keep the cops interested in someone besides herself. Then she added four lines that looked almost like poetry:

The bride got a fortune.
The ex saved his fortune.
The best man saved his theater.
The boy-toy chauffeur became a millionaire, and the groom became a rich kept man.

It looked like everyone had a good reason for wanting Kiki dead. The only one who lost out was Jason. Whatever his motive for cozying up to Kiki last night, it was too soon for him to reap any benefits.

She wondered if writing down the names looked suspicious. She erased the blackboard.

Pace. Pace. Pace. Helen tried to stay calm. She had a bad moment when she was fingerprinted in a room down the hall. Airhead Amy came out of the room as Helen went in.

"They put black stuff on my fingers." Amy dabbed at them with a lace handkerchief.

"At least it matches your dress," Helen said.

The tech explained he needed Helen's fingerprints for elimination purposes, since she'd grabbed the closet door handle.

I have nothing to fear, Helen told herself. My prints aren't on file in St. Louis. She'd never been booked for the assault on her ex-husband, Rob. I'm nobody. There's no way they'll find out I'm wanted by the court in St. Louis.

She wanted to believe that. But she'd also believed Rob would love her forever and they would live happily ever after.

Back in the classroom with the pint-sized chairs, Helen paced and looked at the Jesus Loves Me posters. The cathedral believed in a blond country-club Christ, even though there were few natural blonds in the Middle East. If the real Jesus appeared, would they hand him a mop and make him clean the johns?

The sun was in a late-afternoon slant when Helen finally met the two Sunnysea homicide detectives. They were in the minister's office, a gloomy room full of guilt and power. The dark furniture was designed to overwhelm. Helen wondered how many major donors wrote checks just to get out of there.

Detective Bill McIntyre had the pumped-up body she saw in lots of younger cops. His thick neck and puffed pecs were muscular, but the effect was oddly soft. His dark mustache looked like a woolly bear caterpillar. Helen's grandmother could predict cold weather by the woolly bears. It's going to be a bad winter, Helen thought.

Detective Janet Smith was the scary one. Helen had seen her confront Brendan. She was a thin blonde with a long crooked nose and hard brown eyes. She had yellow nicotine stains on her fingers and no wedding ring.

Smith's hair was sensibly short. Her dark pantsuit was professional but not stylish. Her black lace-up shoes would not come off if she chased a suspect. If I tried to bolt, Helen thought, she'd run me down.

Detectives Smith and McIntyre asked her a million questions, mostly about the room.

What time did Helen get there? Who else was there when she arrived? Were the lights turned on or off when she arrived? Were the doors open, closed, locked, or unlocked? What about the bathroom door? The windows?

Helen's head hurt. The more the two detectives asked, the less she knew. She thought the doors were open—no, closed. She wasn't sure. The windows were definitely closed. Unless they were open.

"That's a nasty scratch on your arm," Detective Smith said.

"A wedding dress got me," Helen said. "I was scratched by the crystal beading."

"Mind if we photograph it?"

Helen let Detective McIntyre take Polaroids of her arm. She hoped she looked calm. She could feel the panic rising inside her, drowning out any reasonable thought.

The two detectives escorted her across the parking lot and back to the bride's room. Techs were still working in the room, and black fingerprint powder was everywhere. Helen felt sick, even though Kiki's body was gone.

"We'd like you to walk us through what you did when you arrived this morning," Detective Smith said.

Helen closed her eyes and tried to remember. "I came in this door. It was open. The light was on. Jeff—he's the wedding planner—had coffee going. He'd set out a breakfast buffet. I checked the room and the bathroom to make sure they were clean. Everything was fine."

She went through the details of that endless day until she said, "I opened the closet door and found Kiki. I don't have to open the door again, do I?"

"No," Smith said.

It was bad enough having to walk over there. It was

an ordinary closet with a couple of padded hangers. Now it yawned, evil and empty, the air around it heavy with hate and fear.

Helen knew this was her imagination, but it didn't help.

"When you opened the closet door, did you touch the body?" Detective Smith said.

"I'm not sure," Helen said. "I tried to catch Kiki when she fell. I think I grabbed her dress."

She saw the skirt flip up again, felt the falling fabric and the tumbling legs. Then the scene shifted and Helen saw Brendan and his buddies lift the body, and Kiki moon the wedding party. It was Kiki's final shot at her ex. Helen started laughing and couldn't stop.

"What's so funny?" Detective Smith sounded suspicious. "Why are you laughing?"

"Because I can't cry," Helen said. She was sick from fatigue, shock, and a day-long stew of ugly emotions.

"Is there anything else you want to tell us?" Detective Smith said.

Helen couldn't think of anything. She couldn't think, period.

It was nearly six o'clock when Helen was finally free to leave. She used the pay phone in the church hall to tell Millicent the bad news: Kiki was dead.

"Damn, I'm sorry," Millicent said.

She was the first person who actually said so, Helen thought.

But then Millicent kept talking. "Kiki still hasn't paid for those dresses. I called her last night and she promised to give you the check this morning. Her daughter heard me, and I wasn't very nice. In fact, I sort of lost it. I can hardly run over there now to offer my condolences and collect the check."

"What's going to happen?" Helen said.

"I'll have to collect the money from the estate," Millicent said. "That may be faster than trying to get it out of Kiki. She liked to play power games with her money—you saw how she treated Chauncey. She may have done me a favor, getting herself murdered."

Millicent sounded almost cheerful when she hung up.

Helen wondered if the wedding reception had been canceled. She didn't care. The wedding was in ruins. The bridal gowns had been bagged and tagged as evidence. The makeup jobs were streaked with tears. The bridesmaids' Vera Wangs were wrinkled and ripe with fear sweat. The miserable day was over.

A crowd of hungry reporters waited on the cathedral steps. Helen ducked out the side door, ran for the shop van, and drove out of the church lot.

Millicent's was closed by the time she arrived. Helen parked the van behind the shop and poked the keys through the mail slot. Then she started walking home barefoot, enjoying the feel of the sun-warmed concrete on her feet. Because it was Florida, no one noticed she wasn't wearing shoes.

Helen was nearly at the Coronado when she realized she hadn't told the detectives about her fight with Kiki.

It's not important, she decided. I just want to go home and get that glass of wine.

This day couldn't get any worse. But Helen was wrong about that, too.

Chapter 9

When she got home, Helen didn't want that drink after all. She wanted the comfort of Phil's arms. She could feel him wrapped around her. She could feel his soft hair and smell his spicy aftershave.

Helen wasn't a woman alone anymore. She had a man who loved her—a faithful man. Phil was nothing like Rob, the rat she'd married.

The day had taken its toll. Helen felt like the detectives had beaten her with a rubber hose. Her hair stuck out in six directions. She was sweaty and shoeless. Her feet were dirty from the city sidewalks, and she limped a bit after stepping on the last bottle cap in America. She needed a shower. Then she needed Phil.

In the Coronado parking lot, Helen saw a woman with long curly red hair struggling with a pile of bulky luggage. She was trying to drag two black wheeled suitcases and a surfboard-sized piece of equipment over the curb and up the sidewalk. Her skin-tight jeans and spike heels made it hard for her to lift the bags.

"Can I help you?" Helen said.

The woman stuck out a taloned hand and said, "I'm

Kendra, the Kentucky Songbird. I have a song on the *Billboard* charts. I'm staying with my husband."

"Warren?" Poor Margery, Helen thought. She was in for a surprise. Her handsome dancing partner had a much younger wife.

"No, Phil. Didn't he tell you about me?"

"No," Helen said. The rest of her words wilted and died.

Kendra gave a gusty sigh. "I don't know what I'm going to do with that man. I told him to let the neighbors know I'll be moving in."

"Moving in," Helen repeated numbly.

"Yes, ma'am," Kendra said brightly. "You must be Helen. He told me all about you. You're a—what? Oh, right, a clerk at a wedding dress shop."

She looked at Helen's dirty bare feet. "Must be one of those hippy-dippy places. Even country brides aren't barefoot and pregnant nowadays."

Kendra's heels were red and glittery. And round, Helen thought nastily.

"I have a gig here in Fort Lauderdale at a big nightclub on U.S. 1, and of course I'm staying with my husband." Kendra's soft country accent was a cross between Billy Ray Cyrus and The Judds.

"Your husband," Helen said.

"Thanks for offering to help carry this. Phil said how nice and friendly you were. He'd said you'd do just about anything for a person when you hardly knew him."

Helen thought about what she'd done for Phil last night. She'd been real friendly. She felt the hot blood rush to her face.

"Sure," Helen said. One word was all she could handle without killing herself or Kendra.

Kendra promptly dumped both suitcases on Helen as if she were a porter. "Here. I'll keep the keyboard. You take these," she said.

It was like moving a pair of refrigerators. Helen staggered behind the woman. On closer inspection, Kendra's hair was orange-red, a color not found in nature unless you were an opium poppy. It reached almost to her round behind, which switched rhythmically back and forth as she walked. Kendra pointed to Phil's apartment. "That's his place there."

Kendra was wearing stage makeup. Her dramatic black eyeliner gave her Egyptian eyes. Her short pink sweater showed her nipples. She moved in a sweet, heavy cloud of perfume.

"I know," Helen said. Last night we made the bedsprings rock, she thought. Phil did absolutely everything, except tell me about you. Oh, wait. He did mention you. He said, "The romance went out of my marriage with the wedding. My ex got caught up in making sure the bridesmaids' ribbons matched the groomsmen's cummerbunds."

"My ex." Not "my wife."

What else had Phil said? Helen searched her shell-shocked brain. "I felt like an afterthought. I never lost that feeling."

I am Phil's afterthought. I'm the fool he screwed while his wife was on the road. Friendly old Helen, providing aid and comfort to lonely husbands. She wanted to hurl Kendra's luggage into the pool. She wanted to throw Phil in after it. She wanted to drag out his drowned body and stomp him into the ground. She wanted to bury him under twenty tons of coral rock. Then she wanted to dig him up, so she could kill him all over again.

"You're a country singer?" Helen said with an odd croak.

"Number ninety-seven on the Billboard country music chart." Kendra thrust out her chest proudly, as if the chart was printed on her front. Her breasts and her dangly earrings jiggled simultaneously. Kendra didn't look like a country singer to Helen. She looked like a man-stealing twit.

"What's your song called?" Helen said.

" 'You Can't Divorce My Heart.' " Kendra's perfume drifted back to Helen in a choking cloud.

"I see," Helen said. And she did.

"Well, here's his place. Don't you want to come in and see Phil?" Kendra said.

"I already have," Helen said.

She dropped the suitcases in front of Phil's door and ran to her apartment. Her hands shook so badly she had trouble unlocking her door. Her ex had betrayed her with their next-door neighbor Sandy. Now Phil, the first man she'd loved in a long time, betrayed her too. She raced to the bathroom and stood in the shower until she was sure the water running down her face was not tears.

She got out, wrapped herself in a big robe, and turned on her hair dryer. She couldn't hear her sobs over the motor's howl. By the time her hair was dry, so were her eyes. When she shut off the hair dryer, she heard the pounding on her door.

"Helen, open up. Please. I have to talk to you."

It was Phil. She wanted to ignore him, but she walked to the door with new determination. She would get this over with. She would get this liar out of her life.

Phil was freshly shaved, with a tiny patch of shaving cream on his throat. Last night, she would have licked it off. Now she wanted to cut his throat. He tried to take her in his arms, but she dodged him.

"Helen, I'm so sorry," he said. "What did she say to you? She twists everything around. She knows I love you. She'll do anything to break us up."

"I don't think she twisted this. She said you were her husband."

"Our divorce isn't final for another month," Phil said. "But believe me, we're divorced. I'll never go back to her."

"Then why is she living with you? And why didn't you tell me?" Helen hoped he didn't hear the hurt in her words.

"I've been tied up in court on that charity orgy case, as you well know. Thanks to me, you're not mixed up in it."

Oh, no. He wasn't going slide by like that. "We spent last night together. Why didn't you say something then?"

"Because I knew you'd act this way." If he'd searched the dictionary, he couldn't find seven words that would make her madder. Phil looked like a high-school kid caught with a roach in his locker.

"Helen, Kendra has an important gig in Fort Lauderdale. She doesn't have enough money to stay at a hotel during the season. I told her she could sleep on my couch."

"Kendra!" Helen said. "What kind of country name is that?"

"She's crossover country." Phil was talking too fast, the way her ex-husband, Rob, did when he was lying.

"Oh, yeah?" Helen said. "What happens when she crosses over to your bed?"

"See? I knew you wouldn't understand," Phil said.

"I understand perfectly," Helen said. "Your wife wants to sleep with you."

"Ex-wife," Phil said. "She's only here for her career. It's all she's ever cared about. You forgot. We're getting divorced."

"You forgot. Divorced people don't live together."

"The solution is simple," Phil said. "I can move in with you. She can have my place."

Helen was outraged. "This is how you propose the next step in our relationship? What am I? A hotel? Maybe you don't take us seriously, but I do."

"This is why I didn't say anything about Kendra last night." Phil was yelling. "You're hysterical."

Helen felt her blood boil and her bleeding heart turn into a black charcoal briquette. The H word was her own personal H bomb. When a man called a woman hysterical, he meant she was crazy.

"I am NOT hysterical," she shouted. "I am justifiably angry." She slammed the door in his face.

There was another knock. Helen opened the door again and said, "I told you I never wanted to—Oh, hi, Margery."

Her landlady was wearing her usual purple shorts set, but now her face was a delicate heliotrope. Margery was mad. "What the hell is going on here? This is an apartment building, not a cat house. Phil's got some redhead moving in with him and the two of you are screaming at each other on your doorstep. I won't have it."

"I'm sorry," Helen said. "But the redhead is Phil's wife."

"What wife? He's divorced."

"It's not final for a month. Her name is Kendra and

she's a country-western singer. She's got a gig here and she can't afford a hotel, so she's staying at his place."

"Dumb bastard. Phil was probably trying to help her out," Margery said. "He's well meaning but not too bright when it comes to exes. Why don't you let him move in with you?"

"Because he's taking me for granted." Helen was gripping her arms so tightly she left red marks on them. "He just assumed he could hang his clothes in my closet and put his toothbrush in my holder. I'm not going to let him."

"You want moonlight and roses?" Margery said. "At your age, you should know better."

But Helen had seen her landlady dancing by the pool with the silver-haired Warren. Margery had romance at seventy-six.

"Come outside by the pool," Margery said. "Peggy's there. We'll have some wine and talk it over. You need to think about this."

"I need to get dressed," Helen said.

"No, you don't. In that big old robe, you're wearing more clothes than Peggy and I combined."

Helen grabbed the box of pretzels from the kitchen counter and obediently followed her landlady to the pool. Peggy was stretched out on a chaise longue, with Pete patrolling her shoulder. Helen gave him a pretzel. Margery gave her a glass of wine.

Peggy took one look at Helen and said, "What's wrong?"

"Phil's wife moved in with him," she said.

"Awwwk!" Pete snapped the pretzel in two.

Helen could feel the tears starting again, but she tried to stop them. "I am not crying over that man. He's not worth it." She downed a hefty jolt of wine. That made her feel safe and warm. "He's living with a country singer named Kendra."

"That's rotten," Peggy said. She'd had her share of betrayal.

Margery set fire to a Marlboro and said, "Helen, it's not that bad. Phil's divorce will be final in a month. He's letting his ex stay with him while she sings at some club in Lauderdale. She can't afford a hotel. He did something stupid trying to be nice. Don't get all bent out of shape. Why are you doing this to yourself?"

"Why didn't he tell me Kendra was staying with him?" Helen cried.

"He was probably scared you'd go ballistic. Which you did."

"I had a good reason," Helen said. "She's so nasty. She made these insinuating little remarks about us, like I was a mercy screw. It was degrading."

"Of course it was," Margery said. "She wanted it that way. She's a sly one. And you're going to leave him alone with a hundred pounds of red-haired temptation? Helen, just let Phil move in with you. He's there almost every night, anyway."

"I would if he said he loved me. But he wants to do it because I'm convenient."

"Helen Hawthorne," Margery said. "If you let a man like Phil get away because you're so stubborn, then you are a fool."

Helen wiped angry tears from her eyes. "He can go to hell," she said.

"Don't worry," Margery said. "He will."

Helen wanted desperately to change the subject. "Phil was just part of this wretched day. There's a lot more. Kiki was murdered."

"Awwk," Pete said.

Margery dropped her cigarette. It glowed in the dusk. She retrieved it and said, "Another murder? How do you get mixed up in these things?"

"Murder is easy at a wedding," Helen said. "Everyone wants to kill the mother of the bride."

"The caterer did it," Peggy said. "Or the photographer. Or the sister with the tattooed boyfriend who was banned from the ceremony."

"Nothing that simple," Helen said. "Ordinary people have those problems. We're talking major money. Let me tell you what happened."

When she finished, Margery said, "How much trouble are you in? Do you want me to retain Colby Cox for you? She's expensive, but she owes me several favors." Colby was one of the premier defense lawyers in South Florida.

"No, there are enough other suspects to keep the cops busy," Helen said.

"The offer stands. I'll call her anytime you need her," Margery said. "Helen? Are you there, Helen?"

Helen was staring at Phil's door. It stayed closed. He had not followed her to the pool. He won't even walk across the yard for me, Helen thought. Damn him. She took a drink, but her wineglass was empty. She refilled it and said, "I'm going to my room to brood."

"Good idea," Margery said. "You've had a dog of a day. If you want company, knock on my door. I'll be out till late tonight, but if you see my light, come on over."

"Going any place interesting?" Peggy said.

"Dancing with Warren." Helen thought Margery smiled like a woman with a secret.

"Warren, now, is it? Is there romance for rent in 2C?" Peggy teased.

"Please." Margery blew a huge smoke screen. "Warren's just for fun. He's one of those rare men who likes women his own age. I go out with three other friends. He dances with all of us. I think he's giving Elsie lessons. She's seventy-eight and having the time of her life—if she doesn't break her hip twirling on the dance floor."

"Never mind Elsie," Peggy said. "What about Margery? Helen could get you a good price on a wedding dress."

Margery snorted. "Young people. You've got one thing on your mind."

"Sex?" Peggy said.

"Marriage," Margery said. "I'm past the marrying stage. Men Warren's age don't want wives. They want a nurse with a purse. I'm not that desperate. He's strictly recreation."

"Awwk," Pete said.

Helen wondered if she'd ever be smart enough to use men that way.

Chapter 10

Phil knocked on her door three times Saturday night. Helen refused to open it. Then, with perfect lover's logic, she was angry that he didn't knock at all on Sunday.

Helen stayed inside all day, drinking cheap wine and brooding. She held a little film festival of failure in her head. Scenes from her marriage played again and again. She relived the afternoon she caught her cheating husband with their neighbor, Sandy. She saw Rob's hairy butt bouncing in the air. How could she have loved a man who needed Nair on his rump?

She saw herself struggling with Kendra's suitcases while that red-haired vixen stabbed her in the back. Now Phil, the love of her life, was shacked up with the enemy.

Helen downed more wine to make the misery movies go away. She was hungry, but she didn't feel like cooking. She ate tuna out of the can. She thought Thumbs would join her for dinner, but he didn't bother. Even the cat didn't want her company.

Finally Helen fell asleep. In her dream, she opened the closet door and Kiki's dead hands reached for her. She was trying to drag Helen into her cold world.

Helen woke up, alone and sweating, dry mouthed and headachy. She stumbled into the bathroom, drank a handful of cold water, and went back to bed.

Now she couldn't sleep. She kept thinking about Kiki, who'd died alone. We made Kiki into some insatiable sexual siren when she was dead and stuffed in a closet, Helen thought. Poor Kiki. She had a lot of sex, but no love. She had millions, but died without dignity. Helen wondered if anyone would mourn her. Who was cruel enough to stuff her in a closet?

Helen's own bedroom closet seemed to pulsate in the dark. The door was white as a tomb. She couldn't sleep staring at it.

Thud! Thud! Thud!

The sound came from the closet, urgent and oddly muffled.

Kiki! Helen thought. She's after me.

"She's dead, you idiot. And you're drunk." Helen thought she said those words out loud. She almost put her fear down to the fantods, when she heard another thud.

Thud! Thud! The door seemed to bulge out from the blows.

Helen switched on the bedroom light and picked up the heavy alarm clock for a bludgeon. Whatever is in there, she decided, wasn't strong enough to open the door. I can overpower it. Helen got behind the door and threw it open, ready to attack.

Thumbs came sprawling out. He stood up, shook himself, and meowed angrily. His giant paws were tangled in an old sweater. He must have fallen asleep in a pile of winter clothes and woke up trapped in the heavy wool. That's why the thud sounded so muffled.

Helen picked him up and soothed his ruffled fur. "I'm sorry, old boy."

Thumbs struggled out of her arms and marched into the kitchen, demanding dinner. Helen opened a can of tuna just for him. Thumbs wolfed it down, took a bath, then followed her into the bedroom and curled up next to her. She was forgiven.

She woke up Monday morning, clutching her cat.

Helen's tongue felt like a knitted tea cozy. Her eyes were an unfortunate fuchsia. The matching zit on her nose was a stop sign in her pale face. She tried to put on makeup, but her lipstick was a bloody slash. Her eyeliner looked like it was done with crayon. She washed her face clean. Millicent would have to take her as she was.

Helen switched on the local TV news while she put on her clothes. The announcer said, "Another bizarre twist in the Blood and Roses Murder. Police say an autopsy has revealed the cause of death for socialite Kiki Shenrad. The mother of the bride was smothered with her daughter's wedding dress sometime after the rehearsal dinner Friday night. A bridal shop employee found her body in a closet at the church Saturday."

Ohmigod, Helen thought. That's me. I'm the employee. This is the biggest murder to hit Lauderdale in years. Kiki was a socialite worth thirty million bucks. Her son-in-law was a movie actor. Her heiress daughter was a new bride. Her death would be national news for sure.

Rob! He'll find me. And so will the court. Helen watched a video clip of the bride and groom leaving the church in a shower of rose petals. Then Kiki's body bag was rolled down the same steps. Helen felt queasy and knew it wasn't from the hangover.

She ran outside for the morning paper. Sure enough, Kiki was front-page news. DEATH COMES TO THE WEDDING:

MOTHER OF THE BRIDE MURDERED, said the morning paper. The free paper, the *City Times*, had a more irreverent headline: ONE DEAD MOTHER.

Millicent's will be swarming with TV cameras, Helen thought. I need a disguise. I have to find some way to get in and out of that shop without being noticed.

Helen remembered that Margery had a khaki work shirt with BILLY on the pocket. She knocked on Margery's door. Helen could hear her landlady's TV going. "... in the Blood and Roses Murder. We've learned that the death dress cost three thousand dollars at Millicent's bridal salon on Las Olas."

Her landlady was wearing her purple chenille robe and red sponge curlers. "Thought that might be you. The TV people are all over your shop, shooting the dresses in the windows," Margery said.

"I'm trying to keep them from shooting me. Can I borrow your BILLY work shirt?"

"Here." Margery handed her the shirt, still warm from the iron. "I've already dug it out. I thought you might need to wear it again. I have to tell you, Billy never worked this hard in his life."

Helen was afraid to ask who Billy was. She took the shirt. Back in her apartment, she put on her khaki pants and sensible shoes. She packed a cardboard box, threw in the *City Times* paper to read at lunch, and taped the box shut. She carried a clipboard under her arm.

Millicent's back parking lot was swarming with TV trucks. They paid no attention to the box-bearing Helen. She rang the doorbell just before nine. "Express package delivery," she yelled.

A harried Millicent answered the back door. "I didn't order—"

"Millicent, it's me. I don't want to turn up on TV."

Millicent gave her a shrewd look. "Come on in. But how are you going to wait on customers in that outfit?"

Helen pulled a dress, her good shoes, pantyhose, and purse out of the cardboard box. "Voila!" she said.

Millicent managed a smile. She'd had a bad weekend, too. Thick concealer couldn't quite hide the dark circles under her brown eyes. Her high heels were scuffed. One bloodred nail was chipped.

"The police interviewed me for two hours," Millicent said. "Desiree told them I had a fight with her mother Friday night."

"Are you a suspect?" Helen secretly hoped she was. She hoped the police had lots of suspects to keep them busy.

"I don't know," Millicent said. "But Desiree found out the cops talked to me. She says the estate won't pay my bill until my name is cleared. She told me, 'It's just a precaution. I don't want my mother's murderer to profit.' "

"That's lousy," Helen said. "After all you did for her."

Including maybe kill her mother.

Millicent ran her bloodred nails through her white hair. "Helen, what am I going to do? I need that money now. What if the cops never catch the killer?"

Helen was saved from answering by a ringing phone.

"It's probably another reporter wanting to see the death dress—that blasted rose gown," Millicent said.

"I'll tell them to get lost," Helen said. "You look like you could use some coffee. Why don't you make us a pot?" Millicent was so upset, she didn't notice her employee was ordering her around.

Helen scrambled for the phone. "Millicent's. How may I help you?"

"You can die, that's how!"

"Excuse me?" Helen said.

"How can you do this to my mother?" the woman shrieked. "I'll ruin you. I swear to God. I'll sue. I'll—"

Helen winced. "Desiree, is that you? This is Helen. What's wrong?" Besides the fact that your mother was murdered at your wedding.

"Don't pretend you don't know. I'm calling about your disgusting ad in the *City Times*."

Helen struggled to make sense of this. The hangover didn't help. "What ad?"

"The ad that makes my mother's murder into a joke," Desiree screeched. "Are you so greedy you have to sell dresses over her dead body?"

Helen wished her head wasn't pounding. She wished this call made sense.

"Desiree, we never advertise in the *City Times*. Let me take a look at the paper. I'll have Millicent call you right back."

"Don't bother," Desiree said. "I'm calling my father. He'll sue you into the next century. Millicent will be lucky if she sells dresses at Wal-Mart when he finishes with her."

Desiree hung up the phone so hard, Helen's ears rang. She needed coffee before she could confront this. The phone jangled again.

"I'll get that," Millicent called from the front room. "Maybe I should tell the reporters yes. Photographing the death dress could be good advertising."

"Millicent, don't! Wait! There's some sort of problem—" Helen ran out to stop her. The pain in her head went all the way down to her feet.

She was too late. Millicent picked up the phone. Helen could hear her saying, "Cancel? Ellen, why would you want to cancel?"

Helen pulled the popular free tabloid from the cardboard box. She found the ONE DEAD MOTHER murder story. Right next to it was a full-page ad framed with ribbons and bridal bells.

MILLICENT'S—WEDDINGS TO DIE FOR! the headline said. Helen felt sick. No wonder Desiree was angry. This was utterly tasteless.

The copy was worse: "Want a beautiful wedding? Tired of ugly relatives? You need Millicent's, Fort Lauderdale's most fashionable bridal salon. See us for all—and we do mean all—your wedding needs."

"Oh, my God." Helen sprinted back inside the store calling, "Millicent!"

But Millicent was on the phone, sounding desperate. "Rebecca, sweetie, you can't cancel. You'll lose your deposit. Of course you care. Three thousand dollars is a lot of money. Rebecca, please listen—Rebecca?"

Millicent stared at the dead phone. "That's the third cancellation this morning."

The phone rang again, shrill and angry.

"Don't answer that," Helen said. "Read this first."

Millicent gave a little shriek when she saw the headline. She was spitting fury by the time she finished. "That bitch at Haute Bridal did this. She's trying to ruin me. I'll sue her. I'll get her if it's the last thing I do."

"We have to find out for sure who placed the ad," Helen said. "I'll call the paper."

"They won't know anything," Millicent said.

"They might," Helen said. "You listen on the extension."

Helen told Eric in the advertising department about the ad.

"Weird. Why would some stranger buy an ad for your store?" Eric said.

"To destroy our business," Helen said. "Do you know who did this?"

"I took the ad myself." Eric sounded nervous now. "Saturday afternoon about three. It was a rush job for Monday. A walk-in at our office. The buyer paid cash."

"Who was the buyer?"

"A woman. She wore a red jacket and black pants. I couldn't see her face real good because she had on these big dark sunglasses. But she had long white hair and really red nail polish, like blood or something."

"Millicent, that sounds like you," Helen said. "How old was she?"

"Old. Older than my mom," Eric said. "I'd say she was about fifty-five."

"I am not." Millicent was outraged. She hung up on Eric.

Helen's head hurt from all the slamming phones.

Millicent paced the pink salon in a red rage. "What did I tell you? It's Haute Bridal. The woman will stoop to anything. And she's older than me. She put on a white wig and placed that ad. She was furious when Kiki came here and canceled the order with her shop."

"How did she find out Kiki was dead? I didn't call you until five."

"It was on the news from about two o'clock on," Millicent said.

Of course. Helen had been holed up at the church all afternoon, but that didn't mean the rest of the world was locked away. She'd seen the TV vans outside the cathedral.

"This is a public relations disaster," Millicent said.

For the first time, she looked old and desperate. "Helen, what am I going to do? I've had three cancellations already. Desiree has refused to pay the balance of

Kiki's order. I'll lose my business. I'm too old to start over again. I've worked so hard for everything and now it's gone horribly wrong."

Millicent put her head down on her desk and began to weep. Helen couldn't stand to watch a strong woman cry.

"Don't!" she pleaded. "I'll think of something."

"What can you do?"

Nothing, Helen thought. I'm a shopgirl. I won't even be that if Millicent goes out of business. I'll have to look for another job, and that's harder work than working. Any job I find won't be as nice as this one.

She recalled some of her previous dead-end jobs. She'd been a clumsy crockery-dropping waitress at a Greek diner. She shuddered when she thought of the owner, his hands fastened on her breasts like hairy suction cups.

She did time as a telemarketer and was cursed from coast to coast. Working at Millicent's was a dream compared to those places. There was only one way to save her job.

"I can find the killer," Helen said. "I've done it before." Her brave words sounded silly.

"Even if the cops catch the killer that won't help us. The damage here is permanent." Millicent waved the "Weddings to Die For" ad at Helen, then threw it down on her desk.

The store was dead. The white wedding dresses hung like shrouds. Helen sat with Millicent like a mourner, while the phone rang and rang and the answering machine recorded one cancellation after another.

Chapter 11

"Customers!" Millicent said, and pulled herself out of the packing boxes like a shipwreck survivor who'd seen help on the horizon. She was starved for business. No bride would come near her store.

"We have customers! It's a couple in their late thirties. Probably a second marriage. Good. She'll be working and have money. She's thin, too. She can wear clothes. I've got just the gown for her."

Millicent spun this fantasy while she picked white threads off her suit and slipped on her shoes. The old fire was in her eyes. She marched confidently down the balcony stairs to the salon, determined to make this sale.

Helen looked over the balcony and nearly threw up on the happy couple. It was homicide detectives Bill McIntyre and Janet Smith. She saw Millicent's shoulders sag as she got closer and recognized them. Helen started down the steps. Her feet felt like cinder blocks.

The Sunnysea detectives sat side by side on the gray husband couch. Both wore suits, but McIntyre's was better tailored. Male detectives seemed to have a streak of vanity the women did not.

"They want to talk to you," Millicent said. Helen could hear the relief in her boss's voice.

Helen took a pink chair and sat down quickly, before she panicked and ran out the door. If I slip, they'll send me back to my old, cold life in St. Louis, she thought. She saw her hands were white from gripping the chair arms and tried to relax.

The pumped-up McIntyre started talking this time. Helen wondered what weights he lifted to get a muscle-bound neck. As he spoke, little muscles moved like a living anatomy lesson. Helen expected his voice to be burly, too, but it was a light, pleasant tenor.

"We want to ask you a few more questions about the day of the wedding," Detective McIntyre said. Even his mustache was muscular.

Helen stalled for time. "Have you found anything interesting?"

"We found some fingerprints on the wedding dress that was wrapped around the victim's head," he said. "Also on the dress the victim was wearing."

"You can get fingerprints from cloth?" Helen said.

"Yes. Some kinds of cloth."

"Do you think the prints belong to the killer?" Helen said.

"We thought maybe you could tell us."

"Whose are they?" Helen said.

"Yours," McIntyre said.

Helen wanted to put her head between her knees, the way the nuns made her when she felt sick at school. She wanted to bolt for the door.

Think, she told herself. You haven't done anything wrong.

"Of course my fingerprints are on both dresses." Helen's voice was shaky and slightly too high. "I helped the bride into her gown during several fittings. I helped Kiki put on the rose dress. I carried both dresses into the church and hung them up."

"Mind telling us where you were between eleven and two the night of the rehearsal dinner?" Detective Janet Smith said.

Helen felt her face grow hot with embarrassment. "I was with my boyfriend at my place."

"All night?" Smith said.

Detective McIntyre sat there like a muscle monument. Helen wished he'd leer or do something human.

"Phil left about seven the next morning."

"Anyone see him leave?" Detective Smith said.

"Probably my landlady. She knows everything that goes on at the Coronado," Helen said.

"And your boyfriend will confirm this?"

"We had a fight and we're not speaking, but yes. You can check with him."

"We will. What aren't you telling us?" Detective Smith said.

"What do you mean?" Helen tried to look her in the eye and failed.

"You know something," Smith said.

I know a lot of things, Helen thought, but nothing I can tell you.

I know the bride didn't want me to open the closet door where her mother's body was stashed. I know her father and the best man virtually forced her into that marriage. I know the groom was determined to be in that Michael Mann movie, no matter what his mother-in-law said. I know the best man will save his theater with the money he inherited from Kiki. I know the chauffeur will inherit a million dollars.

Here's the most important thing I know: I can't afford

to say anything. These people are rich and powerful. They can ruin me.

Maybe she could hint around about Jason. Actors had neither money nor power. Sorry, Jason, she thought, but the sharks are circling. I'm throwing you overboard. She might have felt guiltier if he wasn't such a conceited twit.

"You tested Kiki's body for DNA, right?" Helen said. "She might have been with someone the night of the rehearsal."

"Been with how?" Detective McIntyre said.

"Sexually." The word sounded prim and salacious at the same time.

"Believe it or not, we've heard of DNA," McIntyre said.

"We watch the cop shows, too." Detective Smith had a sarcastic streak.

Say something, Helen thought, but don't babble. "The rose dress, the one Kiki was killed in? She couldn't get into that dress by herself. It had a four-foot-wide hoop skirt."

"Like Scarlett O'Hara?" McIntyre said.

"Exactly," Helen said. "Scarlett had help. So did Kiki. That dress was fragile. It would be easy to step wrong and tear the skirt. Kiki couldn't even sit down in a regular chair. She couldn't put that dress on alone. So who helped her?"

The two detectives looked unimpressed. Helen guessed they didn't understand clothes that required maids.

"Maybe you can explain something else about that dress," Detective Janet Smith said. "We found blood on the skirt. We have a warrant for your DNA."

"My blood?" Helen's voice was a squeak. "You want my blood? You think I killed her?"

"How else did your blood get on that dress?"

"I scratched my arm," Helen said.

"So you don't deny it's your blood?"

"I'm not saying it's my blood. It could be someone else's. But I might have dripped a drop or two on the dress. I didn't think Kiki would notice."

"We think she did," Detective Smith said. "You fought with her Friday night and she threatened to have you fired. You were fighting over that damaged dress, weren't you?"

"No. That's not what it was about. Kiki thought I was eavesdropping on an argument she had with her ex."

"Now you've decided to tell us about the fight. You didn't mention it before," Detective Smith said. "But we heard about it from other people."

Helen remembered the four frightened bridesmaids staring over the wedding planner's shoulder. Did they tell? Or was it Jeff, the wedding planner?

"It wasn't a big deal. Kiki said something nasty, and I refused to take her rudeness. She said she'd buy the bridal shop and have me fired. But she wouldn't spend major money to nail a minimum-wage clerk. It would be bad publicity for Ms. Florida Philanthropist to go after a poor workingwoman."

"Maybe. But if you ruined that dress, she'd make you pay for it," Detective Smith said.

"I didn't ruin it," Helen said.

Smith kept talking. "That dress cost three thousand dollars. You make what? Six dollars an hour?"

"Six-seventy, plus commission." Helen's pay sounded pitiful when she said it out loud. "But—"

"You'd have to sell a lot of wedding gowns to pay for

that rose dress," Detective Smith said. "It would take you three months to make that kind of money, if you kept your job. The victim said she'd make sure you never worked again."

Helen was beyond fear now. She was furious. "It's a lot easier to arrest a shop clerk than someone with thirty million dollars," Helen said. "I'm not the only one Kiki threatened. You'd better talk to Luke. Kiki also told the groom he couldn't take a big part in a Michael Mann movie."

"We heard that, too," Detective Smith said. "But not from you. Now let's get that DNA sample."

"Are you going to stick me with a needle?" Helen said.

"I'm going to run a Q-tip on the inside of your cheek. It won't hurt."

But it did. Helen felt shame, like a fiery brand, where the Q-tip touched her.

Detective Smith dropped it in a plastic evidence bag. "We'll be seeing you again," she said.

It was a promise and a threat.

My sister, Helen thought. I have to warn Kathy. What if she gets a call from the police? Those two detectives could find out what happened in St. Louis. She doesn't deserve this. Helen felt bad that Kathy was mixed up in her troubles. She deserved a better sister.

Kathy was almost perfect. She lived in a white house with a picket fence in suburban Webster Groves. The house needed new plumbing and a coat of paint, but it was an oasis of domesticity. Kathy was different from Helen, but she understood her sister better than anyone.

Kathy was the only person from her old life Helen really missed—and the only one who knew where

Helen was. Helen called her once a month. Her next call wasn't due for two weeks. But she had to talk to Kathy now.

On her lunch hour, Helen ran home like an animal to her burrow. She locked the door, pulled the blinds down, and opened the storage closet. She lugged out the red Samsonite suitcase and dug out the cell phone buried in the pile of old-lady underwear.

Please, please be home, Helen prayed as she dialed. The phone rang four times before Kathy picked up, breathless. "Sorry, I was in the basement. Helen, is that you? Are you OK?"

"I'm fine, Kathy. But if the police start asking questions about me, you don't know where I am."

"Of course. That's what I'd tell them, anyway. No one's been around. Are you sure you're not in trouble?"

"Cross my heart and hope to die." It was their childhood pledge that they were telling the truth. Helen used it when she lied to reassure her sister.

"Something's wrong," Kathy said. "You aren't due to call yet. Did Rob track you down? He's been trying to charm your location out of Mom. He's desperate for money again. Another rich girlfriend dropped him."

"How long did this one take to wise up?" Helen said.

"She saw through him in six months."

"It took me seventeen years," Helen said. "If I hadn't caught him in the act, I would have never figured it out."

"You had a disadvantage," Kathy said. "You were blinded by love."

"I was blinded by stupidity. I let that man live off me for five years while he supposedly looked for work."

"Helen, don't be mean to yourself. When you finally caught that lowlife, you made him skip."

"Skip naked," Helen said. "I wish you could have seen him."

Rob had been buck-naked with their neighbor, Sandy. First, Helen saw a lot of pink skin. Then she saw red. Helen picked up a crowbar and started swinging. Rob abandoned his lady love and ran for the protection of his Land Cruiser. Helen bought that for him, too.

She hit Rob where it hurt the most—right in the radiator. She reduced the Land Cruiser to rubble while Rob cowered inside. By the time the police arrived, the SUV was totaled. Rob and Sandy refused to press assault charges.

"It's the court, right?" Kathy said. "They've tracked you down."

"Ah, yes, the judge," Helen said. "The man who was dropped on his head at birth."

Helen filed for divorce. But a slick lawyer convinced the judge that Rob was the victim, a house husband who put up with a crazy career woman.

His lovers testified that Rob provided invaluable services. He did, too. He serviced them all. Helen wanted her lawyer to ask the women if they'd had sex with Helen's husband. The lawyer refused. He was too much of a gentleman.

The judge said Helen made six figures because of Rob's love and support. He gave Rob half the house, even though Helen made all the payments. She had steeled herself for that. Then the judge awarded Rob half of Helen's future income, because her worthless husband made her career possible "at the expense of his own livelihood."

Rage flowed through her like molten lava, wiping out her old life forever. Helen grabbed the familiar black book with the gold lettering and said, "I swear on this

Bible that my husband, Rob, will not get another nickel of my salary."

The Bible turned out to be the Missouri Revised Statutes. But Helen considered the oath binding.

She left the next day, zigzagging across the country before winding up in South Florida. Now she worked dead-end jobs to stay untraceable.

"It's your new job, isn't it?" Kathy said. "You're in trouble again."

"I wouldn't call it trouble exactly," Helen said. "One of our customers died. The police have been asking questions. I don't want them asking anything about me, that's all. How's Mom?"

"That was a subtle change of subject," Kathy said. But she suddenly sounded too cheerful. "Listen, Helen, I'm glad you called. I have some news. Mom's getting married again."

"Oh, no. Mom's not going to marry Lawn Boy Larry," Helen said.

"They've been dating for almost a year, Helen. The wedding is next week."

"I can't believe she's marrying that old buzzard. All he wants to do is get his hands on her grass."

"Helen! She's been a widow for ten years. And she's lonely. She's having a wonderful time planning the wedding."

"Tell me about this wedding."

"Well, she's got this guy from the senior center to sing 'Oh, Promise Me.'"

"Mr. Carmichael?"

"That's him."

"I don't believe it. She wanted to inflict him on my wedding," Helen said. "He's this horrible ice-cream tenor. We had a big fight about it."

"You had a big fight about everything."

"I couldn't be perfect like you, Kathy. Mom hated my bridesmaid dresses."

"Orange harem pants were unusual, Helen."

"It beat baby pink formals."

"That's what Marcella, Mom's maid of honor, is wearing."

"Let me guess," Helen said. "The reception is at the Knights of Columbus Hall. It's a buffet with mostaccioli, roast beef on dollar rolls, and a sheet cake from Schnucks. The band is six guys in iridescent tuxes and one of them plays the accordion."

"How did you know?" Kathy said.

"My mother is having my wedding."

"Helen, I'm sorry you can't come back for Mom's wedding."

"Kids shouldn't go to their parent's wedding. It's unnatural," Helen said. "I don't know why she's getting married, anyway. She said sex at her age was disgusting. What's the point of getting married if you're not having sex?"

"Our generation is obsessed with sex," Kathy said. "The Victorians didn't have our hang-ups. I just read this novel where the couple had a 'white marriage.' It meant no sex. It could be very romantic. It's possible to marry for companionship."

"She could get a cat," Helen said.

"You forgot. Mom is allergic to cat hair."

"Well, Lawn Boy Larry is hairless."

"Helen!" Her sister laughed. Helen laughed. Then the two of them couldn't stop laughing.

When she hung up, Helen realized she was crying. She was intensely lonely for her old, safe life. When she was an executive, the police never threatened her with jail.

But my old life was a prison, too, she thought. I served time in a boring job. I closed my eyes to an unfaithful mooch. I'm much happier in Florida, if I can stay out of jail.

But the police already have part of me. They took my DNA.

Next they'll take me.

Chapter 12

It was a cold day for a funeral.

The temperature dropped to forty-eight degrees the morning of Kiki's funeral. Lizard-blooded Floridians shivered. They'd become sun creatures who couldn't take the cold. But it wasn't the weather that gave Helen the shakes.

"I don't want to go to Kiki's funeral," she said.

"You have to," Millicent said. "I finally convinced Desiree I didn't have anything to do with that awful ad, but I can't go to the church. I'll be a constant reminder. You were there on her wedding day, Helen. You should be at the funeral."

"Millicent, Kiki hated me. She tried to get me fired the night she was killed. Desiree's wedding was the worst day of her life. That poor bride doesn't want to see me again."

"She likes you. She asked if you were coming. You found her mother's body. You have to go, Helen."

"Really? Maybe we should ask Miss Manners: 'What is the proper etiquette when one finds a body? Should one attend the funeral and the burial service?'"

"You don't have to go to the cemetery. Just the church." Millicent said it as if she were offering Helen a bonus.

"Isn't this awfully quick for a funeral?"

"Her family pulled strings and got her autopsied fast," Millicent said. "If they can push the medical examiner around, what do you think they'll do to me? You have to go as the store's representative. Look . . . I'll pay you."

"I should get combat pay," Helen said.

"You should, but I can't afford it."

That's when Helen said yes. Millicent hadn't had a sale since Kiki's death, and the cancellations were piling up. Her unstoppable energy had evaporated. Her supreme confidence was gone. Millicent was stoop shouldered with discouragement. Her white hair turned an odd, dispirited gray.

"The service is at eleven. It's not like I'm overwhelmed with customers. I'll give you the shop van."

Normally, that would have been a perk. It was a long bus ride to the Coco Isle Cathedral in Sunnysea. Today Helen wasn't sure she wanted to be driving anything with "Millicent's Bridal Salon" on the sides. She hoped the van wouldn't be keyed.

At the church, Helen parked at the farthest end of the lot, behind the Dumpster. It was one of the last spaces left. She panicked when she saw the hordes of reporters outside the church, but they were too busy interviewing the local celebrities. Helen slipped into the cathedral unnoticed.

Kiki had quite a turnout for her funeral. Give the public what they want and they'll show up, Helen thought, then regretted her meanness. Kiki's dead and I'm sorry. I'm also sorry I've been dragged into this mess.

Helen watched the people filing into the cathedral. Floridians laughed at the tourists for their garish vacation togs, but they looked just as silly in winter dress. We don't waste money on cold weather clothes we'll wear maybe one day a year, Helen thought.

She could smell the mothballs wafting on the wind. She could feel the locals' resentment. They'd moved down here to get warm. They could have had these rotten temperatures up north.

You could tell when Floridians first arrived in the state by the cut of their winter coats. Helen saw lots of shoulder-padded eighties styles, a few straight-line seventies numbers, even some garish sixties coats. There was also that Florida phenomenon, flip-flops and fur, a fashion statement that said, "I'm wearing the coat because it's cold, but I have on sandals because I'm in Florida."

Helen found a seat in the back of the church, next to an older woman in an ancient pink-and-orange coat that went oddly with her dyed red hair.

Helen thought Kiki would have been disappointed by the shortage of hunky male mourners. Helen suspected the scattering of sleek women in their fifties probably served on charity boards with Kiki. A few well-dressed older men sat by Kiki's ex-husband, Brendan. The wedding party was also near him. The bridesmaids' short black dresses went better with cocktails than caskets.

The bride wore black: a dowdy high-collared dress and a mourning veil. Helen had seen pictures of the First Lady in a similar veil at John F. Kennedy's funeral. Helen couldn't see Desiree's face behind her crepe curtain, but she could hardly walk up the aisle. Saturday she'd marched up that same aisle, furious at her mother. Today she seemed almost paralyzed by her grief. Desiree had to be helped by her friend Emily, flapping in black fringe, and Luke. She clung to her husband as if he might escape. Luke wore a dark suit and a stunned expression.

When Desiree saw the casket, her knees buckled and she wept bitterly. Helen wondered if she cried for her mother or for the maternal love she never had.

The casket stood in the center aisle, its dark polished wood covered with dozens of red roses. It looked beautiful, if coffins could be described that way. To Helen, it also looked sinister.

"She loved her mother so," said the red-haired old woman at her side. She laid a soft, liver-spotted hand on Helen's arm. "Look at those gorgeous roses. There must be ten dozen on that casket."

Helen knew that wasn't love. It was revenge. Kiki had sneered at roses as something for shopgirls, and now she was buried under them.

"And a closed coffin. Such dignity." The woman patted Helen again.

She would have hated that, too, Helen thought. Kiki never missed a chance to be on display. To be locked in a wooden box for her last public appearance would be hell.

"Darling Desiree. Such a sensitive child. I bet she chose her mother's final outfit with care."

"I bet she did, too," Helen said.

It would be carefully chosen to annoy her mother for all eternity. What horror would Desiree pick? A cheap polyester dress? A conservative gray suit? Maybe she'd wrapped her mother in a sheet. Helen had a vision of Kiki facing her Maker with a sheet gathered around her like a large bath towel. She struggled to suppress a giggle.

"I see she asked her mother's oldest friends to be pall-bearers," the woman said.

Another slap. Desiree had chosen six of the oldest men in Florida—and that was saying something. The poor old dodderers were having trouble rolling out the casket, even with the help of the funeral-home employees. Kiki would have wanted six young studs to carry her body.

"It was the perfect funeral," her companion said.

"Yes, it was," Helen said. Perfectly malicious. She wondered if Desiree would ever bury her hatred of her mother.

Helen stepped out into the cold winter sun, eager to find the shop van and leave.

"Returning to the scene of the crime?"

Detective Janet Smith blocked Helen's way. Helen hadn't seen her at the funeral.

"I'm representing the shop," Helen said, and gulped. Damn Millicent. Why did she make her come to the funeral? Helen knew her attendance looked odd. She was no friend of Kiki's.

"Good way to see what's going on," Detective Smith said. "Enjoy the drama. Feed on the grief. A lot of murderers do that. That's why we tape the mourners. You are mourning her death, aren't you?"

"Are you accusing me of anything?" Helen said, her heart pounding.

"Should I?" Detective Smith smiled. "Have a nice day."

She's trying to rattle me, Helen thought as she climbed into the van and dropped her keys on the floor. She's succeeded, too. Helen decided not to tell Millicent about the detective's sideswipe in the parking lot. She was getting an uneasy feeling about her boss.

It was one o'clock when she returned to the bridal shop. Helen was so tired, she felt like she'd been digging ditches. She took off her coat and flopped into a pink chair. There were no customers.

"How was the funeral?" Millicent said.

"Indecently quick. Nobody cried but Desiree. Nobody fainted. Nobody fought on the parking lot."

"Anyone mention me?" Millicent said.

"They hardly mentioned Kiki," Helen said. "The minister talked briefly about the brevity of life. No one else gave a eulogy. Maybe they couldn't think of anything good to say. After some prayers, they shoved her body in the hearse. My old cat Missy had a longer funeral—and more people cried."

"Kiki deserved better," Millicent said. "I know you didn't like her, Helen, but Kiki was born too soon. Today she'd be a senator or a CEO. Her family forced her into a traditional woman's role. She wasted herself on sex and society parties."

"In theory, I feel sorry for her," Helen said. "In fact, she was a bitch. Things any better here?"

Helen knew she shouldn't have asked. The empty store was answer enough.

"I haven't sold a ribbon," Millicent said. "Look, I should warn you. If business doesn't pick up soon, I'll have to let you go. I don't want to, but I can't make the light bill at this rate."

At two o'clock, the doorbell chimed, and two twenty-something women came in. One was a tall, skinny blonde. The other was a short, buxom brunette. The brunette held her left hand in the newly engaged position, ready to display a diamond the size of a peach pit.

Helen stood up. Millicent surged forward, eager to sell. She never asked, "May I help you?" Millicent knew the answer would be, "Just looking." Instead, Millicent talked about the weather until the women felt they had a friend. Then she said, "When is the wedding?"

"I've just got engaged!!" The bride extended her hand to show off the rock. "I'm Cassie. My best friend Toni's going to help!!" Everything Cassie said had at least two exclamation points.

"She's going to do it," Toni giggled.

"I've already done it, silly!! Now I'm going to get married!!"

Helen's heart sank. Newly engaged women visited every bridal shop in three counties. Many went to expensive shops like Millicent's first, tried on the ten-thousand-dollar dresses to see what styles suited them, then bought the two-hundred-dollar knockoff at Bob's Bridal Barn.

"When is the date?" Millicent said.

"June, 2006," Cassie squealed. "I can't wait. I can't wait!!"

Another bad sign. She had eons to look for a dress. But Millicent was too desperate to discourage her. "What style do you prefer?"

"Don't know. I haven't tried anything on yet. Let's try them all!!"

Oh, boy. This was going to be a long day.

Cassie had shiny black hair that curled to her shoulders, fine white skin, and a firm bust. Her figure was a little chunky by current standards, but she'd look smashing in a simple strapless A-line.

Millicent tried to steer her toward slim styles that would flatter her figure. But Cassie didn't like those dresses. "Too plain," she said. "It's my day. I want to look like a princess in ribbons and lace."

For four hours, Helen and Millicent dragged dresses

back to the fitting room. Cassie settled on a white satin dress with a full skirt layered in lace. The chunky bride looked like a cotton ball. But this was the dress she'd dreamed about since her first Barbie wedding.

"I love it, I love it, I love it!!!!" Four exclamation points this time. "I know it's the one for me, just like I know Bernie is my man."

"It's perfect," her friend Toni said.

"Does it make me look fat?" Cassie said.

"Of course not," Toni said, loyally.

"How much would you like to put down for a deposit?" Millicent said.

"I'm almost ready to buy," Cassie said. "But I'll have to bring back my sister and show her."

"Don't wait too long," Millicent said. "It won't be here forever."

It may be repossessed, Helen thought.

"She'll come back," Millicent said when Cassie left. "No bride buys the first time."

"Of course," Helen said. Like Toni, the loyal friend, she said what Millicent wanted to hear. They both knew she was telling polite lies.

Helen and Millicent were discouraged when closing time rolled around and there was no need to balance the cash register.

Helen walked home toward the Coronado. She passed the Blue Note. The little bar off Las Olas was no fashionable hangout. It was a dark hole for getting drunk, and it fit her black mood. Helen stood in the doorway breathing in Pine-Sol, bug spray, and fried food. Then she saw someone she recognized sitting at the bar.

Rod the chauffeur was drinking himself into a stupor. He didn't seem a happy new millionaire. His face was loose, rubbery, and wet with sweat. His eyes were glassy. He was sloppy drunk.

"Rod, are you OK?"

"No, I'm not." His words were slurred. His breath was sour with beer. He squinted at Helen in the dim light. "Do I know you?"

"I work at Millicent's."

"Oh, yeah. The water lady. You brought me a bottle of water when I was standing in the sun and I chased you off like a total asshole. Only human I met in that job, and I was mean to you. I'm sorry. I'm so damn sorry."

Rod's handsome face crumpled, and he started to cry.

"Rod, it wasn't that big a deal. What's wrong?" Helen ordered a beer and drank it out of the bottle. It would be cleaner than the bar glasses.

"The will was read after the funeral." He stared morosely into his beer.

"Congratulations," Helen said. "Now that you're a millionaire, will you get yourself a chauffeur?"

"I'm not a millionaire." He belched. "I'm not in the goddamn will. Kiki promised me a million bucks. She said that to all the boys. I knew that. But I thought I was different. Turned out she lied. She never had any of us in her will. She wasn't going to waste money on legal fees every time she got a new fucking chauffeur. Or a fucking new chauffeur."

He took a drink, then looked confused. "Where was I? Oh, yeah. I'm out of the will. All that for nothing. I'm just another dumb hooker."

"I'm sorry," Helen said.

"Not as sorry as I am," he said. "You didn't stick your—"

"Uh, did she lie to everybody?" Helen interrupted quickly.

"Whadya mean, everybody?" Rod said, turning belligerent. "Who you calling everybody?"

"She was supposed to leave a hundred thousand dollars to Chauncey for his playhouse and thirty million to her daughter."

"Chauncey got his. Never had to screw her, either. Just kiss her ass. Desiree got hers, too. That means Luke has it all—and no mother-in-law."

"Kiki was some mother-in-law, all right."

"Huh, you don't know the half of it. She wasn't going to let Luke make that movie."

"I heard," Helen said. "That was his big break."

"Kiki said no son-in-law of hers was going to play a retard on the big screen. Only reason Luke was marrying that girl was to get enough money to take his career to the next phase. Luke was so mad he wanted to kill Kiki."

"How do you know that?"

"I heard them arguing. But he would have told me. We were like this." He made a circle with his thumb and forefinger and stuck his shaky finger through it.

"You and Luke were lovers?"

"Yeah. We met at the theater. I decided to take this role as a chauffeur and act like I enjoyed banging an old bag. He played Romeo to the dreary daughter. We both whored for money. But he got it and I didn't. He's a good whore. I'm a bad one." His self-contempt was corrosive.

"When did you hear the fight?"

He belched and stared straight ahead until Helen brought him back. "The fight, Rod. Where was it?"

"In the restaurant parking lot after the rehearsal dinner. Desiree was still inside with her bridesmaids. Luke and Kiki were out by the Dumpsters. Good place for trash like her. You know she never wore panties?"

"Yes," Helen said.

"Me, too. The hard way. Hard way. That's a joke." His laughter sounded more like crying.

"About Kiki."

"Kiki. I hope she's somewhere hot and it isn't Florida. You want to hear something really pathetic? I actually liked her. No, I'm drunk. I should tell the truth. In beero veritas." He had another gulp of beer. "I started out doing it for the money, but I ended up loving her."

Helen stared. She couldn't imagine anyone loving Kiki.

"I'm not bullshitting you. That little woman had big balls. She made me feel like a stud."

"We thought the two of you were having marathon sex in the Rolls the morning of the wedding," Helen said. "What were you doing in there, anyway?" She figured Rod was drunk enough he might tell her.

"Oh. That." Rod belched delicately. "She didn't come home the night before. The housekeeper and I thought Kiki spent the night with some guy. She did that more and more. I drove to the church, figuring the guy already took her there. I sat in the car, getting up the courage to go inside and see if she was with her new chauffeur. I ran the air conditioning in the Rolls. I wasn't supposed to do that if she wasn't in the car. But I wanted to look good. I was afraid she'd lost interest in me. What a fool. She never cared in the first place. She was one hot geezer babe, too. Joke's on me. The hot old babe left me cold. Didn't give me a nickel. Did I tell you that?"

"Yes," Helen said. "I'm really sorry. You were talking about a fight with Luke?"

"Oh, yeah. She told Luke no movies. Luke said then there would be no wedding. Kiki said if he didn't marry her daughter, she'd ruin him with every agent and acting company from Miami to New York. She could do it, too."

"And if he did marry, he'd never act again," Helen said.

"Riiiiiiiight. Oh, he could go back to it after Desiree got her own money, but that would be ten years, and the momentum would be gone. His looks, too. Luke's career was starting to take off. If he handled things right, he could go national. Movie parts and theater roles in national companies. If he waited ten years, he'd be doing local stuff the rest of his life. Kiki gave him one of those choices—the lady or the tiger."

"This time, the lady was a tiger," Helen said.

"Riiiiiight. Except he picked door number three. A dead Kiki. Solved everything for everybody, except me."

"Do you think he killed Kiki?"

"If he didn't"—he hiccupped—"he should have. But it could have been that other guy she had the fight with."

"What other guy?" Helen said.

"Didn't see him. Didn't hear much, except he was real mad. That one was at the church. I had to take the Rolls back over there. Then she sent me home.

"She's an evil little woman. Looking all sad and talking all soft. Had me thinking about crazy stuff I never would have considered. Almost did it, too."

Rod suddenly stood up. "I'm gonna be sick." He sprinted for the bathroom.

"You better go, miss," the bartender said. "I'll make sure Rod gets home."

Chapter 13

The cops thought she was a killer. Her romance was on the skids. Her job was drying up. Her mother was going to marry Lawn Boy Larry.

Helen had one consolation: It wasn't snowing.

This morning was a sunny seventy-two degrees. Helen poured herself a cup of coffee, grabbed the paper, and sat by the pool.

A soft breeze playfully flapped the front page as she read the headlines. Kiki's murder had been preempted by a vicious snowstorm that hit the East Coast. Like all Floridians, Helen read the reports of stranded motorists, ice-slick roads, and power outages with satisfaction.

Her life might be a mess, but she didn't have to shovel her car out of a snowbank.

The day seemed less sunny when she read the want ads. In some ways, an arrest would solve her problems. She'd have a place to sleep and three meals. Helen knew Millicent would probably have to fire her. There was still no business.

What was she going to do? More than a quarter of

Florida workers were "working poor," people who made less than eight dollars an hour. Helen was one of them. When she lost her job, she'd be just poor. All she had was seven thousand dollars stashed in a Samsonite suitcase. That wouldn't go far.

The want ads had plenty of high-paying jobs for exotic dancers, escorts, and lingerie models. Keeping your clothes on didn't pay nearly as well. The best Helen could find was an ad for "medical receptionist, must be bilingual, $7 an hour." Helen doubted her high-school Spanish counted as a second language.

A job in a dentist's office promised "competitive pay to commiserate with experience."

I'd like someone to commiserate with my experience, Helen thought.

Wait! This job looked promising: "Ground-floor opportunity in the advertising industry. No training required. $6.25 plus commission and meals."

The pay was less than she made now, but free meals would make up for it. Helen wondered if the company would pay her in cash under the table. It was worth checking. She needed Margery's phone.

Her landlady was hosing purple bougainvillea blossoms off the pool deck.

"Margery, I have a shot at an advertising job," Helen said. "Can I use your phone to call for an interview?"

"I'll be finished here in a minute." Margery wore a new plum shorts set and flirty kitten-heel slides.

"You look chipper this morning. Out dancing with Warren last night?" Helen said.

"Till three o'clock." Margery gave a little grin. "Elsie and Rita folded early, but Warren and I stayed out late. Might as well enjoy it while I can. His new condo will be ready soon and he'll be moving."

"You won't have any trouble renting 2C again," Helen said. "The paper says it's supposed to be a cold winter. The first big snowstorm hit up north already. The Midwest and East Coast were slammed with a foot of snow."

"Oh, good." Margery dropped the hose and headed for her place. "I have to find my list."

"What list?"

"I keep a list of all the people who call me when a hurricane's heading this way and say, 'I don't know how you can live in Florida with the hurricanes, the bugs, and the heat.' Now it's my turn. Watch."

Helen followed Margery into her kitchen. Her landlady started dialing her purple princess phone. Her voice oozed concern. "Hi, Betty, I thought I'd find you inside today. I heard about your ice storm. I'm sitting out by my pool and thought I'd give you a call.

"How's Ed? He's shoveling snow? Oh, Betty, he should be careful. I don't know how you can live in Michigan: the icy roads, the cold, the snow. I heard six people died in snow-related accidents, and that doesn't count all the snow-shoveling heart attacks.

"What? You have an ice problem? I have one, too. It keeps melting in my glass.

"She hung up," Margery said. "OK, make your call."

The man who answered sounded like Helen's idea of an ad man. He was a fast talker and a little slick. "I'm calling about your ad in this morning's paper, the ground-level advertising job," she said.

"Can you get here by eight thirty?"

Helen checked her watch. It was seven thirty. "Sure."

"If I like your looks, I can start you out tonight. Dinner's included. Ask for Frank."

Frank gave her an address in a new shopping center on Federal Highway, a brisk ten-minute walk.

"I think I have a live one," Helen said. Margery waved good-bye absently. She was tormenting a snowbound friend in Connecticut.

As Helen passed Phil's place, she couldn't resist peeking through his half-open miniblinds. She was relieved to see Kendra sleeping on the couch instead of sharing Phil's bed. The Kentucky Songbird's mouth was wide open. She was drooling.

Probably drooling over Phil, Helen thought. She slammed her own door hard and hoped it woke Kendra.

Helen dressed quickly in a dark suit and heels and arrived at her job interview five minutes early. It was a pink stucco building with a "Hot and Ready Pizza" sign.

The man who unlocked the front door looked like he'd been put together from pizza circles: a small white doughy one for his bald head, a large one for his round gut, a medium for his oddly round hips. His flaming orange T-shirt said, "I'm hot and ready."

"I'm Frank." He looked Helen up and down like he was going to stamp Grade A on her rump. "You'll do. Got any red shorts?"

"Is that the office uniform?" she said.

"You won't be working in an office. You'll be out on Federal Highway with this sign."

Frank unrolled an orange banner that said, "I'm hot and ready for six bucks!" There was no mention of pizza.

Helen was appalled. She'd be a walking double entendre. "You want me to hold up that thing on the highway? I'll have to put up with every creep in a car."

"That's why we pay the big bucks," Frank said. "You'll make a dollar more than the industry standard. Plus, you can have any leftover single-topping pizza. We'll charge you fifty cents for each additional topping. And don't forget your commission. You get twenty-five cents if a guy comes in and says he saw you. They're bound to notice you. With those legs, you should get an extra two or three bucks a night."

The guy really thought he was offering her a good job. Helen was hot and ready to set him straight. "You can take your pizza sign and put it right"—Frank's eyes were now circles, too—"in the middle of the road."

She walked to Millicent's, wondering if this was her last day. The salon seemed so refined after her encounter with Hot and Ready.

But Helen was a realist. Millicent hadn't had a single sale since that awful "Weddings to Die For" ad. She'd love to know who placed it and why. Millicent swore her competitor, Haute Bridal, planted the ad. Helen didn't believe that. She thought it was tied somehow to Kiki's murder.

The person who bought the ad had long white hair and red polish like Millicent. But anyone could put on a white wig and red polish. Even a man. Especially an actor. Helen thought someone wanted to ruin Millicent.

They might have succeeded, if it wasn't for the shower-curtain dress. When Helen entered the store at nine that morning, she was surprised to hear voices. Customers, at long last.

A short, dark man in a too-tight knit shirt was shopping with his wife. She was a size sixteen squeezed into a size-twelve dress. Her long curly hair was dyed dead black. She balanced her thick body on teeny black heels

with big red bows. Her hands—and his—were loaded
with diamonds. Their necks were heavy with gold
chains.

Mob money, Helen thought.

Lou, the husband, did not sit on the gray couch and
read *Forbes* magazine like most men. He personally
picked his wife's clothes. So far, he'd rejected everything the woman put on. Helen could see the panic in
Millicent's eyes. She had to make this sale to save the
store, and she was running out of choices.

His wife, Patti, came out of the fitting room in a
black lace dress. Helen thought it was attractive. Lou
didn't.

"It don't look like the money," he said. "It looks like
a nightgown."

"It's twenty-three hundred dollars," Patti pouted.

"We're looking for something unique—like you
won't see on every broad."

"Well, I do have a special dress," Millicent said. "But
it takes a certain kind of customer to appreciate it."

One with no taste at all, Helen thought. Millicent
had hit rock bottom. She was going for the shower-
curtain dress.

Millicent had exquisite taste. But occasionally, for
reasons Helen never understood, Millicent would buy
a dress of breathtaking ugliness. The shower curtain
was hideous. The blue polyester fabric was so shiny it
looked like plastic. The pink rosebuds looked like a
rash. The lumpy overskirt added ten pounds to the
slimmest figure.

The first time Millicent showed her the dress, Helen
said, "Where did you get that: Bed Bath & Beyond?"

"I know. It looks like a shower curtain," Millicent

said. "We should accessorize it with a sponge and a soap bar. What was I thinking when I bought this?"

Millicent kept the shower-curtain dress hidden. She only brought it out when she thought someone might like it, which wasn't often. Today she was desperate.

Lou examined it from the neck to the hem. "Now this is very unique," he said.

"That it is," Helen said.

Millicent kicked her. "I promise you no one at the wedding in Jersey will have a dress like that," she said.

"Try it on," Lou commanded his wife.

A few minutes later, Patti teetered out in the shiny dress. It rustled noisily and hung in bunchy folds at her waist. But it showed off the woman's huge chest.

"I love it," Lou said. "How much?"

"Twenty-seven hundred dollars." Millicent had doubled the price. She knew her man.

"See?" Lou said. "It's better than that black nightgown thing. We'll take it."

Millicent waited until the couple drove off in their black Lincoln Town Car. Then she did a triumphant dance around the store. "Yes! I can't believe I sold it. And to a mob wife. It's perfect. Who's going to tell Lou his wife's dress is ugly? They'd wind up in cement shoes. It's gone. I'm free."

Until Millicent bought the next ugly dress she had to get rid of.

But sales is about confidence. Millicent was on a roll. She sold dresses all day long. If a bride even walked down the block, she was sucked into the shop and bought a dress.

The only one who didn't buy was Cassie. The chunky little bride had come back three more times. She'd tried on her dream dress for her sister, her mother, and her maid of honor. She still hadn't bought it.

Now Cassie showed up with a tiny wrinkled woman in black. "This is my grandmother!!" Cassie said. "I want to show her my dress."

Helen thought it was getting a little gray from all the try-ons, but she brought Cassie's lacy dress to a fitting room once more.

"Grandma loves it!!" Cassie squealed, when she came out. "There's just one more person I need to show it to."

"You should charge her rent on that dress," Helen said.

"She's about ready to buy," Millicent said.

"I'm about ready to win the lottery," Helen said. "As soon as I buy a ticket."

Millicent's most haunting sale that day was to Becky. Thirteen-year-old Becky had a doelike softness. Her mother had the same face, except it looked freeze-dried.

Becky wanted a special dress for her bat mitzvah, the coming-of-age ceremony for Jewish women. She tried on an electric-blue gown that was perfect for her dark hair and eyes. The style was right for her. So was the price.

Her mother started picking it apart. "The color's too bright. I don't like the material." On and on she went, finding flaws in a flawless dress.

Becky apologized for her mother. "She doesn't mean it. She's a careful shopper."

"You need to try on more dresses," her mother said. Millicent dutifully brought them back. None were as electrifying as the blue dress.

"We need to see some selections at another store," the mother said.

"But, Mummy . . ." The girl was near tears.

"Let's go, Becky," her mother said.

"Please, don't sell my dress," Becky told Millicent. "I'll make her come back today. I promise."

"We'll never see her again," Helen said.

"Wait and see," Millicent said.

Two hours later, Becky was back. "You've come for your dress," Millicent said.

Becky nodded shyly and smiled.

"Not so fast," her mother said. "I want her to try on the black satin suit again. And the pink outfit."

Becky tried them both. Then she said, "Mummy, I've tried on every dress in the store. I want this one. I feel like a princess."

Becky got her electric-blue dress. She carried it like an actress clutching her Oscar.

"That's one determined little girl," Helen said, as Becky left with her prize. "What happens to girls like that?"

"She'll either grow up like her mother and become mean, controlling, and critical," Millicent said. "Or she'll rebel and turn out totally different. If that happens, she'll have a hard fight on her hands, poor child. I don't know if the girl will be strong enough. But she did get her dress. Maybe there's hope."

Helen wondered if there had ever been any hope for Desiree. In some ways, the bride seemed more helpless than thirteen-year-old Becky.

Chapter 14

Millicent was saved. Helen was not.

Her job was safe, but how long would she have it if the cops arrested her for murder? Helen felt a sick, twisty feeling. She'd been inside a women's prison, all cinder block and steel. She'd talked to her best friend through a Plexiglas partition. Helen couldn't bring her flowers, chocolate, or comfort. She'd watched her wither away in jail.

I have to get help, Helen thought. I can't do this by myself. I'm too scared to think straight. Peggy was at work. Margery was wrapped up in Warren. And Phil. She didn't want to think who Phil was wrapped up in. Helen sneaked back to the shop's office and called the one friend who helped her see problems clearly.

"Helen!" Sarah said. "What's happening?" She sounded cheerful, but then she had a home office overlooking the beach.

"Lots of things," Helen said. "None of them good."

"Then we need to meet," Sarah said. "When can you do lunch?"

"Tomorrow is my day off." Helen said those words

with satisfaction. A few hours ago, she'd been facing a permanent unpaid vacation.

"Wear black," Sarah said. "We're going to South Beach."

"I've never seen you in anything but bright colors," Helen said.

"I don't want to be mistaken for a beach ball."

Sarah was a woman of size. Helen couldn't imagine her any other way. She had a Kewpie-doll face and energetic brown curls. She also had a shrewd money sense. Sarah had made a fortune in Krispy Kreme doughnuts and adult diaper stock.

That was why she picked up Helen the next afternoon in a green Range Rover. Helen settled into the luxurious leather seats with an appreciative sigh. The bridal-shop van had all the comfort of a welfare office.

As Helen's guts knotted into a rope, she tried to pretend she was going to South Beach on a sunny day. She soon ran out of chitchat. The traffic was the only subject left.

"Is this a street or a parking lot?" Helen said, as they crawled along Ocean Drive. "We've gone one block in the last five minutes."

"It's South Beach in the season," Sarah said. Suddenly she swung into a side street and pulled the SUV sharply to the curb.

Helen gripped the armrest to keep from sliding sideways. "What happened?"

"A miracle," Sarah said. "I've found a parking space near the restaurant."

"Where are we going?" Helen said.

"To the closest thing South Beach has to a shrine: The News Cafe."

Inside were tables, a newsstand, and a bookstore that

catered to the crowd who read Thoreau for fun. Outside was a sidewalk cafe with a breathtaking view of the beach beauties. Thongs and Thoreau were an unbeatable combination.

Sarah and Helen felt doubly lucky when they spotted an empty table outside under a green umbrella.

"Is this where Versace went before he was gunned down?" Helen said.

"Such a shame," Sarah said. "It wasn't fair to him or the restaurant."

Helen wondered if Versace had once warmed her seat. It was the closest she'd ever get to his clothes.

She was dining with the rich and beautiful. The air seemed to glow with money. Then the wind shifted. The money glow was replaced with something rank and powerful, like a high-school gym on a hot day: unbridled body odor.

They were downwind from four exquisitely dressed strangers. Their stink was a noxious cloud.

"Who are those people?" Helen said. "They're wearing couture, but they don't have two bucks for deodorant."

"Eurotrash," Sarah said. "A South Beach hazard. They infest all the restaurants. They think deodorant is for the masses."

"So is breathing," Helen said. "I see why our table was open."

"The good news is, they're leaving," Sarah said.

The four striking, smelly strangers rose. Their BO got up and went with them. Their table was quickly cleaned, and the Eurotrash were replaced by a very young woman and a very old man. His yellowish skin was so scored with wrinkles it looked like it had been cut with a razor. His eyes were flat and dead.

Now Helen thought she smelled sulfur.

The young woman had an angelic face and a burning desire for corruption. She almost thrust her high white bosom into his trembling old hands.

"Whatever he has, she wants it bad," Helen said.

"You don't want to know," Sarah said. "This is South Beach. We can watch the show or we can talk. Why don't you tell me what's wrong? You've worked hard to avoid the subject."

Helen's insides were tied so tight, she could hardly talk. "I'm mixed up in a murder, Sarah, and I'm scared."

There. She said it.

A waiter with a chiseled chin arrived, giving Helen a brief reprieve while they ordered lunch. Helen wondered if he was an actor, a model, or just another beautiful waiter. Everyone seemed to be seriously thin and glamorous. Helen felt fat and frumpy. She ordered the fruit plate as penance. Sarah wanted the Caesar salad with fried calamari. Helen wished she had her friend's culinary courage.

After the waiter brought their food, Helen began the story of Kiki's murder. Sarah started dismantling her salad with gusto. But as Helen talked, her friend's appetite waned. By the time Helen got to the DNA demand, Sarah abandoned her fork.

Helen knew it was serious if her friend wasn't eating. "You need a lawyer, Helen," Sarah said.

"A lawyer will run up bills I can't pay and tell me not to talk. If the cops arrest me, I'll be stuck in jail." Helen shuddered as she pictured herself in a prison jumpsuit on the other side of the Plexiglas.

"Then you need to solve the murder," Sarah said.

Helen could feel her guts rotating into new knots. "How?" she said. "I don't have the police resources. I don't have their forensic knowledge. I can't make people talk to me. I don't know anything."

"Sure you do. You know the time of death, right?" Sarah said.

"Well, I overheard the cops talking. They guessed Kiki had been dead about twelve hours. I saw that she'd been smothered. The police mentioned petechiae. You should have seen her face. It was like . . ."

Sarah turned as green as her salad. "I don't need to know that," she said quickly. "But you're wrong, Helen. You already know two important things: the time and the cause of death. Do you think a man or a woman killed her?"

Helen saw Kiki's doll-like corpse again. It had seemed so small. "The killer could have been a woman. Kiki weighed about a hundred pounds. A strong female could have thrown her facedown and smothered her. A big man could have done it easily."

Helen thought she hadn't eaten anything, but her plate was empty. How did that happen? "It's the cut nails that got me," Helen said. "They were a mutilation."

"Kiki must have scratched her killer," Sarah said. "Why else were her nails clipped? The police photographed your scratch, right? Did anyone else in the wedding party have scratches on their arms or neck?"

"Desiree had a long scratch on her arm," Helen said. "She said the cook's cat did it. Her father had some nasty scratches, too."

"That cat gets around," Sarah said.

"It's odd," Helen said. "Desiree doesn't live with her father."

"Maybe you need to look into that," Sarah said.

Helen's guts unkinked a notch. Perhaps this wasn't

hopeless after all. "Someone else had a scratch," she said. "I remember hearing about it, but I can't remember where."

"It will come to you," Sarah said confidently, as she speared a chunk of calamari. She was eating with enthusiasm again. "Here's something else: Who locked the church after the rehearsal and who opened the doors in the morning?"

"Good question," Helen said. "Kiki locked up after the rehearsal, but I heard her make a date to meet Jason in the church after the rehearsal dinner. She said churches made her hot."

"Nice lady," Sarah said.

"I don't know who opened the church. Jeff, the wedding planner, would. He was there when I arrived the morning of the wedding, directing a flock of florists."

There were swarms of people involved in this wedding: hairstylists, makeup artists, caterers, and guests. There must have been four hundred guests. Just the wedding party alone was huge. Sixteen attendants preceded the bride and groom to the altar. How many of those people hated Kiki?

The gut twisting started again. "What's the use?" Helen said. "It's too much for one person. I don't have anything."

Sarah pointed her fork at Helen. A crispy circle of calamari hung on the end. "You have one major advantage. You knew Kiki intimately. You heard her fight with her daughter, her ex, and other people the police may not know about. You have insights into her character they don't. The police have to find that out secondhand."

"True," Helen said. "I even saw her naked. Do you

know she had her pubic hair waxed into a dollar sign?
What do you think that says?"

"Sex and money. It's a dangerous combination. But
that's what I mean. You knew the victim alive. The police only saw her dead."

"Victim," Helen said. "That's a funny word for Kiki.
Tormentor would be more like it."

"Would anyone she'd tormented want to kill her?"

"Everyone," Helen said. Her guts twirled like a fork-
ful of spaghetti. But Sarah wasn't going to let her slide
back into despair.

"So there is no shortage of suspects. Tell me the main
ones," Sarah said.

"The bride, the groom, the father of the bride, the
best man."

"Killer wedding party," Sarah said.

"I'm not finished. There's the chauffeur. And maybe
Jason, the groomsman she was chasing at the rehearsal
dinner. But why are we even making this list? I can't interview them. Do you really think Desiree will talk with
me?"

"Yes," Sarah said. "You bonded with her. You were
her surrogate mother on her wedding day."

"What about her father, the lawyer?"

"Well, no, I don't think you can talk to him." Sarah
chewed some lettuce thoughtfully, then said, "I doubt if
the police can, either. But I bet you could worm your
way into his office for some background."

"How? I don't know anybody important."

"That's your strength, Helen. You're a clerk, one of
the invisible people who do the work. You can talk to
his office staff. They'll know more about him than anyone, including his wife."

"How do I see the others? I can't call up Chauncey. He's a big local theater director."

"Theaters always need volunteers," Sarah said.

"I have two tickets to *Richard the Third* tonight," Helen said. "It's Luke's last performance in that play before he does his movie. I can start there. Then I can call the theater and say I was impressed by the production and want to help. Would you like to go with me to the show?"

"Sorry, can't make it tonight. What about Phil?"

"He's dumped me for his ex."

"He hasn't dumped you. And you haven't dumped him. You're waiting for him to come to his senses. When does his ex leave town?"

"Margery said her run's been extended another week."

"Oh. Well, that's good. You need to work on this," Sarah said briskly. She polished off the last of her calamari. "I think you're on to something with that rose dress. Why would Kiki be wearing it? She was saving it for the reception. It was for her grand entrance, right?"

"Yep. It was way over the top for a mother of the bride, but she wanted to be a star at her daughter's wedding."

"So why was she wearing the rose dress when she died?" Sarah said.

Helen saw what Sarah was getting at. "Kiki wanted to impress someone with her fabulous gown. It had to be a man. A woman would be turned off by a sexy dress. It wasn't her chauffeur. Why would Kiki need to impress an employee?"

"So she wore it for a man, possibly a young one," Sarah said. "But would a young man be impressed? You said Kiki looked like an aging movie actress around the bridesmaids. She was no match for their youth and beauty."

"But she had one thing they didn't," Helen said. "Money."

"Which young men needed money the most?"

"The chauffeur, but we've ruled him out," Helen said. "Luke could get money from his wife. That leaves another actor—the handsome twit Jason. He's in the production, too. Guess I'm a theater volunteer."

"Unless . . ." Sarah said thoughtfully.

"What?"

"Unless Kiki wore the dress to get her ex back. Brendan might be impressed with a glamorous older woman."

"Her ex-husband?" Helen said. "No way. He has a new trophy wife."

"Maybe the young wife has worn him out. Young wives can be high maintenance. They need lots of money, attention, and time in the bedroom. Besides, if Brendan married Kiki again he wouldn't have to worry about money."

"But they fought the night before she died," Helen said. "I heard them."

"That fight sounds like jealousy to me, and where there's jealousy, there's still love. Brendan didn't want Kiki throwing herself at some young stud."

"I can see the advantages for him," Helen said. "But why would Kiki want to go back with Brendan? What could he give her? She had all the money and no-strings sex she wanted. Why cater to an older man with empty pockets and a big ego?"

"Ever talk to a twenty-year-old?" Sarah said.

"I wouldn't waste time talking to Rod," Helen said.

"After a while, you get tired of bimbos, male or female," Sarah said. "Chasing young studs was making Kiki look silly, and society's opinion was important to her. Maybe she wanted to settle down and quit being a scandal. She made a play for Jason at the rehearsal dinner, but she did it to make Brendan jealous. Her ex was her real target. If she remarried Brendan, she'd get a smart, respected man and a presentable escort."

"Do you think Brendan killed her out of jealousy?"

"That's one possibility," Sarah said. "Or maybe she made a promise to a younger man that she couldn't keep if she went back with Brendan."

"Interesting," Helen said. "But there's something else that bothers me. My boss, Millicent. She got in a fight with Kiki over money. She made me go to the funeral. And there's that weird ad in the *City Times*. The person who placed it looked like Millicent. But it could have been an actor impersonating her."

"All it would take was a white wig and red nails," Sarah said.

"Maybe I should get a better description of the buyer," Helen said.

"Sounds like you have a plan," Sarah said.

"Would you like dessert?" The beautiful waiter was back with more temptation.

"A cappuccino," Helen said.

"Chocolate mousse cake with a scoop of vanilla on the side," Sarah said.

"Ice cream *and* chocolate mousse?" Helen said.

"Kiki died thin," Sarah said. "Look where dieting got her."

"I'll take the cheesecake," Helen said. "Hold the ice cream." Sarah was the only person who made her feel virtuous when she pigged out.

Their conversation had been so intense that Helen

had lost track of where she was. Now she saw the South Beach scene again. The old man and the young woman were gone. Sitting at their table was a quiet man carrying a long leather case with a triangular bottom.

The hair went up on the back of Helen's neck. "What do you think he has in that case? A shotgun?"

"It's too narrow for a shotgun," Sarah said. "How about a pool cue and two balls?"

"It's not wide enough for pool balls. If this was my neighborhood, I'd say he was a shuffleboard hustler. They use a long, forked stick. Maybe the waiter knows."

The waiter was carrying Helen's foaming cappuccino and two wicked pieces of cake.

"Pssst," Helen said. "What's that man got in that case?"

"His broom," the waiter said. "He had the case custom-made."

There was nothing more to say.

Chapter 15

Helen heard the pop of a champagne bottle near the pool, then the clink of glasses.

Peggy and her policeman must be enjoying a little afternoon delight. Their voices carried in the soft, subtropical air. Helen tried not to listen, but she couldn't help it.

The man said, "You are so beautiful."

The woman said, "I love it when you lie." Her laugh was light and sophisticated. Helen heard the couple kiss.

The woman had a low, throaty voice, intimate and teasing. She didn't sound like Peggy. Was it Kendra?

The man definitely wasn't Phil. She'd know his voice anywhere. That was a relief. She hoped Kendra was with another man. Maybe she'd go away and forget about Phil.

Helen moved closer to listen. This was demeaning. She'd sunk to spying on a lowlife like Kendra. She had to get out of there. She had to stay. Helen stood behind the thick bougainvillea near the pool gate. She couldn't see anyone, but she could hear better.

"I'm not lying," the man said.

"Of course you are. I'm a wrinkled old bag." Good God. Now Helen recognized that voice. It was Margery. The man must be Warren. Look where her jealousy landed her.

"You are a woman of experience," Warren said. "The life you've lived only makes you more beautiful."

The Margery Helen knew would have snorted. This Margery gave a sexy little chuckle.

Helen was mortified to be eavesdropping on her landlady. She backed slowly away and fell over a folding lawn chair. Helen made more racket than twelve raccoons in a trash can trying to untangle herself. She wound up flat on the grass, bruised and embarrassed.

"What the heck was that?" Margery said. Now she sounded like her old self.

Her landlady popped up behind the bougainvillea. She was holding a champagne glass. Her hair was in that elegant French twist so unlike her usual pageboy. Her royal purple off-the-shoulder blouse had slid off even farther than the designer intended, revealing good shoulders and a firm bosom.

Helen blushed and stammered. "I'm really sorry. I didn't know you were there. I wanted to ask you if you'd like two tickets to *Richard the Third* tonight."

It was the first excuse that leaped into her head, and it was lame. If Margery said yes, Helen would have to buy herself a ticket for another performance. Her murder investigation was off to a great start.

"What are you doing on the ground?" Margery said. "Never mind. I don't want to know. The answer's yes. I'd love to see the play."

"Good," Helen lied. "You'll be taking Warren, of course."

"Nope, he's working at the studio tonight. I'm going with you. You need a keeper."

Warren stood up, holding a bottle of Piper-Heidsieck by the neck. The man could wear a safari jacket and not look silly. "Would you care to join us for champagne, Helen?" he said.

"Three's company. I mean, it's a crowd," Helen said. "Pardon me. Alcohol and stupidity don't mix."

Margery and Warren laughed and toasted her, clinking their glasses again. "See you tonight at seven," her landlady said. "We'd better go early. And I'll drive."

Helen started to say thanks, but she saw Warren nibbling Margery's neck. It was time to go.

By seven o'clock, Margery looked like her old self again, with her purple shorts and plain gray pageboy. They arrived almost forty-five minutes before the show, but there were no parking spots on the playhouse lot. Margery circled the side streets.

"Good thing the tickets Luke gave me are reserved," Helen said. "At least we'll have seats."

"This must be some show," Margery said. "The sign says it's sold out."

"The show may be good, but that's not why they're here," Helen said. "It's the first night the theater's been open since its benefactor's death—and the last night that Luke is playing Richard. Look at that. Three TV trucks and who knows how many newspaper reporters. This is the sort of story that winds up in *Vanity Fair*."

"The millionaire movie star," Margery said. "That's what the TV anchors are calling Luke. Kiki's death was a good career move. He hasn't even made the movie yet, and he's a star. I guess the rest are the usual ghouls who want to see the chief actors in the Blood and Roses Murder."

"I wonder if Desiree will be here," Helen said.

Margery swung her car into a spot on the street behind the theater. "Is that her? The little woman creeping in the stage door?" Margery pointed to a hunched black figure.

"Yep," Helen said. "She's only twenty or so, poor thing. She looks like an old woman."

But she moved like a young one. When a TV reporter approached her with a microphone, Desiree sprinted through the door at a speed that Jackie Joyner-Kersee would envy.

Helen and Margery elbowed their way through the crowd and found their seats. The Sunnysea Shakespeare Playhouse was the grand name for a small theater in an old supermarket three blocks from Sunnysea beach. The chairs were molded white plastic, the sets were amateurishly painted, and the props seemed to be from the actors' homes. Helen's heart sank. It was going to be a long night. Maybe they could sneak out after the first act.

Helen had an even greater desire to run when the actors filed onstage for the first scene. It was Shakespeare in modern dress. Richard and his men wore jackboots and trench coats with Nazi insignia. The women wore 1930s evening dresses.

"I didn't realize they had Goodwill in the fifteenth century," Margery said.

"Why do directors have to tinker with Shakespeare and make him modern?" Helen said.

The dark-haired woman sitting in front of them turned around and glared. Helen thought she looked like one of the actors in Richard's entourage. Oops. Had she insulted someone's son or husband? After that, Helen didn't dare say what she thought about Richard himself. She looked for Desiree and didn't see her in the audience.

Luke, as the clubfooted noble, wore a black trench coat and a modern walking cast to "show his crippled spirit," the program notes said. In case the audience still didn't get it, he carried a cane. The hollow thumping he made on the old wooden floor was distracting.

Soon Helen didn't notice. Luke glowed onstage. From the first familiar words, "Now is the winter of our discontent made glorious summer by this sun of York . . ." Helen could not take her eyes off the man.

Luke had seemed so handsome in the bridal salon. Now he was twisted with hate and malice. When Luke said he was "cheated of feature by dissembling nature, deformed, unfinished . . ." he really did look ugly.

How did he do that? Only the best actors were not afraid to make themselves unattractive for a role. Luke might well be a major talent. Helen reveled in his words. His voice was rich, without the orotund phoniness that afflicted so many Shakespearean actors. Helen was completely under the spell of the future Richard III.

"He's carrying his cane in the wrong hand," Margery said.

"Who?" Helen was jerked back to reality.

"Richard," Margery said.

"I hadn't noticed."

But now she did. It was no longer Richard III onstage, but Luke stumping around, saying that he was "so lamely and unfashionable that dogs bark at me."

"Actors!" Margery snorted. "Look at that. They always get it wrong. Only one I know who gets it right is the crippled coroner on *CSI*."

"Shush," Helen said. The woman in the row ahead

was glaring at them again. Helen could hear nearby theatergoers stirring restlessly in their seats.

"He's supposed to carry the cane on the side of his good leg, not the bad one," Margery said. "I see it wrong in plays and movies all the time. Even the major names do it. Makes me crazy."

"You're making me crazy," Helen said to her. "I want to watch the play."

"Quiet!" commanded the glaring woman. Even Margery shut up. Helen happily entered the world of make-believe murder, until the lights went up at intermission.

"That Luke is one hell of an actor," Margery said, as they strolled to the lobby. "He's got quite a future."

"Now that his mother-in-law doesn't." Helen regretted her words as they slipped out. "What did you think of the other actors?" she said quickly. "Elizabeth, King Edward's queen, seems quite good."

Margery checked her program. "Name is Donna Sue Hawser. She's better than good, but I'm guessing she's on the shady side of forty. Donna Sue's lost her chance for the big time. Must be hell, knowing she could have made it and didn't. All she needed was a little luck."

Must have been hell for Luke, knowing he was about to lose his main chance, Helen thought. But he was lucky. Conveniently lucky.

Helen was really glad she didn't say those words. She felt a tug on her sleeve and jumped. Desiree appeared soundlessly at her side. The new bride was drowned in black. Her shapeless mourning clothes seemed to swallow her. Her eyes had dark rings under them.

Desiree grabbed Helen's hand and pulled her away from Margery. "I must talk with you. After the show," she said in a tense whisper. "Someplace where the people here won't go."

"There's Lester's Diner," Helen said. "But I'm with a friend. She's my ride. Can Margery come with us?"

"No, I want to talk to you about my mother's death," Desiree said. Her eyes had a frantic, feral look. "It's important. Don't worry. I'll take you home. Meet me in the lobby after the show." She vanished through the backstage curtains.

"What was that all about?" Margery said.

"Desiree wants to meet with me and talk about Kiki. She wants someplace where the theatergoers don't usually go. I suggested Lester's Diner."

"You're asking a woman worth thirty million dollars to go to Lester's?" Margery said.

"It will be a new experience for her."

"That's for sure," Margery said. "Well, I don't mind. I like Lester's pancakes."

"She doesn't want you there. She wants to talk to me alone. She insisted and I said yes. She might tell me something useful."

"I don't like this," Margery said. "Let me follow you. I won't even come in. I'll sit in the parking lot. I can keep an eye on you through Lester's plateglass windows."

"No! Desiree will see your car and get suspicious." Margery drove a white Cadillac the size of a sunporch. It was hard to miss. "She'll bring me home. She's not going to hurt me, Margery. She knows I'm telling you where we're going. Her request is a little weird, but she's perfectly safe."

"Helen, that woman scares me," Margery said.

"She scares me, too. But she might know who killed her mother."

"Probably just has to look in the mirror," Margery said.

"Do you really believe that?" Helen said.

"I believe she is one sick chick. I don't like this," Margery said. "If you're not home by midnight, I'm calling the police."

"Good," Helen said. "That's exactly what I want."

Chapter 16

Everything about Lester's Diner was huge: the gray booths piped in red, the plateglass windows, even the coffee cups. They held fourteen ounces of java and looked like soup bowls with handles.

The china was thicker than an alderman's head. Helen loved the diner's shiny metal and neon. It was bright, noisy, and reassuring.

Helen needed its cheerful comfort after the trip there. They drove through stop-and-go tourist traffic. The conversation was also stop-and-go: strained chatter punctuated by awkward silences. Desiree drove a black BMW, a modest car by her mother's standards. Luke sat in front, drained by his performance.

Helen tried to praise Luke's acting, but he cut her off in midcompliment. "I was okay," he said. "I don't think that audience cared much about Shakespeare."

"You were better than okay," Helen said. "You were the real thing. It was a privilege to watch you."

Luke shrugged. He seemed to need her praise and despise it at the same time. "The rest of the cast was first-rate," Helen said. "Especially the woman who played Edward's queen."

"Oh, you mean Donna Sue," Desiree said. "She works for my father. She's a secretary." Dismissed.

Helen filed that information away. She now had an in at Brendan's law firm. After that, all three gave up trying to say anything.

Helen wondered why the heiress wanted to talk to her. She'd never known a rich woman who cared what a poor one thought.

Helen was grateful when they finally pulled into Lester's lot. Heads turned when Luke walked into the diner. The man had star power. No one noticed his tiny, chinless bride.

Luke seemed attentive to Desiree, but Helen couldn't tell if it was true love or a good act. His new bride clung to Luke. When his cell phone rang, which was every three minutes, he had to pry her fingers off his arm to check the number.

"Is this place real?" Desiree asked Helen.

"What do you mean?"

"Is it one of those new diners made to look old?"

"No, Lester's has been around since 1967."

"It's a hoot," Desiree said.

The hostess showed them to a booth the size of a motel room. Their waitress called them honey, poured coffee, and took their orders. Luke drank his coffee black. He asked for a salad with lemon juice and a hamburger with no bun—the diet of an actor facing the camera.

Desiree wanted a three-egg omelet, pancakes, extra-crisp bacon, and a side of sausage. She added enough cream to turn her coffee beige, then three packets of sugar.

"I wanted to thank you for your help when—" Desiree stopped and took a deep breath. "When my mother was found. I don't think I'll ever get over it."

Luke patted her hand on cue.

"I'm sorry," Helen said.

"I didn't get to tell Mother good-bye," Desiree said. "We didn't part on good terms. I'm learning to forgive her and bury my resentment."

Helen flashed on Kiki's rose-covered coffin. You buried something, she thought. But it was a knife in your mother's back.

The waitress arrived with platters of food, most of them for Desiree. Helen caught Luke staring longingly at the crispy bacon. He didn't look at his wife with the same hunger. Desiree poured an astonishing amount of syrup on her pancakes. The woman craved sweetness.

Helen pushed her single egg around on her plate, too nervous to eat.

"An actor friend used to work at that bookstore with you," Luke said. "He said you solved a murder."

"He was wrong," Helen said. "I didn't do anything." She didn't want any connection with that mess.

"We need your help." Luke batted those long lashes and handed her a card with the couple's phone number on it. "The police aren't doing enough about Desiree's mother. We thought you might know something."

Helen knew he wouldn't pay her for that knowledge. Luke was a user.

"You're probably closer to the investigation than I am," Helen said. "Who do you think killed Mrs. Shenrad?"

"Well, I don't want to say anything bad about another actor, but Jason's behavior at the funeral was unacceptable."

"He was disgusting," Desiree burst out. "He cornered me at the funeral and said it was Mother's last wish that I give him twenty thousand dollars. Can you believe that?" Helen knew the bride was upset. She'd quit eating.

"I can believe anything about Jason," Helen said. "Did you tell the police?"

"No, it was too embarrassing."

Embarrassing? Why would that be embarrassing? Unless lover boy's request was blackmail. Maybe Jason had photos of the naked philanthropist getting a big contribution.

Would Jason blackmail Desiree at her mother's funeral? Well, the guy would have sex in a church.

Luke's phone rang again. He checked the number and said, "Excuse me. My agent in California. I have to take this one." He headed outside. Desiree went back to her abandoned plate. Her bacon crunched like bones.

This was Helen's chance to get some information from Desiree. "It must be exciting to have your husband in a major movie," Helen said. "I don't know why your mother objected in the first place."

"I think my marriage made Mother feel old and frightened. She tried to get control any way she could."

Helen wondered if that soothing theory came from a shrink.

"It's so terribly sad that our last day together was that dreadful wedding rehearsal." Desiree paused at this solemn thought, then attacked her bacon again. "I was humiliated by Mother's behavior. How would you like that to be your last memory of your mother?"

Helen had enough trouble thinking about her mother and Lawn Boy Larry. She wondered if he wore that flat cap to bed.

"You're not your mother," Helen said. "You're not responsible for her behavior."

Desiree dabbed at her eyes with a tissue. Was the bride so beaten down she needed a shop clerk's good opinion? Or was she an actor, too? Helen studied the dark circles under Desiree's eyes. The left one was slightly smeared. Desiree had enhanced her grief with makeup.

Luke was still pacing the parking lot and talking on the phone.

"Desiree, do you really think Jason killed your mother?"

"I don't know." Desiree shifted uneasily and looked around for her husband. She was lying, Helen thought.

"Is there anyone else you think might be the murderer?"

"Yes," Desiree's eyes turned flat and mean. "Millicent."

"My boss? You think Millicent is a murderer?" Helen started to laugh, then saw Desiree was serious.

Helen waited while Desiree slit three sausages. "Millicent placed that awful ad. I know she did. It was revenge. She was furious when Mother forgot her checkbook. Millicent stormed over to the rehearsal dinner."

Hmm. Her boss didn't mention that.

"She threatened Mother at the restaurant. She lured her outside, away from the other guests. I saw her."

Oh, boy. No wonder the police questioned Millicent. "Threatened her how?" Helen asked.

"Millicent said if she didn't get the check by Saturday morning, she'd rip those dresses off my bridesmaids' backs."

"That doesn't sound like much of a threat," Helen said.

"Then she said, 'After all I did for you, Kiki Shenrad, you are the biggest ingrate in Broward County. I could strangle you with my bare hands.'"

"People say things like that all the time," Helen said.

"But the people they threaten don't turn up dead. Mother said she'd bring the check the morning of the wedding. Then Mother told Millicent to leave the premises immediately or she'd call the police. She left after that."

She'd have to, Helen thought. A police report of an altercation with a prominent customer over money would ruin Millicent.

"I could see where she might be angry. But why would Millicent kill the woman who writes the checks?"

"Mother always paid, but she was in no hurry," Desiree said. "She delayed as long as she could. People with means do that. It would be faster and easier for Millicent to collect the money from Mother's estate. But I'm going to make sure she has a very hard time. And you can tell her that."

Desiree pushed her empty plate aside and looked out the window. "It's Luke. He's waving to me. He wants me to come outside. He must have good news. I'll meet you at the car."

"But—" Helen said.

Desiree threw down her napkin and ran out. She wrapped herself around Luke's waist while he talked on the phone.

Helen paid their bill.

If Luke's call was good news, he didn't share it with Helen. Nor did the couple thank her for picking up their dinner tab. Helen guessed she should be grateful they gave her a ride home.

As she sat in silence in the Beemer, Desiree's accusation worked its way through Helen like a slow poison. Little distrustful memories stabbed at her: Why didn't Millicent say that Kiki would give her a big check at the wedding? She could have left a message at Margery's.

Because she knew Kiki was dead, an ugly little voice whispered.

Helen could see an enraged Millicent following Kiki to the church, waiting till Jason left, then fighting over money and smothering Kiki with the dress she wouldn't pay for.

Unless Jason killed her.

Or maybe it was Desiree, the little bride with the big fake bags under her eyes. Desiree had to paint on her grief. Her husband Luke was some actor—but so was his wife.

"I turn left off Las Olas?" Desiree said.

"Then right," Helen said. "It's that big white building."

The Beemer pulled in front of the Coronado. Helen wished that Desiree did not know where she lived.

As she walked to her apartment, Helen saw a shadow figure on Phil's closed blinds. The woman swayed, swung her long hair, and sang, "You can't divorce my heart. It's the part that will always love you."

Kendra.

Was she rehearsing—or giving Phil a private performance?

Helen slammed the door to her apartment, but she couldn't shut out Kendra's song. All thoughts of murder—Kiki's murder, anyway—vanished. She was tormented by jealousy, loss, and love.

It's your fault, she told herself. You drove Phil away.

Why didn't he tell me about her? Helen's heart cried. She paced restlessly as the rooms grew smaller. Tonight her cozy apartment seemed claustrophobic. She couldn't sleep. She couldn't sit out by the pool. She might run into Margery and Warren, or Peggy and her policeman. Everyone had a lover but her. Even Kendra. Especially Kendra.

Helen couldn't stand being shut up with her thoughts. Although it was midnight, she found herself walking—no, stomping—through the dark streets. Helen knew it was foolish to wander alone in the poorly lit lanes. But she couldn't bear the laughing couples and bright lights of Las Olas. She was too angry, and though she wouldn't admit it, too wounded.

Her ex had betrayed her so badly, Helen swore she'd never trust a man again. Until she met Phil and learned to love him. Then Kendra showed up and wrecked Helen's life all over again.

She stumbled on the uneven sidewalk. Helen stopped to wipe away her tears. Damn him. Damn all men.

Suddenly, she was aware of footsteps behind her. Heavy footsteps, not the light click clack of heels. Someone was following her. Helen looked around the street. The bright-painted Caribbean cottages were dark. The porch lights were off. The Bahamas shutters were down. No dogs barked.

Where was she? How many blocks had she gone?

Helen reached in her pocket for her key ring. Her car had died, and she couldn't afford to fix it. Now its only use was the dubious protection of a pointed car key in a stalker's eye.

The footsteps drew closer. She walked faster, saw a street sign, and made a quick turn toward the lights of Las Olas. They were three dark blocks away.

"Helen!"

She jumped. It was Phil.

"Helen, wait up!"

She walked faster, long-legged strides that ate up a whole sidewalk square at a time. But Phil was determined. She heard him running. Then he was beside her.

"Helen, please! Let me talk to you."

Phil stepped in front of her, which was like stepping in front of a charging lioness. "Listen to me, Helen Hawthorne. I love you. I can't live without you."

Then his warm lips were on hers. She felt her foolish anger dissolve.

"I'm counting the days until Kendra's gone," he whispered, as he kissed her face and then her throat. She ran her fingers through his long silky hair, then down the muscles of his shoulders. He felt so strong.

"I was wrong. I should have never let her stay with me," Phil said. "It was the second biggest mistake of my life."

"What was the first?" Helen asked and was instantly sorry. Phil stopped kissing her to answer.

"The day I married Kendra."

Helen wanted to go back to kissing, but she needed some answers. "How did you meet her? Kendra doesn't seem your type."

"She wasn't. But I had a long undercover assignment in Kentucky. She was the prettiest girl in town and I was lonely."

"So you really went undercover."

"I knew it was wrong when we stood at the altar," Phil said, "but it was too late. I tried to make the marriage work, but it was hopeless. Now that she's staying with me, it's worse than hopeless. I'd forgotten what a slob she is. This morning, I found wet pantyhose in my shower, dirty dishes in my sink, and an open jam jar on the counter. You can't leave food out in this climate. Now I have ants."

His commonplace domestic complaints gave her a little thrill.

"I promise you that she means nothing to me," Phil said, as she let him fold her into his arms. The soft fabric of his shirt was almost like suede.

Helen remembered that her ex-husband had said the same thing about Sandy. She kissed Phil until she smothered that memory.

Chapter 17

It was the morning of the lost men.

They sat on Millicent's gray husband couch like sailors stranded on a desert isle, dazed and bleak. Helen thought the couch cast a spell on men, sucking out their money and their hope.

One couch castaway was in his late twenties. Mark was a lawyer who looked like he was wearing a tie even when he had on a Polo shirt. His bride, Courtney, was in butt-sprung shorts and broken-down mules. Helen wouldn't wear that outfit to take out the trash.

The bloom was off that rose, she thought. Helen saw the couple in twenty years, gone to seed and planted in matching recliners.

"I haven't given Courtney the ring yet," Mark said. "She's picking out the dress. I guess we have to get engaged."

He sounded so hopeless, Helen said, "You don't have to. It's not too late."

"I don't have any choice," he said.

The bride marched out of the dressing room, flushed with triumph.

Millicent followed with a plastic-shrouded gown. Courtney paid for the dress, then dragged her not-yet-fiancé with her like a newly captured slave.

"How do you pick out the dress before you get the ring?" Helen said when the couple left.

Millicent was rehanging Courtney's rejected gowns. "Are you kidding? I get brides in here who don't have the groom yet. If a woman wants to marry, she will. She goes out and gets herself a man. Don't believe that stuff about women waiting for the man to pop the question. In my experience, women do the picking. The smart ones let the guys think it was their idea."

Courtney's quick march through the store had left a gaggle of gowns tangled on their hangers. Helen pried them apart carefully, protecting the delicate fabrics.

"That groom sounded awfully trapped."

"He trapped himself," Millicent said. "Mark wants to make partner at a big Lauderdale law firm. He's marrying the boss's daughter."

"How do you know this?"

"Courtney told me."

"She doesn't care?" Helen dropped a heavy duchesse satin in surprise. Good thing Millicent didn't see it hit the floor.

Millicent's white hair had disappeared into the snowy gowns, making her look headless. Now she faced Helen, using a bloodred nail to emphasize her words.

"Listen. Courtney is getting what she wants—an ambitious husband. Mark is getting what he wants—a partnership in a big firm. People always get what they want, Helen. They just don't realize it."

Helen wondered if Millicent got what she wanted, and how she got it. She wished she'd never listened to Desiree. Helen thought last evening was the start of the investigation that would clear her name. Instead, she was more confused than ever. The little bride was sly. Her accusations insinuated themselves into Helen's mind. Did Millicent really murder Kiki in a fit of rage to get her money from the estate? Did she place that shocking "Weddings to Die For" ad?

The ad was a brilliant move. Oh, not at first. Millicent endured cold shoulders and cancellations. But now the shop was deluged with brides and their mothers, all buying. The ad was outrageous, and Floridians reveled—or wallowed—in their own bad taste. Kiki's death brought new life to Millicent's business.

Millicent hung up the last dress, pulled a bottled water out of the fridge, and dropped into a pink chair.

"Put your feet up a minute, Helen. This is the last free time we have until six o'clock. We've got appointments the rest of the afternoon. I've got so much business, I may have to hire another salesperson."

"Because of that ad?" Helen said.

"Yes. The TV coverage didn't hurt, either."

Helen lowered her voice, even though the store was empty. "Millicent, it's just us girls. I swear I'll never tell. Did you place that ad?"

"Of course not." Millicent looked indignant, but her bloodred nails crawled nervously in her lap.

"The *City Times* ad taker said it was bought by a woman with white hair, red nails, and a red jacket," Helen said.

"So? Anyone can dress up like that."

Anyone could. But did they? Helen needed to know for sure. Truth was the only antidote to Desiree's poison. Fortunately, the answer was right down the street.

"OK if I go out for coffee?" Helen said.

"Go ahead. Just be back in half an hour."

"Can I get you anything?"

"I'm fine. Leave." Suddenly, Millicent seemed relieved to have her out of the store.

The *City Times* office was ten desks, bales of tied papers, and a bundle of energy behind the counter. The small brown-haired receptionist darted about like a hummingbird.

"Eric is in the ad department, around the corner," she said, and zipped off to answer the phone.

Eric had a soul patch, a pierced eyebrow, and a lot of attitude.

"I'm from Millicent's," Helen said. "We're still trying to find out who placed that ad."

"Hey, it's not my fault. I just took the money." He shrugged. Helen thought about grabbing him by his eyebrow ring.

"You took the money to ruin our business. I don't want to cause trouble, Eric. Answer my questions and I'll go away. Give me grief and I'll be back with a lawyer."

That got his attention. Helen's bluff worked.

"Could the person who placed the ad have been a man dressed as a woman?"

"Not unless he had his Adam's apple shaved," Eric said. "We get transvestites in here with ads for the clubs." He was impressed with his own esoteric knowledge.

"You said she was about fifty-five?"

"Yeah. My mom's fifty-one and this lady looked older."

"Could this person have been wearing a white wig to make herself look older?"

"Maybe," Eric said. "But she had those freckles on her hands—what do you call them?"

"Age spots." Helen had been trying to convince herself those brown spots on her hands were big freckles.

"Her neck was crinkly, too," Eric said. "I guess you could artificially age yourself if you were in a movie, but it would be pretty hard to pull off otherwise."

Helen sighed. Eric was right.

She went sadly back to the salon. Now she knew. Millicent had placed that ad and lied about it. Helen felt sick. She'd admired her boss as one tough, smart businesswoman.

Millicent was hauling new stock out of the back room. She towed a rack of heavy dresses as easily as a child's wagon. Her biceps bulged through her suit sleeves. Her fingers were strong. Millicent could have easily smothered tiny Kiki.

"Here, Helen, hang this dress on the front rack." Helen took a beaded gown from Millicent's lightly liver-spotted hand.

"Millicent, I've got to talk to you before the next round of appointments."

"So talk," Millicent said.

"I saw Desiree last night."

"The deadbeat bride," Millicent said.

"She said you went to the rehearsal dinner and threatened her mother."

"She's a liar," Millicent said hotly. "I never went near that rehearsal dinner. I wondered where the police got that story. She sicced the cops on me. I ought to sue her. I yelled at Kiki on the phone. They can check my cell phone records."

So what? Helen thought. That wouldn't stop her from driving to the restaurant. "Desiree says you wanted to strangle Kiki."

"Of course I wanted to strangle her," Millicent said. "I

also wanted to shoot her, stomp her, and chop her into little pieces. But give me some credit for customer relations. I didn't say it. I asked her to pay the bill, and she promised to bring a check Saturday morning. Now her debt-dodging daughter wants to get out of paying me. That's what this is really about."

"Where were you the night of the rehearsal dinner?" Helen said.

Millicent pointed one bloody nail in Helen's face. "That's none of your business. But if you think I'm a murderer, Helen Hawthorne, you can walk right out that door."

Helen couldn't quit. She needed the money. She also needed to keep an eye on Millicent. Maybe Desiree was lying about that rehearsal dinner. But Helen didn't think so.

She'd already caught Millicent in one lie.

For the rest of the afternoon, while Helen wrestled with white silk and satin, she made her decision. Tonight was the night. She would ask Phil to move in with her. She was ready. She couldn't change her lying boss, but she could fix her love life.

Last night with Phil had been wonderful. When he'd gotten out of her bed at two a.m., she'd wanted him to stay. Not just for the rest of the night, but the rest of her life.

Phil said he had to get up early to meet with the lawyers again. Helen felt a small twinge of delight when she thought of Phil stumbling through his front door and accidentally waking up Kendra asleep on his couch. He'd have Helen's scent on his skin, her lipstick on his shirt. That would teach Kendra to move in on her man.

But Helen knew it was stupid to leave a man as fine

as Phil alone with a schemer like Kendra. That's why she would ask him to live with her. Eventually they'd need a bigger place. Maybe they could move into 2C when Warren went to his condo. They would break the curse on that apartment forever.

She ran home to tell him. She started to knock on Phil's door, but it was open. A good sign. He was waiting for her.

"Phil," she said softly. She didn't want the whole apartment complex to hear her. Margery knew too much about her love life already.

There was no answer.

"Phil?" Helen stepped inside.

She smugly noted that the living room was a welter of women's clothes, pizza boxes, and dirty coffee mugs. Kendra had not gotten any neater. She stepped around a sparkly red bustier on the floor. Cheap, just like its owner.

"Phil?"

He must be waiting for her in bed. He'd done that before. He knew when she got off work. Phil had sexy black silk sheets and a silver champagne bucket. Helen sighed at the memory of their champagne nights and picked her way around Kendra's pink spike heels.

The bedroom door was shut. Phil definitely planned to surprise her.

Well, she had a surprise of her own. She tiptoed back across the room, stepping over purple hot pants. Did anyone wear those tacky things anymore? She slipped the chain lock on the front door. Kendra was probably at the club by now, but Helen didn't want her walking in on them.

Helen checked herself in the mirror. Not bad, considering the day she'd had. Her hair looked pretty good, and she'd put on fresh lipstick before she left work. Her white blouse and black pants were boring, but she'd take care of that. Helen unbuttoned her blouse and saw that her white bra was gray. Ugh. She flung the blouse and bra on top of Kendra's trashy clothes. The boring pants followed. The black lace panties could stay. They looked sexy.

Much better, Helen decided. She was forty-two, but she had a good body. Lifting heavy wedding dresses had given her firm upper arms and a perky chest.

Enough of Miss Proper. Helen could be dead as Kiki tomorrow. It was time she lived a little.

"Surprise, Phil!" She flung open the bedroom door.

Phil looked stunned.

He pulled himself away from Kendra. The Kentucky Songbird was clinging to him like ivy on a college wall.

"Helen, it's not how it seems," Phil said.

"Let me guess," Helen said. "She was giving you mouth-to-mouth resuscitation."

"No, she was trying to get me back."

"She doesn't have to try," Helen said. "She can have you."

Kendra stood there with a little catlike smile. She was wearing clothes. Helen was not. She grabbed her pants, bra, and blouse and yanked open the front door. The chain lock flopped it back.

Helen ripped off the chain, holding her clothes over the vital spots. She was humiliated enough without getting dressed in front of Phil and Kendra. She only had to scamper next door.

Phil blocked the door. "Please don't go. Remember last night. Try to see this sensibly."

"I don't want to see it at all," Helen said. "Get out of my way."

She pushed past him.

"Helen!" Phil cried, but she slammed the door in his face. The ten-foot sprint to her place was screened by tropical plants. She made a running start and ran smack into Margery.

"Nice to see you," her landlady said. "All of you. Are you taking up nudism?"

"It's not funny," Helen said. "I caught Phil with Kendra. All men are unfaithful bums."

"Get dressed," Margery said, "and meet me at the pool. I'll have Peggy there."

"I don't want to show my face ever again."

"You've shown everything else," Margery said. "Put your clothes on and meet us by the pool. You can't stay holed up inside in the mood you're in."

Helen put on her dingy bra, dull blouse, and boring pants. She gave her cat Thumbs some food and an indifferent pat, picked up a pretzel for Pete, and headed for the pool.

Her landlady was in lavender tonight. There was nothing sensible about her clothes. Margery's shorts had a flirty ruffle around the hem. The pointy toes on her lavender T-straps would have killed Helen's feet. She handed Helen a cold glass of wine.

Peggy and Pete were both in brilliant green. The dieting parrot munched morosely on a celery stick.

"I brought him a pretzel," Helen said.

"He can't have it," Peggy said. "He's gained another ounce. The vet says he has to lose weight."

"Forget Pete," Margery said. "What did that bird-brain Phil do?" She lit a Marlboro.

"I caught him with Kendra. She was all over that man like a cheap suit."

"Like a cheap tart." Peggy was the sort of friend who took your side.

"I finally trust a man after my ex," Helen said, "and Phil does this. I loved him. I really did." Her throat was clogged with tears.

"Awwwk!" Pete snapped his celery.

"Go ahead and cry him out of your system," Peggy said. "That's awful."

"It gets worse," Helen said. "I was going to surprise him. I was standing there in my slightly wrinkled birthday suit and Kendra was fully dressed."

Margery blew out enough smoke to set off a fire alarm. "Wait a minute," she said. "Kendra was dressed?"

"Yes," Helen said. "In black spandex. With rhinestones."

"Anything disarranged or popped out?" Margery said.

"No," Helen said. "Why do you care what that little tramp was wearing?"

"What about Phil? What was he wearing?"

"Jeans and a blue shirt with rolled-up sleeves." The shirt matched his eyes, Helen wanted to say, but didn't. She sniffed back more tears. She was a sucker for rolled-up sleeves. She was a sucker, period.

"His shirt was tucked in and buttoned?"

"Yes," Helen said.

"Any signs of life in the zipper area?"

"Margery!" Helen said. "No. Why are you asking these disgusting questions?"

"Because Phil may be telling the truth. Kendra could have ambushed him. It's possible she heard you come in and threw herself at him. She knew how you'd react."

"What were they doing together in the bedroom with the door closed?" Helen asked.

"She could have shut it when she heard you stumbling around in the living room. Was the door closed all the way?"

"I don't know. Is it important?"

"Yes," Margery said. "Try to visualize the scene."

Helen took another slug of wine to fortify herself. She closed her eyes and replayed one of the more embarrassing moments in her life. She saw herself chucking her clothes and heading for Phil's bedroom. She felt her hand on his doorknob. It opened at her touch. She didn't have to turn it.

"It was closed, but not completely shut. It wasn't locked, that's for sure."

"How close was Kendra to the door?" Margery said.

Helen saw a fiery waterfall of hair and a short black skirt. "I almost hit her with it. I wished I had."

"The only thing he's guilty of is stupidity," Margery said. "Phil was duped."

"I don't understand," Helen said. "He's a private detective. He's done undercover work with mob bosses and drug dealers, but he's outsmarted by his ex-wife?"

"Yep," Margery said. "That takes a different kind of smarts."

She poured Helen more wine. "You're going to need courage. I gather your marriage wasn't the best. It gets harder to love as you get older. Your new man has to live with the mistakes of the old—and he doesn't even know it. Don't make Phil pay for something your ex-husband did."

Helen wanted to believe her. But she saw herself slut naked in front of Kendra.

Her heart shriveled with shame.

Chapter 18

The bride was a young Grace Kelly in a simple white strapless gown.

"She's beautiful!" Millicent said.

Molly was touchingly, heartbreakingly beautiful. The pale blonde was alight with love. Molly's mother was as handsome as Chanel and a good salon could make her, but she'd never been as lovely as her daughter. Now maternal pride made her beautiful, too.

While Helen buttoned the bride into the gown and Millicent pinned the hem, Molly talked about Eric, the accountant she was marrying in four months.

"Last night, Eric brought me a rose and teddy bear for our anniversary," she said.

"Which anniversary is this?" Helen asked.

"We'd been engaged exactly one hundred eighteen days, six hours, and seven minutes. Eric doesn't like to celebrate conventional dates. Eric says . . ."

Molly's mother interrupted the Eric ecstasies. "Put on the veil, please, so I can see the full effect."

Millicent dusted off her knees, stood up, and pinned the gossamer veil to the bride's chignon. It floated around her, a silken aura. Molly did a dramatic twirl that ended in a happy little skip.

Two tears ran down her mother's cheeks. "My baby is really getting married," she said. "It wasn't a wedding dress until you put on the veil."

Millicent wiped her own eyes with a red-lacquered nail. This tender scene seemed to erase all the hysteria, fights, and harsh words heard in her salon. "This is why I sell bridal gowns," she said.

Helen felt tears forming, too, but hers were bitter. She ran for the small dressing room, locked herself in, and wept silently. She cried for Kiki, who could only compete with her daughter. She cried for Desiree, who had oceans of money and not a drop of her mother's love. She cried for Molly and the inevitable loss of her young love. She hoped it would change into something strong and mature.

Finally, Helen cried for the woman she used to be, the one who wanted to love Rob forever and fled when that love failed. The woman whose life was shattered again last night.

Then she shook herself like a wet dog, blew her nose, and decided she'd had enough dramatics.

Helen could not believe that Millicent, who wept for her beautiful brides, was a murderer. It didn't make sense. Helen's brain had been infected by her dinner with Desiree.

I have Mad Bride Disease, she thought. The craziness that affects weddings has seeped into my head. Helen had seen perfectly normal women have fits because their bridesmaid dresses were the wrong shade of cranberry. I'm the wackiest of all, if I think Millicent is a killer. The only cure was to prove Millicent was innocent. Maybe

her appointment book would say where she was the
night of the rehearsal dinner.

Millicent was still working with Molly and her
mother. Helen slipped into the back office and checked
the appointment book. It was blank for that Friday.

Then Helen opened the filing cabinet and pulled out
Kiki's folder. The bills were staggering: almost seventy
thousand dollars, including the special-order dresses, express delivery, and seamstress overtime. She found a
copy of Kiki's check for half the amount, but no other
record of payment.

Then she found one other thing: an application for a
home-equity credit line on Millicent's home. She'd mort-
gaged her house to front this order. Helen had Millicent's
motive for murder.

She put the file back, then pulled it out again and
wiped it with a clean cloth. If the cops arrested Millicent
for murder, she didn't want her prints on the papers.
Next she wiped down the file cabinet. She hoped Windex
killed fingerprints.

"Good!" Millicent was standing in the doorway. "This
office needs dusting. I'm glad you're doing it."

"I'll stay back here for a bit," Helen said. Her heart
was beating so fast she was afraid she'd slide onto the
floor. "Yell if you need me out front."

As soon as Millicent went back to work, Helen called
Jeff. There was nothing odd about that. Bridal salons and
wedding planners talked constantly. Besides, Jeff was so
soothing and sensitive.

"Oh, my *God*, Helen, are you all right? Did you survive that horrible, horrible *day*?"

"I'm fine, Jeff," Helen said. But she couldn't keep the
weariness from her voice. "It was bad, wasn't it?"

"That poor *family*." Helen could see Jeff's boyish face.

Even his freckles would seem sympathetic. "I feel so *bad* for them. When I came home, I told my partner, Andy, don't expect me to cook for you tonight, because I am *wiped out*. Andy called for Chinese takeout and then he rubbed my feet. I hope your honey did something *special* for you."

"Very special," Helen said. "He made sure I went out and had a few drinks."

I'm not lying, she thought. After I met up with Phil's almost ex-wife, I ran out and got plastered.

"Aren't we *lucky*? Both of us?"

"Yeah, Jeff, real lucky. I've been wondering about something ever since the police questioned me."

"How *long* did they keep you there, Helen? The police let me leave about two."

"Till five o'clock."

"That's *terrible*. I made the calls about the reception and then I gave that cute Detective McIntyre my name and phone number. Don't get me wrong, Andy's a keeper, but the cop was a hunk-a-rama. His *mustache* is like a little pet."

Jeff's voice became confiding. "You do know the family *canceled* the reception?"

"That must have cost a fortune," Helen said.

"One-ninety a plate for four hundred people. The family will have to eat all of it."

Helen saw Desiree, Luke, and Brendan stuffing down hundreds of dinners.

"I mean the *cost*, not the food," Jeff said. "They wanted to donate the food to a homeless shelter, but the hotel insurance and the health department regulations wouldn't allow it.

"Still, *canceling* that reception was the right thing to do.

They couldn't be dining and dancing with that poor woman *murdered*."

"One-ninety a person," Helen said. "You must be some planner. What were you serving for a dollar ninety—peanut butter? My wedding buffet was fifteen a person almost twenty years ago."

"You're such a kidder," Jeff said. "You know it's a hundred and ninety *dollars* a person."

Helen did the math. The reception dinner would come to almost eighty thousand dollars with taxes and tips. That would buy a nice condo.

"I know some people think that's a *lot* of money," Jeff said.

Like me, Helen thought. Nearly six years' salary for one dinner.

"But they don't *understand*. Desiree is a *princess* and a royal wedding must have a *feast*. It's expected in their position."

Poor Desiree. A princess could not have a private life.

A few notes of the Wedding March chimed in the background. "Oops," Jeff said. "Here comes another bride. Gotta go."

"Wait! Jeff! Do you know who locked the church Friday night and opened it Saturday morning?"

"I know Kiki had the key. She paid some *huge* deposit for it. She said she had to go back there for a little something after the rehearsal dinner."

Yeah, Helen thought. Little Jason.

"I assumed she'd lock up after that. She was going to send someone to open the church for me at six a.m. I found the door open when I got there."

There was a loud silence.

"Helen, do you think it was open *all night*?"

"I do," she said.

*   *   *

One call down, one question answered. But before Helen could do more investigating, she had to deal with more customers. Millicent was caught up in the bridal chaos. She even smiled when Cassie came in, towing a short, shy woman.

"This is my Aunt Nita!!" Cassie said. "She wants to see my dream dress. Nita's like my second mom. I couldn't buy it unless she approved."

Helen hauled the wedding gown back to the dressing room one more time. Maybe she should just leave it there, Cassie was in so often showing it off.

"Aunt Nita loves it!!" Cassie said, when she came out of the dressing room. Aunt Nita nodded and smiled, but stayed silent. "I just have to show my dream dress to one more person!!" And she was out the door, Aunt Nita obediently following.

"Her dream dress is turning into my nightmare," Helen said.

"She'll buy," Millicent said.

It was another hour before Helen was free to call the Shakespeare Playhouse office.

"We can always use volunteers," said the woman who answered the phone. "In fact, could you usher this evening?"

Helen was startled. "So soon? Well, uh—"

"If you can't, we'll try to find someone else. We've had two ushers call in sick."

"No, of course, I'll be there."

"Good. Wear a black skirt or pants and a white blouse. Be here at six."

Helen checked the time: twelve forty-five. Perfect. She called the law offices of the bride's father. "Could I speak to Donna Sue Hawser?"

She was transferred twice before she heard, "Donna Sue here."

"My name is Helen Hawthorne. I saw you last night at the theater. I just wanted to tell you that you were terrific as the queen."

"Really? Why that's so nice. But how did you get my number?"

"From Desiree." It was only a little lie.

Helen waited for the telltale silence, but there wasn't any. Donna Sue apparently liked the bride. "Well, wasn't that sweet? That poor little thing. There she is, her mother just buried, and she took time to compliment me."

That wasn't quite how it went, but Helen didn't straighten her out. "I was so impressed, I'm volunteering. I'm ushering tonight."

"Good. Although with Luke out of the show, we may not get the crowd we had last night. So what can I do for you?"

Helen took a deep breath. This was the big lie. "I talked with Desiree and Luke the other night. They asked me to look into their mother's death."

Well, they had.

"Isn't Luke the greatest actor?"

"Yes," Helen said, glad to be telling the truth again. "I wondered if I could come talk to you."

"Are you like a private detective or something?"

"Yes," Helen said. She was something, all right.

"And you're definitely helping Desiree?"

"Trying to," Helen said.

"Well, I'm in favor of that. I think what her father did is rotten. Why don't you meet me in half an hour at the office? We can talk in the conference room. He'll be out until two thirty."

Helen hung up. That was one strange conversation.

The office of Shenrad and Gandolf, known to insiders as Shag and Gonef, looked like a men's club with filing cabinets. Helen wondered what the attorneys told the decorator when they ordered dark wood and wing chairs: "I want a law office that looks so successful I can charge four hundred an hour."

Donna Sue was about ten years older than she'd seemed onstage: fifty-something with thick dark hair going gray and good cheekbones. She'd been heavily made up for the play. Today she wore only a little lipstick. Her gray eyes were startling. Her skin was acne-scarred, the occupational hazard of stage makeup.

Helen poured on the praise. "You were a brave queen. That was a nice bit with the lace handkerchief. You were good."

"Thanks," Donna Sue said. "Excuse the salad. This is my lunch hour." Helen's stomach growled. This interview and an energy bar were her lunch.

"I'm proud to be part of the production," Donna Sue said. "But it won't be the same without Luke. He's special. He left to do that movie with Michael Mann. Some people get all the breaks."

"You didn't," Helen said. "You're good enough for New York."

Donna Sue colored with pleasure. "I used to think so. But I fell in love with a lawyer in Lauderdale. I put him through school and he dumped me. The old story. You can't go to New York with two kids. I'm getting back to acting now that my youngest is in college.

"I'm sure you didn't come to hear about me. I want to be up-front with you. I'm leaving here. I've got a better job. I want to help that poor little girl. She's always been nice to me, unlike some people I could name. It's so unfair. She's his daughter, after all. She can't help who her mother is."

Helen began verbally feeling around. "I was at the wedding. I found her mother's body at the church."

Donna Sue's eyes grew wide. "You did?" She lowered her voice. "Was it horrible? Was there lots of blood?"

"Kiki didn't look bad," Helen said. "She was definitely dead and she wasn't prettied up like at a funeral parlor, but she wasn't horrible."

Helen saw that rigid corpse again, the clipped claws reaching for her, and shuddered.

"Are you cold?" Donna Sue said. "I swear the men in this office turn the air-conditioning up till it's a meat locker."

"No," Helen said. "I lied. There wasn't any blood, but finding her was still awful. It makes me shiver just thinking about it. The day before Kiki had been so alive."

"And driving everyone crazy."

"You knew her?" Helen said.

"I knew she called Mr. Shenrad twenty times a day and chewed him out," Donna Sue said. "He had his new wife screaming at him on line one and his old wife yelling at him on line two."

"What was his new wife screaming about?" Helen wondered if Donna Sue would hesitate to reveal inner-office secrets.

"Money," Donna Sue said. She must really be ticked at Brendan. "Shannon, his new wife, didn't get enough. She didn't get enough of something else, either, if you ask me. Brendan fired the pool service a couple of months ago. Said the guy didn't need to come to his house twice a week. Shannon came here nearly hysterical. You could hear them arguing all over the office."

My, my. Brendan had himself a regular soap opera.

Donna Sue had a Shakespearean interest in murder. "Was anyone around when you found the body? Did people scream and faint?" Her eyes were bright with curiosity.

"The whole wedding party was there," Helen said. "The bride, the groom, Mr. Shenrad. Everyone was screaming. I felt so sorry for Mr. Shenrad. It must have been a terrible shock."

"Are you kidding?" Donna Sue said. "He practically did cartwheels around this office."

"I know Kiki's death saved him a bundle," Helen said. "And he gave her a lot of money to get free."

"He owed her, you ask me," Donna Sue said. "He left Kiki for a trophy wife twenty years younger. He gave Kiki a big settlement and the house. But it wasn't just the divorce. Brendan has been teetering on the verge of bankruptcy for months. I was afraid he'd close the office with no warning. That's when I started looking. Friday's my last day, and good riddance."

"Brendan has money trouble?" Helen asked. "How did that happen? I thought lawyers were money machines." She thought she'd get more information playing dumb.

"They are," Donna Sue said. "Especially class-action lawyers like him. But he spends it as fast as he makes it. Private jet, a yacht, a shooting lodge in North Carolina. All the lawyer toys plus an expensive young wife. The yacht's for sale now, if you have a spare million."

"I don't get my commission money until Friday," Helen said.

Donna Sue laughed. "Brendan was doing okay until

three months ago, when he lost this big securities case. He thought it was a sure-bet win. He'd spent several million lining up clients and running ads on TV. You know the kind."

She intoned: "If you've been ripped off by your brokerage firm, we can help. Call 1-800—"

Donna Sue went back to her regular voice. "He needed money and Kiki was driving him to bankruptcy. On top of all he'd shelled out for the settlement, he agreed to pay half his daughter's wedding expenses. He expected the wedding to cost about two hundred thousand, but Kiki ran the bills past three hundred thousand dollars, with no end in sight.

"Kiki signed for everything for that wedding. All the bills. Florist, hotel, limos, you name it. The two of them were supposed to split the cost, but her signature was on the receipts. Now Brendan says there's nothing in writing, so Kiki's estate will have to pick up the whole wedding tab."

Helen was shocked. "But the estate goes to Desiree. That's his daughter's money. He's making her pay for her own wedding."

"I think it's lousy," Donna Sue said. "He says Desiree can afford it. I say he should pay. A man shouldn't abandon his family."

Helen suspected Donna Sue's ex had abandoned her, and that's why she felt sorry for Desiree.

Helen sneaked a look at her watch. It was two fifteen. She wanted to be out before Brendan came back. "Listen, I know this sounds crazy, but do you think there's any chance Kiki and Brendan might have gotten back together?"

"I don't think it's crazy at all," Donna Sue said. "A couple of times I accidentally picked up the wrong line, and I'd hear him talking real soft and she was being really sweet. Then next time they'd be screaming at each other. I wouldn't have been surprised if he married her or killed her, either one.

"I see a lot of couples like that in the theater. They're at each other's throats one minute, lovey-dovey the next. They get off on the drama. Me, I like peace and quiet. Guess that's why I never remarried."

A voice came from behind a dark wood door. "Donna Sue! Is that you yakking out there? Get your ass in here."

"Is that him?" Helen lowered her voice.

"Charming, isn't he? Must have snuck in the back way."

"I better run," Helen said. "I don't think he's in a good mood for a condolence call."

"He's never in a good mood," Donna Sue said. "That man's got a temper like a stepped-on snake. I can't wait to tell him good-bye."

Chapter 19

Clink. Clink. Clink.

It was the first act of *Richard III*. The evil Richard began his powerful speech. "Now is the winter of our discontent made glorious summer by this sun of York—"

Clink.

Jason, the production's new Richard, paused. The tiny noise had distracted him. He recovered quickly. "And all the clouds that—"

Helen heard the small sound all the way in the back of the theater. After she'd seated the last latecomers, she'd propped herself against the wall. The house was sold out.

From his first words, she knew Jason was no match for Luke. Helen missed Luke's crazy energy and high emotion. Luke's Richard was crippled in mind and body, bent on revenge for imagined slights, hungry for power.

Jason was correct but dull. The only good thing was his speeches seemed much shorter. Otherwise, Helen felt trapped in a PBS special.

Clink. Clink. That sound. There it was again. Where was the stage manager?

Helen tiptoed across the empty lobby and slipped through the velvet curtains to the backstage entrance. A table in the narrow hall was piled with props: a crown with glass jewels, an evening purse, a dagger.

She threaded her way through a fire marshal's nightmare of costume racks and stacks of scripts. Sagging gray curtains divided the men's and women's dressing rooms.

Clink.

The sound was louder now. Helen thought it came from the other side of the dressing rooms. She slid past a bearded actor going over his lines, his costume damp with flop sweat. He didn't notice her.

A plywood partition was just beyond him. Helen peeked around it. Chauncey was sitting on a kitchen chair at an old wooden desk, a bottle of bourbon in front of him. He picked up the bottle and poured sloppily into a water glass, hitting the rim with a loud clink. His shirt was open almost to his waist and there was a bandage on his neck.

Helen felt a cold hand touch her shoulder and stifled a scream. It was Donna Sue, in a black gown and silver crown. She raised a finger to her lips, brushed past Helen, and held out her hand with a regal gesture.

Chauncey sheepishly surrendered the glass. Donna Sue poured the bourbon into a foam coffee cup and gave it to him. Helen wanted to applaud.

Chauncey stared at the foam cup moodily. His too-red lips trembled, then sagged. He poured his next drink in silence.

Helen followed Donna Sue through the plywood passages to a small kitchen. The counter was cluttered with half-eaten veggie subs, bottled water, and boxes of doughnut holes. Actor food, all of it.

"What—" she said, but Donna Sue shushed her. Helen watched as she rinsed Chauncey's glass in the sink, then pulled a lighter and a pack of Virginia Slims out of a purse and slipped out the back door.

Helen followed her into the chilly night. There was no one else in the bleak staff parking lot, but a mound of cigarette butts and a rank nicotine odor said this was where the pretend princes and peasants smoked between scenes.

Donna Sue the actress was more self-assured than Donna Sue the secretary. The theater was her world. "Sorry to shut you up." She took a deep draft of her cigarette. "But sound carries backstage. We can talk out here."

"I didn't know that Chauncey drank," Helen said.

"He doesn't," Donna Sue said. "Well, every so often, he goes on a bender when the pressure gets too much. The production isn't the same without Luke."

"It's the first act of his first night," Helen said. "Jason may get better as he warms up."

Donna Sue shook her head. "We knew there was trouble in the rehearsals. Jason forgets lines like crazy. He missed about a third of his speech in that last scene, and forgot the cue line. Ben—he's the Duke of Clarence—covered for him, thank God."

"I hardly noticed it," Helen said. "Really."

"But you did, just the same. Jason's memory gets worse and worse. I don't know what's wrong. Chauncey spent hours rehearsing him. Poor Chauncey. All that, on top of Kiki's death. No wonder he hit the bottle."

"Literally," Helen said. "I could hear the clinking in the back of the theater."

"I figured," Donna Sue said. "That's why I took the glass away. You're wondering why I didn't take the bottle, too?"

Helen nodded.

"I've seen Chauncey like this before. In a day or so, he'll come back apologetic and hungover with some clever way to fix the play. It's how he works."

"Why did Kiki's death upset him?" Helen said. "I saw that woman publicly humiliate him. Besides, she left him lots of money."

"Humiliation is no big deal for anyone in the theater," Donna Sue said. "Some of us even like it. I know a few cast members who are into S and M. Chauncey depended on Kiki. She was his patroness. She brought big donors to his shows. She was a good critic. She could watch the rehearsals and tell him where the weak spots were. She spotted Luke's talent and made him a leading man. Of course, she didn't expect him to audition for son-in-law."

"Was she upset when he got the role?" Helen said.

"I don't think she liked it. But Desiree could do a lot worse than Luke, and Kiki was smart enough to know that. I was there the night Desiree met him. Her mother had dragged her to a production of *Midsummer*. She sat there like a bundle of old clothes. Then Luke came onstage. I think he had a small role as the changeling boy. Desiree couldn't keep her eyes off him."

"Did Luke see her?"

"Oh, yeah. He saw her all right—as his meal ticket." Donna Sue took another drag.

"Kiki may have helped Chauncey in the past, but she was withholding money lately," Helen said. "Chauncey said the theater would fold unless she gave him five thousand dollars. She refused. I heard her."

Donna Sue shrugged. "It was a game they played. At the last minute, after he begged her hard enough, she'd give him the money. She always did."

But what if this time she didn't? Helen wondered. What if the game went too far? Masochists died when their games went wrong.

"What happened to Chauncey's neck?"

"Cut himself working on the set. It's just a scratch." Donna Sue blew out a long curl of smoke like a forties movie actress. Helen thought she'd smoke if it made her look as romantically world-weary.

"How'd he do that?" Helen asked.

"I didn't see it, but I think it happened late Friday night. Chauncey is obsessive. He'll come back to the theater at two a.m. and rearrange the set. Makes the set designer crazy, not to mention the actors. We'll get our parts blocked and he'll move all the furniture and we'll have to reblock. But he's not bad, as directors go. I've seen some throw chairs or scream at actors until they cried."

"Does Chauncey have a temper?"

Donna Sue ground out her cigarette on the stucco wall, careful to keep from breaking the half-smoked butt.

"I hope you're not measuring Chauncey for a frame," she said. It sounded like a line from a play. "Because Kiki was worth more to him alive than dead."

She turned her back on Helen and walked inside, like the queen she was.

*   *   *

Donna Sue would not talk to Helen during the intermission after the first act. But the actress didn't hold a grudge. After the second act, Helen found an excuse to make conversation with her backstage.

"What's in that locked cabinet?" Helen asked.

"That's where we keep the stage knives, sword canes, and guns," Donna Sue said. "The stage manager has the key. Actors love them, especially the sword canes, but they can get killed playing with those things. The actors can use them only if they sign a release and take special training. I need a smoke. Want to join me outside?"

The actors' parking lot was a desert of broken asphalt with a rusty chain-link fence. Helen thought she saw something interesting. She wanted to examine it alone.

Three actors were huddled at the far end of the lot, puffing on their cigarettes. Donna Sue waved at them, then lit her half-smoked butt.

"I should quit," she said. "Funny, I don't smoke at the office. But get me onstage and I crave nicotine."

All the cars on the lot were clunkers, except one. A black Eclipse was parked beside the battered Civics, Neons and rusting Toyotas.

"Who owns the hot new Eclipse?" Helen asked.

"Jason." Donna Sue spat out the word.

"He must have a good day job."

"I don't think he has any job at all," she said.

"Really? Where's he get his money? It can't be from acting." Helen hoped she wasn't pushing too hard again.

But Donna Sue had no protective instincts toward Jason. "Don't know. I stay away from him. I don't like touchy-feely creeps. His hands are all over the younger actresses, and they're too dumb to see past Jason's good looks. I call him the Green-Eyed Monster."

"Those green eyes are compelling."

"He doesn't bother flashing them at me. He likes younger women. Real young. Some of his dates have lollipops."

Jason liked younger women? Then why was he hanging all over the much older Kiki?

The outside light flicked three times, the signal to return. "Gotta go," Donna Sue said. "Are you coming in?"

"No, thanks," Helen said. "Think I'll enjoy the night air."

Donna Sue tossed the butt into the pile by the door, then went inside. The other actors followed. Helen waited a few minutes, then examined the cast's cars. Young actors lived in their cars, sometimes for real when they couldn't make the rent. Looking in their cars was like peeking into their homes.

Helen saw piles of scripts, demo tapes, photos, and resumes. There were college textbooks, old carry-out bags, and whole wardrobes, from skirts and jeans to high heels and running shoes.

Jason's Eclipse stood out from this sorry pack. The sleek outside was polished. The interior was pristine. There were two odd touches: dozens of stuffed animals were in the backseat—bears, elephants, kittens, even a fuzzy fish. A bouquet of lollipops was stuck in the drink holder.

Jason was not in touch with his inner child. He was selling Ecstasy. Helen knew the drug left people extremely sensitive to touch, especially soft, plush surfaces. The suckers relieved the clenched teeth it could cause. Jason must hand them out to his customers. Dr. Feel Good gave a little extra relief.

"Some of his dates have lollipops," Donna Sue had said. Not because they were young. They used X.

She remembered Lisa's taunt at the rehearsal when another bridesmaid mentioned a newly thin friend: "It's the South Beach Diet—Ecstasy and Corona. Right, Jason?"

Helen slipped back inside as the actors were taking their final bows. She stayed to clean up. "You are the greatest," the stage manager said when she found Helen vacuuming the lobby rug. "I wish all our volunteers were like you."

No, you don't, Helen thought, and gave a traitor's smile. She wasn't there to help. She was planning a little drama of her own tonight, as soon as Jason showed up. The elements were worthy of Shakespeare: Money, murder, sex, and blackmail. If she succeeded, it would be curtains for the struggling playhouse.

Helen was out to prove their new leading man murdered their major benefactor—then blackmailed her only daughter.

Chapter 20

Jason materialized in the backstage blackness, green eyes glowing like a cat's. He was wearing the softest sweater. Helen wanted to pet it. Once again, she was startled by his good looks. His face had a perfection Luke's lacked. But his beauty seemed without animation. Jason wanted to be admired.

Helen followed him to the back door. "So how long have you been selling X?"

"I don't know what you're talking about." Jason tried to push past her. She blocked his way.

"I could call the cops and let them jog your memory," Helen said. "Based on what I saw in that car, they could get a search warrant." Helen was bluffing. She didn't think stuffed animals and suckers counted as drug paraphernalia.

Jason's green eyes burned with anger, lit by an odd fire she never saw onstage. "So what? It's recreational. I'm only helping my friends."

"Let's ask the cops what they think about your help."

"What do you want from me?" Jason's perfect mouth was distorted by hate.

"I want to know what happened after you left the rehearsal dinner."

"I went home. Alone."

"Liar," Helen said. "You went back to the church to have sex with Kiki. I bet the police don't know that. But I do."

Jason shifted uneasily. Helen had won that bet. She remembered what the chauffeur said: He'd heard a man arguing with Kiki at the church. It was time to gamble again. "You fought with the murder victim the night she died, didn't you, Jason?"

Jason looked frightened now. He didn't ask how she knew. "It wasn't how it sounds. Kiki said she could help me. She knows—knew—the whole theater community. She had the bucks. I thought I should make nice. I agreed to meet her at the church. Just for a talk."

"That's not what I heard. Kiki said doing it in church made her hot."

Jason's green eyes opened in surprise.

"I've got a witness," Helen said. "You didn't want to screw on the steps."

"She wanted me to fuck her, okay? In the church. She thought it would be a hoot. That's what she said. A hoot."

"And was it?" Helen said.

He stared at her, defiantly silent.

"Jason! Tell me or tell the cops. What happened next?"

"Nothing. She was old."

"You didn't think so earlier that evening," Helen said. "You were all over her."

"Maybe I was. But during the rehearsal, the church was dark. So was the restaurant. When we went back to the church, she was drunk, stumbling around and giggling. She wanted to put on that stupid rose dress for me.

"We went upstairs to the bride's dressing room and she flipped on the overhead lights. They were real bright. She took off that gold dress and that's when I saw how old she was—old like my grandmother. She had wrinkles on her neck. Her stomach was flabby. Her tits sagged to her knees. It was gross. She wanted me to kiss her again, but she had these lines around her mouth. She started screaming at me. I said she was a hag. I left her there. She could find her own way home."

"You killed her because she insulted your manhood."

"My what?" Jason laughed. "What century are you in, lady? I wasn't insulted. I don't screw grannies."

"You had to shut her up. She could ruin your career."

"What career? I'm a character actor."

"You've got the lead now," Helen said.

"Not for long. I'm a stand-in until Chauncey can find someone better. That's what he told me tonight."

Helen heard the sad truth in his words.

"To be honest, Kiki couldn't do me any damage," Jason said. "She'd look silly if she tried to pressure some director not to hire me. I'm not worth going after, and that's the truth."

In Helen's experience, when people mentioned the truth a lot, they were lying.

"Why did you ask Desiree for twenty thousand dollars after the funeral?"

"You're nuts, lady. I'm leaving." But Jason stayed.

"Were you trying to blackmail Desiree? Did you have photos of her mother?"

He laughed contemptuously. This time, her gamble didn't pay off. She'd guessed wrong. "You have no idea what you're talking about."

Still Jason didn't storm off. Helen tried again. "Where did Chauncey go when he sneaked out of the rehearsal dinner?"

A sneer disfigured Jason's handsome face. "An evening with the breeders makes Chauncey nervous. He went to a gay bar to get in touch with his inner boy."

"You don't think he came back to the church and killed Kiki?" Helen said.

Jason gave a nasty, braying laugh. "He's an old queen. He wouldn't touch a fly—unless it was unzipped."

Unzipped. "Did you unzip Kiki out of that rose dress?"

"What? I told you. I walked out. I didn't care if she spent the rest of her life in that dress."

"That's exactly what she did," Helen said.

Helen waited for Jason to leave first. He was furious at her, and she'd be walking alone down a deserted street. When she heard his car start up, she shut the door sadly behind her. Helen could never go back to the Shakespeare Playhouse. Not after that scene with Jason.

She crunched across the theater parking lot, heading for the bus stop. A car pulled into the lot and blocked her exit. It was one of those plain sedans that might as well have "Unmarked Police Car" painted on the door.

Detective Janet Smith got out of the driver's side. She looked lean and mean. Her partner, Detective Bill McIntyre, looked malevolent and muscular. The two of them stood side by side in gray suits, their arms folded.

Helen could hear the blood rushing in her ears. How did they find her?

"Just thought I'd give you the results of your DNA test," Detective Smith said. "We found your blood on the dress. We also found your fingerprints on the dress and the closet door."

"Of course you did," Helen said, trying not to panic. "I helped put the dress on Kiki. I hung it in the closet."

"And the blood?" Detective Smith said.

"I told you. I cut my hand and bled on both dresses— the wedding gown and the rose dress."

"We checked the wedding gown. We didn't find any blood," Smith said.

"That's because I cleaned it off. Then the bride threw hot coffee all over the dress."

"We should have found traces," Smith said. Helen wondered if the detective was telling the truth. Maybe she should get that lawyer Colby Cox. Helen had about seven thousand dollars stashed in her suitcase. That should buy her a few hours of help. Right now she'd give it all to make these two disappear.

"How did it feel when you cut the victim's finger-nails?" Detective Smith said.

Helen saw those pathetic gold claws again and nearly threw up.

"Are you going to arrest me?" she asked.

"Let's just say we're a step closer," Detective Smith said. "Don't leave town." Detective McIntyre said nothing, which was even more ominous. They got into the car and drove off.

As Helen waited for the bus home, she couldn't stop shivering. Her encounter with the cops frightened her. Her DNA was in all the wrong places. Was anyone else's blood on that dress? She should have asked. But they probably wouldn't have told her.

If the police weren't scary enough, there was Jason. He frightened and confused her. Helen knew he was lying, but she also thought he was telling the truth. He believed Chauncey was no murderer. Donna Sue, whose opinion she respected, thought so, too.

The fight scene with Kiki probably happened pretty much the way Jason described it, Helen decided. But she thought he was leaving something out.

Did Jason murder Kiki in an impotent rage? Or did he stalk off and leave her, tipsy and trapped, alone with her killer? Kiki couldn't run away in that hoop skirt. And why would Jason ask Desiree for money at her mother's funeral?

It was almost midnight when Helen got to the Coronado. It was a warm night for December. She went by the pool, hoping for some company. Margery and Warren were drinking champagne in the moonlight.

"Come join us," Margery said.

This time Helen did. She didn't want to be alone. She didn't want to think about the cops, Jason, or Phil. She wanted to believe that people could live happily ever after and have real love at age seventy-six. Her landlady sat on the chaise longue next to Warren, smoking a Marlboro. She had the smile of a satisfied woman.

Warren filled a flute with champagne and handed it to Helen. She toasted the couple, then took a sip. The bubbles tickled her tongue.

"Do you dance, Helen?" he said. His tanned skin was like fine old leather, and he had interesting crinkles at the corners of his eyes. Margery had herself quite a catch.

"I grew up in the dreaded disco era, Warren. I just bounce up and down."

"You should take dancing lessons. Many young people do." It didn't sound like a sales pitch. Warren seemed to believe dancing was good for people. It had done wonders for Margery.

"I give lessons to brides and grooms," Warren said. "Many couples dance together for the first time at their wedding. They're afraid of tripping or looking foolish. A lesson or two from me, and they have a beautiful start to their married life."

"I'm not planning to get married anytime soon," Helen said.

"You never know. You're certainly in the right business. I gave the most unusual lesson of my life at your store. An emergency dance lesson, if you will."

"My store? You mean Millicent's?"

"Yes, Millicent had a gay couple in the shop after hours. She sold the bride—a female impersonator named Lady George—a lovely dress. An Oscar de la Renta, if I remember correctly. It had this deep-pleated ruffle running down the back. Very graceful. The groom's name was Gary. The couple admitted that they were nervous about dancing together at their reception.

"Millicent tried to send Gary and Lady George to my studio, but they didn't want to be seen learning to dance where others could watch. I have those large windows, you know.

"So Millicent called me, and I came to her store. We went upstairs to the fitting area so the couple could have privacy, and I gave them dancing lessons. It took awhile, but they finally caught on. I think they'll dance beautifully together, now that Lady George has mastered that ruffle.

"They danced until nearly three in morning. They were so touching. Your Millicent was magnificent. I knew she wanted to go home. It was a Friday night after all, and she'd just put together this big wedding as a special rush job. But she stayed there for them."

"A Friday night?" Helen said. "In early December?"

"Yes. I asked after you, but she said you were at the rehearsal. Millicent opened the shop specially for Lady George, so the bride could make her dress selection with no observers."

Now Helen understood Millicent's secrecy. Society brides would not buy a gown if it had been tried on by a transvestite. Lady George would not feel comfortable undressing near women with all the factory-installed equipment.

Helen could imagine what Desiree's snotty brides-maids would say about Lady George. They'd flayed poor flapping Emily, and her only fault was a few extra pounds.

Millicent stayed late at the store to give Lady George the privacy she needed. Then she kept her customer's secret. And what a secret it was. Helen could see the couple now, dancing among the dressmaker's dum-mies.

I thought Millicent was a murderer. Instead, she was a decent person and a good businesswoman. Helen felt small-minded and mean. She wanted to creep away and hide.

Helen finished her champagne and said, "Good night. Thanks so much. And Warren, I'm really glad I talked with you."

The moon lit her way back to her room. Millicent was innocent. She'd eliminated one suspect. Suddenly, she felt so tired. She tiptoed past Phil's window, but she wasn't quiet enough. He opened his door.

For a moment Helen was struck silent with longing. The light shone on his silvery hair and outlined his broad chest. He was wearing another blue shirt. She was a sucker for blue shirts and blue eyes.

"Helen, what's going on? Two homicide detectives

came here today, checking your alibi for that wedding rehearsal night."

"What did you tell them?"

"That I was with you all night and left about seven in the morning."

Helen couldn't hide her relief.

"I've been so worried." Phil's eyes were soft with concern. "Why are the police asking about you?"

Phil's sympathy almost melted her anger. But then she saw Kendra, wrapped around his trunk like poison ivy. To hell with his sympathy. She'd give him the facts and that was all.

"A customer at the bridal shop was murdered," Helen said, as if there was nothing odd about that sentence. "The police found my fingerprints and DNA at the crime scene."

"My God," Phil said. "Please let me help you. I know a lawyer, a good one. I can investigate for you. I'll do it for free. I have contacts with the police. I can talk with them—"

He reached out for her, but she stepped away, trapped in her shame, lost in her ancient anger at another man.

"Good night, Phil." She unlocked her door.

"Helen, don't be like that. Helen—"

She shut the door on his protests and double locked it.

Chapter 21

Helen locked her door to keep Phil out—and herself in.

She longed to run out and throw herself into his arms. She missed him so much. Helen felt like he had been torn from her—no, amputated without an anesthetic—and she was bleeding all over everything.

Margery said she needed courage to forgive Phil and learn to trust men. Helen thought she needed an eraser to get rid of her awful memories. They replayed endlessly in her mind: Once again, she saw Kendra's dyed red hair, cheap short skirt, and catlike smile as she clung to Helen's man.

And Phil—he was standing in his bedroom like a gigged frog.

Let's not forget your role, Helen told herself. She'd popped in half-naked and yelled "surprise" like a hooker at a bachelor party.

Helen had worked herself into a meltdown rage when a blue envelope came skidding under her door. She opened it and read the note: *I love you*, it said. *Please let me help—Phil*.

She crumpled the note into a ball and threw it against

the wall. Thumbs jumped off the couch and batted it around the floor, doing flips and leaps. Helen sat down for a moment in her turquoise Barcalounger to watch the big cat play.

She woke up at three A.M.

Ugh. She hated when she did that. Her face was greasy with old makeup. Her mouth was dry. It hardly seemed worth going to bed when she had to be up in another three hours, but Helen dragged herself to her bedroom.

As soon as she hit the mattress, she was wide-awake. Helen stared at the ceiling and thought of her champagne nights with Phil. What would he drink with Kendra: Ripple? Cold Duck? Mad Dog 20/20?

Finally she cried herself into a restless sleep.

The morning didn't look any better and she looked worse. Helen winced when she glanced in the mirror. The bags under her eyes were prizewinners. She could haul bowling balls in them.

Helen fished two ice cubes out of the freezer, put them on her bags for a bit, then checked the mirror again.

Great. Now the bags were bright red. She looked like she had eye hives. Worse, her concealer didn't stick well to semifrozen bags. She quit trying to paint over them and got dressed.

As she slipped on her right shoe, Helen felt something in the toe. She pulled out Phil's crumpled note. Thumbs had dropped it in her shoe.

I love you. Please let me help—Phil.

I love you, too, she thought, but you can't help me until you help yourself. I've been a fool, but so have you. I'll have to save myself.

Helen wondered if Margery had talked with the

homicide detectives yet. She'd better warn her. Helen knocked on her landlady's door. It was opened by a fluffy old woman in pink hot pants. Her orange mules matched her hair. A snug green sweater bared her substantial midriff.

Helen blinked. The woman was kind of cute in a surreal way. She reminded Helen of a punked-out Miss Marple. She even had the same soft, dithery voice.

"Oh, you must want Margery," the woman said. "I'll get her. You just wait here."

Margery came out in a purple bathrobe, trailing a cloud of cigarette smoke. She moved like a hibernating bear that had been awakened two months early. Last night's champagne must have taken its toll.

"Another hard night of dancing with Warren?" Helen said. "Did you two go out on the town after I went to bed?"

"I've had my last dance with that old coot," Margery said. "We've got problems. Elsie's in trouble and it's Warren's fault."

Elsie's middle bulged a bit, but Helen was pretty sure she wasn't pregnant.

"What happened?"

Elsie folded her liver-spotted hands on her pink lap and looked like a contrite schoolgirl. "I signed a bad contract," she said in her fluttery voice. "Margery's going to help me get out of it."

"So far, I haven't been much help," Margery said.

"I should have listened to you before I signed," Elsie said. "You were afraid Warren ran one of those dance studios that signed people up for lifetime contracts."

"Which at our age is about six months." Margery lit another cigarette. It glowed like a red eye. Helen felt there were enough of those in the room already.

"I checked like she told me," Elsie said. "It was only a two-year contract. But I should have read the rest of it. I couldn't make any sense out of that legal gobbledy-gook. My Jim used to do that for me. Now that he's gone, I'm not so good at coping."

"The contract was only for two years," Margery said. "But the payments were two thousand dollars a month for twenty-four months."

Helen was stunned. "Two grand a month for dancing lessons? That's a mortgage payment."

"Elsie signed a contract for forty-eight thousand dollars in dance lessons."

"I had no idea it was so expensive until I got the first statement," Elsie said. "I had two free lessons. Then I paid only fifty dollars for the first month. I thought I was paying fifty dollars a month for two years."

"That's outrageous," Helen said.

"It's an old scam," Margery said. "I checked it out on the Internet."

"You have a computer?" Helen said.

"Welcome to the twenty-first century," Margery said. "Got my own Hotmail account, too. I use the library's computers. Best time to go is early afternoon. All the old farts are napping and the kids are still in school. I did a search on the Net and found out how these phony dance schools operate. They give the victim some cheap dance lessons, sign her up for a contract, and then she learns she's committed to thousands of dollars."

"How do they hide those outrageous prices in the contract?" Helen asked.

"They don't bother," Margery said. "Con artists know people rarely read the fine print. At our age, we can't see it without a magnifying glass. That's how they got Elsie for nearly fifty grand."

"I don't have that kind of money any more," Elsie said. "I made some bad investments." She dropped her voice and said the dreaded words: "Enron. And World-Com."

Helen shuddered. She'd done the same thing. "That's terrible. You need a lawyer."

Elsie hung her head. "My son is a lawyer. That's the problem. Milton will find out if I go to one. He knows everyone. Fort Lauderdale is such a small town. He's been trying to get me into one of those assisted-living facilities. If Milton knew what a fool I was with those dance lessons, he'd put me in a home for sure and get power of attorney over what's left of my money."

Elsie's chins trembled. Her young clothes made her seem older and more helpless.

"Milt's a bit of a stick," Margery said, her cigarette glaring at Helen. "He wants his mom to put on a shawl and sit in a rocking chair."

"He's a good boy," Elsie said, loyally.

"I didn't say he wasn't," Margery said. "But Milt wore pin-striped diapers."

"Takes after his father," Elsie said. "Except Jim enjoyed my wild side. Said I had moxie. Milton says I embarrass him."

"I warned you about wearing that leather miniskirt to his firm's Christmas party," Margery said.

"The legs are the last thing to go on a girl," Elsie said. "Mine are still worth showing off."

They were pretty good, Helen thought, but the thighs drooped a bit.

"We've got to help Elsie," Margery said. "I introduced her to that crook. I'll get her out of this if it's the last thing I do. Elsie, you go on home. I need to think."

Elsie tottered out on her orange mules.

"What do you want?" Margery snarled at Helen. "I know you didn't come over to meet Elsie."

"Were the police by to speak with you yesterday?"

"No, I was out all day with Warren, that son of a bugger. I drank champagne with him until two. What kind of trouble are you in now?"

"None," Helen lied. Her voice went too high and Margery looked at her sharply. "The police are checking my alibi for the night of Desiree's rehearsal dinner, that's all."

"You were with Phil from eleven o'clock on. He left about seven a.m."

"Jeez. Were you watching?"

"I know everything that goes on here," Margery said. "Peggy's still dating her policeman, but I think that romance is about over, thank God. Those two would sneak down to the swimming pool at midnight and wake me up. Thought if they turned off the pool lights I wouldn't know what they were doing in the water."

Helen's cheeks burned at this revelation about her friend.

"Cal is currently in Canada. He says he wants to spend Christmas with his grandchild, but he's really worried about his residence dates. He needs to spend more time in his home country. No Canadian wants to lose that national health insurance."

"Amazing," Helen said.

"Oh, yeah. I know everything. Except that Warren rooked my friend with his dance lessons right under my nose. Are you working today?"

"One o'clock to six," Helen said.

"Good," Margery said. "Warren leaves about nine thirty to open his dance studio. You can wait with me until he's gone. I have a passkey. We need to look at his apartment."

Margery changed into purple shorts and red tennis shoes. "The rubber soles will give me traction if I have to run for it," she said.

"What exactly are you expecting to find?" Helen asked.

"Something that will help me nail his crooked hide to the wall."

They drank coffee in a heavy silence. At nine thirty-three, Warren went whistling down the walk to the parking lot, golden sun shining on his silver hair.

"What a waste," Margery said. "There aren't many men his age with their own hair and teeth, and this one turns out to be a con artist."

At nine forty-five, Margery used her passkey to open 2C. Helen followed her into the furnished apartment. Like many bachelors, Warren wasn't big on dusting, but the place was tidy. There were racetrack programs on the coffeetable, a coffee maker and a can of cashews on the kitchen counter. A jai alai schedule was posted on the fridge. Helen looked inside: deli turkey, hamburger buns, mustard, hot sauce, a jar of olives, and a bottle of champagne. The freezer had two frosted champagne glasses.

"The old geezer keeps it on ice all the time," Margery said. "So much for our special night."

"What?" Helen said.

"There's no fool like an old fool," Margery said, "and I don't mean Elsie."

The woman with the throaty laugh and the elegant French twist was gone forever, Helen thought sadly. Margery would never again dance with a man in the moonlight. Warren had committed a double crime: He'd stolen Elsie's money and taken the last of Margery's youth.

The two women searched for dance lesson contracts and other papers. "I haven't turned up anything more incriminating than his grocery and gasoline receipts," Helen said.

"Gas prices are a crime, but he didn't commit it," Margery said.

In the bedroom, Helen found a locked closet. "Ha," she said. "He's up to something, and he doesn't want the women he's dating to find it."

"Dating," Margery said. "That's a nice old-fashioned word for what he's been doing. I've got keys to the closets, too."

Margery unlocked the closet door. They saw the heads—two of them. Helen gave a little shriek of surprise.

One foam head had a beautiful shock of silver hair. The other was empty.

"Well, I'll be damned," Margery said. "That pretty silver hair is a rug. I never guessed—and I ran my fingers through it."

She turned the toupee over. On the inside were round metal eyelets. "He's got an expensive one. The hooks are embedded right in his head. He attaches the toupee and gets the best fit."

Helen winced. She could feel the hooks sticking out of her head.

Margery shoved the toupee in her pocket. "Got him. His ladies won't think he's such a stud when they see him with hooks in his bald head. I'm so happy about this, I feel like dancing."

"Me, too," Helen said.

"We'll take my car, in case we need to make a quick getaway," Margery said.

Warren's Studio of the Dance was in a pink stucco storefront off Las Olas. Warren was waltzing a woman of about eighty around the room. They were both graceful dancers.

"He's fun to watch, I'll give him that," Margery said. "He put me through my paces." Helen could hear the layers of hurt and bitterness under her light words.

The studio was furnished with a couple of couches, a few potted palms, and photos of dancers from Fred and Ginger to Tommy Tune. There were black footprints painted on the floor in intricate patterns. Helen knew she'd fall over her feet if she ever tried them, but Warren and the dancing woman moved through the routines with practiced swiftness.

Margery wasn't watching the couple. She was examining the framed items on the walls.

"Time's up, Shirley!" Warren said when the music stopped. "See you next week."

Shirley changed out of her ballroom shoes and headed for the door. Margery waited in the shadows until Shirley left.

When Warren saw her, he gave a glittering smile. "Margery! Have you come for those advanced lessons after all? A little rumba, maybe? Or a cha-cha?" He swiveled his hips expertly.

"Nope, this is going to be a cakewalk." Margery whipped out the silver toupee.

"Margery! How could you? You stole that," he said indignantly. "You entered my apartment illegally."

"And you stole forty-eight thousand dollars from my friend, Elsie. You better tear up that contract."

"I can't. It's a legal document. It's way past the three-day cancellation period."

"Dance studios are supposed to be registered with the state of Florida," Margery said. "Your registration certificate should be prominently displayed up there with Fred and Ginger."

"A minor oversight," Warren said.

"Yeah, well, I'm overseeing this toupee." She shook it like a dead rat. "I'll come back for the other one and tear it off your bald head. Let's see how attractive those gullible old biddies find you then." Helen knew who the most gullible biddy was. Margery was gleefully destroying their moonlit nights.

"That's stalking! I'll get a restraining order." Warren's craggy face was unpleasantly flushed.

"You might stop me," Margery said. "But you can't stop every old woman in South Florida. You'll never know when one of my friends will come in here, start dancing, and snatch you bald. They won't be gentle, Warren. They might tear some hooks out of your head. Especially when they think about what you did to a sweet widow woman like Elsie."

"Margery, please, can't we talk?" Warren pleaded. "Doesn't our time together mean anything?"

Helen winced at Warren's sappy words.

Margery's smile was savage. She held the toupee like a fresh scalp. "Nope. I got me a wild hair. Let's go, Helen."

They left Warren flatfooted in his dance studio.

Chapter 22

"So how's your investigation going, Sherlock?" Margery was weaving in and out of the tourist traffic on Las Olas. Warren's captured toupee lay between them like a dead pet.

Helen did not want to have this conversation. But if she didn't, Margery would ask about Phil. She wanted to discuss her love life even less.

"Why do you think I'm investigating anything?"

"Your customer's been murdered, the cops are asking the wrong questions, and you want me to give the right answers."

Margery slammed on the brakes to avoid hitting a man in a parrot shirt. "Blasted brain-dead tourist. Did you see that? Walked right into the traffic. I should run him down to teach him a lesson."

Warren's toupee slid across the seat. Now it was nuzzling Helen's leg. "I could talk better if you'd get rid of that creepy hairpiece," she said.

Margery picked it up by its scruff and stuffed it in her pocket.

"Speak," she said.

Helen did. When she finished, Margery said, "Was that wedding held in a briar patch? Why is everyone scratched?"

"Not everyone," Helen said. "Just three people. The cops think Kiki may have scratched her murderer. That could be why her nails were chopped off, to get rid of the incriminating DNA. Or maybe her killer was kinky. I saw her hands. They looked bizarre."

Those clutching dead-child hands flashed in her mind again.

"Hello, Helen, are you there? Who else is scratched?" Margery said.

Helen shook off the memory. "Chauncey has a scratch on his neck, but Donna Sue says he got it at the theater. Desiree has a scratch on her arm. She says it was a cat. Her father's not saying how he got the scratches on his hands."

"All these scratches aren't natural," Margery said.

"One isn't natural," Helen said. "The others just happened. Everyone gets scrapes and scratches."

"Yeah, right," Margery said.

"What's that on your right hand?" Helen pointed to a long red scrape.

"I was trimming the bougainvillea and it bit me," Margery said.

"I rest my case," Helen said.

"Watch it or I'll get out that toupee again," Margery said. "Have you checked that Jason guy for scratches?"

"No. Come to think of it, he was wearing a sweater with long sleeves. Of course, it was chilly."

"He could be hiding something," Margery said.

"He is hiding something. Ever since I talked with him at the theater, I've been trying to figure out what it is. I know he sells Ecstasy. I suspect he's also using his product. One actress said he's real touchy-feely. He wore this super-soft sweater, cashmere or something. X makes you sensitive to touch, so users crave hugs, stuffed animals, soft things."

"What else do you know about Ecstasy?" Margery said.

Like everyone in South Florida, Helen considered herself an expert on street drugs. "It gives you endless energy," she said. "You can dance all night. It makes your teeth clench, so some people use suckers to relieve that symptom. Jason had a bunch in his car."

"Is it addictive?"

"I guess so," Helen said.

"How?" Margery said. "Does it mellow you out like pot? Does it make you crazy like angel dust? Do you try to fly off buildings like with LSD? Or do you think you're putting a stake through a vampire's heart when you're really killing the mother of the bride?"

"I don't know," Helen said. "But I'd better find out. Could you drop me off at the library? I have time to do some Ecstasy research before I go to work."

"I'll go with you," Margery said. "After you do your research, we'll see Jason and check him for scratches."

"He won't be at the theater until six," Helen said.

"Who said anything about the theater? You can get home addresses on the Net."

I'm losing my edge, Helen thought. Too much time with chiffon, not enough with computers. "Glad somebody's thinking," she said. "We have a good chance of catching him at home before noon. Drug dealers are rarely early risers."

Helen put her name on the computer list at the library. Twenty minutes later, she was typing in "Ecstasy addiction."

"Bingo," she said. "This article says X users may encounter problems similar to amphetamine and coke users, including addiction."

Helen scrolled down the story. "Wow. Jason is using it for sure. Listen to this: " 'The designer drug Ecstasy, or MDMA, causes long-lasting damage to brain areas that are critical for thought and memory. . . . Researchers found that four days of exposure to the drug caused damage that persisted six to seven years later.' No wonder Jason was dropping lines in *Richard the Third*. The other actors were complaining about it."

"That boy's in big trouble," Margery said. "Actors depend on their memory for their living."

"Here's a list of where to get help," Helen said. "Florida has a major rehab industry. Jeez. Clean doesn't come cheap. A top rehab center costs as much as a good college."

Margery checked her watch. "Your computer time is about up. Did you look up Jason's home address?"

"Yes. He lives in a town house in Dania," Helen said.

Half an hour later, Margery pulled her white whale of a car into The Gardens at San Andrino. Florida developers loved to give subdivisions splendid names. The semi-Spanish town houses had an impressive entrance and a velvety green lawn.

"Margery, paranoia is a symptom of Ecstasy addiction," Helen said. "Jason may think the two of us are ganging up on him. I'd better talk to him alone. Would you mind waiting in the car?"

"OK. I can grab a smoke. If you're not out in fifteen minutes, I'm coming in after you."

Margery sounded like a late-night movie, but Helen felt a little safer. Jason had a nasty streak for a guy taking a huggy drug.

Jason's town house was one of six set around a tropical courtyard. Helen knocked on his door. No answer. She knocked harder and a voice called out, "I'm coming. I'm coming."

Jason swung open the door and blinked at the bright light. His face was puffy from sleep, but startlingly handsome. He wore a blue velvet robe and nothing else. His chest was perfectly tanned and toned. Helen wondered if he waxed it.

Jason's beauty was only skin deep. He had an ugly mouth. "I said I didn't want to talk to you, bitch," he snarled. "Beat it."

A small, determined woman in her sixties came out two doors down. She stood on her porch, cell phone in hand, and glared at Jason.

Helen lowered her voice. "You can invite me in for five minutes or I can tell your neighbor there how you make your money. I don't think she'll be happy living by a drug dealer."

Jason reluctantly opened the door. His right wrist was wrapped in an Ace bandage.

Helen waved at the woman as she stepped through the door. Her protector nodded but didn't budge from her porch or put away her cell phone. Good. She'd be listening for sounds of mayhem.

The cold air hit Helen immediately. It was like walking into an upright freezer. She caught a glimpse of a kitchen sink piled with dirty pots. That was the last normal sight in the town house.

The living-room walls were covered with dark blue velvet. The couches were dark velvet, too, a fabric way too warm for Florida. No wonder Jason had the air-conditioning set at subzero.

Midnight-blue curtains blocked the light. In the soft

velvety darkness, the white marble fireplace had a graveyard glow. Over the mantel, in place of a picture, was a flat-screen TV.

Helen felt like she was trapped inside a jewelry box. The dark velvet made Jason's green eyes glow like emeralds. His face was cold white stone. He made a grab for Helen's arm, but she stepped back and put a velvet chair between them. She picked up a black marble candlestick from the mantel and hefted it.

"Nice," she said. "And heavy."

Jason backed off. "All right, bitch. What are you doing here?"

"What happened to your wrist?" Helen said.

"I sprained it during a sword fight at rehearsal," he said.

Helen saw blood spots on the bandage. Sprains didn't bleed. "When did that happen?" she said.

"None of your frigging business. You want to tell me what this is about?"

"I saw your performance as Richard."

"And you came by for my autograph?" A nasty sneer disfigured his face.

Helen knew how to wipe it off. "You're losing your memory."

He shrugged. "It happens to actors."

"It happens to X users," Helen said. "Ecstasy destroys memory. You're using your product."

His Adam's apple bobbed up and down. He opened his mouth to deny it, then burst out with, "I didn't know it did that. Nobody told me. I didn't find out until too late. At first, all I knew was X gave me energy. I could rehearse till midnight, then party till dawn. I felt like a god. I'd discovered the secret of the universe. The other actors were working shit jobs and struggling to pay their bills. X made me all this money. It gave me all this energy."

"Then it took it." Helen said.

"It took everything." Jason's voice was sticky with self-pity. Were those tears in his eyes? He'd gone from threats to tears in eighty seconds. If he'd shown that range onstage, he'd have been a great actor. He had no trouble remembering his lines for *The Tragedy of Jason I.*

"Ecstasy took my memory. I started dropping my lines. It took my confidence. People talked about me behind my back."

"Paranoia is a symptom of addiction," Helen said.

"I saw that Web site, too." That sneer again, a rictus of hate. But Helen remembered something else from the Web site. The last piece fell into place.

"That's why you were all over Kiki at the rehearsal. You wanted her to bankroll your rehab. A good rehab center would cost you twenty thousand bucks."

"She owed it to me as an artist. She had the money. It was nothing to her."

"Wrong, Jason. Money is everything to the very rich. They want value for their money. What could you give her?"

"What do you think?" He thrust his pelvis forward. Helen prayed the robe stayed closed. She'd seen enough of Jason. "Where would an old bitch like her find a young stud like me?"

Helen laughed. "Boys like you are on every street in Florida. Kiki had her boy toys drive her Rolls. Besides, she wouldn't hand you the cash. She'd make you crawl until you hated her and hated yourself—then you wouldn't get the money, after all. That's what she did to her chauffeurs."

Jason petted his velvet sleeves. "Do you think it's

easy selling X? There's not that much money. I don't have a Miami penthouse and a Mercedes. I'm in Dania, driving an Eclipse. It's not even a convertible."

The addict's whine. Helen hated his self-pity. "Any struggling actor would love to live here and wear expensive clothes like yours."

The self-pity dried up. The sneer was back. "They're from Sawgrass Mills Mall, moron. Whoever heard of a drug dealer shopping at an outlet mall?

"Look, I admit it. I asked her for help. So what? Do you understand how time-consuming drugs are? They take energy, effort, and careful planning. Kiki was my last hope. I begged her. She didn't understand. No one does. Having an addiction is like hiding a beautiful damaged child in your home. I hate it. I hate it." He was sniveling again.

"You love it," Helen said. "You called your addiction a child, not a burden or a monkey on your back. You'll never let go of this baby—and it will never let go of you. You thought Kiki would set you up in a nice apartment, maybe even pay for your rehab. You poor schmuck. I thought only women fell for rescue fantasies."

Jason gave a mean laugh. "Hey, Helen, you know what they say about you older women? You don't swell, you don't tell, and you're so grateful."

Helen wanted to slap him. "Kiki never heard of gratitude. She turned you down and laughed at you. So you killed her."

Jason was sweating heavily now, despite the room's freezing temperature. His hair was plastered to his forehead. Sweat slid down his tanned chest.

"Are you crazy? I couldn't even fuck her, much less kill her."

Helen felt the acid of his bottomless self-contempt.

"You tried to hit up Desiree for the rehab money the day of her mother's funeral, didn't you?"

"She owed it to me," Jason said. "But she wouldn't give it to me. And I didn't kill her, did I? Just like I didn't kill Kiki."

Helen left him alone in his velvet box, hugging himself.

Chapter 23

"This wedding dress makes my hips look fat!" The bride was so skinny, Helen could have pulled her through a wedding ring.

"Stacey, you don't have any hips!" Helen snapped.

Stacey's sunny little face clouded.

"I mean, you're lucky to be so thin," Helen said. "Most brides would kill to be as slender as you." The rest would be treated for anorexia.

Stacey's smile returned. She bought the dress. But Helen's patience was shredded. She was tired of hearing: "My butt's too big." "My gut sticks out." "I have cellulite on my thighs."

Each statement was pronounced in the tragic tones usually reserved for, "I have terminal cancer."

What irritated Helen was that these young women didn't have an ounce of extra fat. They were model thin, with thick glossy hair and sweet, firm skin. But they didn't appreciate their natural gifts. They also didn't realize how soon those gifts would be gone.

Helen wanted to strip off her clothes and say, "This is cellulite, sweetie. This is fat. In twenty years, you'll look like me—if you're lucky. Most women my age look even worse."

Stacey barely had her nonfat thighs out the door before Helen had the celadon affair.

Lindsey, a fragile redhead, came in to inspect her celadon bridesmaid dresses. Celadon looked like plain old celery green to Helen, but two-thousand-dollar dresses couldn't be the color of a common vegetable.

Helen thought the pale green dresses would look like an Impressionist's dream on Lindsey's redheaded sisters and cousins. She expected the bride to go into raptures.

Instead, Lindsey fished two pale green carpet fibers out of a miniature purse. They looked like something the police picked up with tweezers at Kiki's crime scene.

The bride put the two fibers against the celadon dresses. Her rosebud mouth turned down. "They don't match," she wailed.

"They don't?" Helen squinted at the carpet bits. She could hardly see them.

"The color scheme is wrong, wrong, wrong," the bride cried. "The dresses are supposed to match the hotel carpet exactly."

Helen saw Lindsey sneaking into the hotel and snipping off the carpet fibers. She wondered if the rug had other bridal-induced bald spots.

"My whole color scheme depends on this." Lindsey sounded desperate. "The dresses have to match the carpet and the carpet has to match the chair covers."

Privileged brides rented chair covers so their guests wouldn't see the naked metal legs.

"Everything is ruined." Two tears ran down Lindsey's unlined face. "We'll have to send back the dresses."

Helen saw an ugly shade of red. No way, missy, she thought. You'll take those celery dresses if I have to chop them up and feed them to you. Helen summoned the last of her sanity and said, "Let me get Millicent."

Millicent was hauling white gowns out of brown boxes in the back room.

"Another crisis," Helen said. "Lindsey is crying because the dresses don't match the carpet. I can't believe anyone would make an issue out of something so stupid."

"Helen, take a deep breath," Millicent said. "I know it seems trivial to you, but it's vital to her. I'll handle this." She ran her hands through her white hair, adjusted her black suit, and headed out to the salon floor.

"Lindsey, darling," Millicent said. "Please don't tell me you want an exact match. That's so Kmart."

Lindsey's green eyes widened in horror. Helen could see the flashing blue lights.

"You want something in the same color family, but it should be at least two shades off." Millicent picked up a celadon dress. "This is perfect, like everything else in your wedding. Now have your bridesmaids call me for their fittings."

Lindsey put the fibers up against the dresses again.

"See?" Millicent said. "Two shades. Precisely."

Lindsey sniffled. "You've saved my wedding."

"That's my job, darling." Millicent hugged her goodbye.

"Move over Henry Kissinger," Helen said. "If you were in the diplomatic corps, we'd have peace in the Middle East."

"World peace is not as important as celadon dresses,"

Millicent said. "I'm unpacking stock in the back. Watch the store."

The shop was blessedly empty. Helen sank down in the pink chair. She was tired of the problems of people who had no problems. "Who cares?" she wanted to shout at the brides. "In twenty years, you'll be divorced, anyway."

Like me, she thought. Had she ever shed tears over wedding trifles? She vaguely remembered some flap over baby's breath and daisies. But it was almost two decades since she'd married Rob. She'd cried a river since then.

The doorbell rang. Helen saw a woman of about forty sporting a plum-sized stone on her left hand. Hallelujah! A mature bride. They were usually easier to deal with. This one turned out to be a doctor with good sense and good money.

Helen soon had the doctor bride in the fitting room with three gowns. Millicent was measuring another bride's train. The doorbell rang again. It was Nora, a nervous mother of the bride.

"Have a seat, Nora, and I'll be right out with your dress," Millicent said.

But Nora didn't sit. She slipped by Helen and Millicent and found her dress in the back. She tried it on by herself in an empty fitting room. Millicent never let a woman alone with a salon mirror and her own insecurities. Now Helen saw why.

Nora stumbled out wearing fuzzy-ball tennis socks and a five-thousand-dollar red gown. She stood in the salon shrieking: "It's too big. I hate it. My husband will hate it. It's a disaster."

Tears flowed. Makeup ran. Millicent charged out. "Nora, sweetie, it's not a disaster. It's a minor alteration.

I know my business. I ordered it a little big because you're so well-endowed. Our seamstress will take it in at no charge."

"It's dragging down my chest," Nora cried.

Mother Nature did that, Helen thought.

"It just needs a little adjustment," Millicent soothed. "Let me pin it for you. It will be fine. You'll see."

Millicent led a sobbing Nora back to the fitting room. In a short time, Helen heard giggles. "You are one hot mama," Millicent said.

"I love it," Nora said. "Can you ever forgive me?"

Once again, Millicent had worked her magic. No wonder her hair was snow white.

Helen waited on the next mother of the bride. Rosemary was a tall woman with hair like iron and a backbone of steel. Helen thought Rosemary could walk across the salon with a book balanced on her head.

"I'm supposed to pick out a black dress," Rosemary said. "I have no say-so in the matter. I've been told it's not my wedding—by my own daughter."

Helen could see the bitter hurt in the mother's eyes. "Would you like something strapless or with a sleeve?"

"I don't know," Rosemary said. "My daughter's getting married on the beach. It could be cold. It could rain. I don't care. It's not my problem. It's not my wedding. Oh, hell. Make it sleeveless. If my arms are flabby, who cares? I'm sixty-two."

Helen sold Rosemary a handsome black knit, but she couldn't do anything about her hurt feelings.

Simone, the next mother of the bride, was a scrawny face-lifted blonde. "I don't want to compete with my daughter," she said, as she picked out a flashy rhinestone number.

Helen translated that as, "I *do* want to compete with her."

Poor Simone. She was expertly nipped and tucked, but a fifty-five-year-old could not upstage a woman thirty years younger. Not even if she went to the wedding naked. Especially if she went naked.

Helen sighed. Some women could not let go of their youth, even though it left them long ago. This store didn't need a salesclerk. It needed a shrink.

Kiki's murder didn't surprise her. Helen was amazed every wedding didn't end with a killing. Family neuroses were painfully exposed, often in the middle of the shop. Right now, Millicent was refereeing a family fight.

The father of the bride was sleek as a panther in black Armani. The mother of the bride wore matronly blue lace. Mr. Panther curled his lip at the blue lace.

"Are you trying to make me look bad?" he said. "That's a five-hundred-dollar dress. It looks it."

"I'm trying to be practical," the mother of the bride said.

"There's nothing practical about a reception at the Biltmore," he said. "We're having it there because I am successful. My wife must reflect my success. Don't come out in anything less than two thousand dollars."

"Come, dear," Millicent said. "I have something that will look smashing with your hair."

Helen wondered what it was like to fight with a man because you didn't spend enough money. Probably like any other fight.

The mother of the bride appeared next in a six-thousand-dollar dress the color of old money. She smiled tentatively.

"That's more like it," Mr. Panther said.

Helen hoped they would leave soon. I feel like one

big exposed wound, she thought. I'm rubbed raw by other people's unhappiness. All this money, all these plans, and half these marriages will fail. Just like mine.

But it wasn't only her unhappiness that haunted Helen. She was afraid. Each day, fear tightened her gut. Each night, it invaded her dreams.

She wondered how much longer the police would be able to ignore the pressure to make an arrest for Kiki's murder. I'm an easy suspect, she thought. My fingerprints are in all the wrong places. My blood is on the victim's dress. I had a fight with her the night she died.

Every time the doorbell rang, she expected to see Detectives McIntyre and Smith. If I can't find the killer, I'm going to jail, she thought. If by some miracle I'm not convicted, my ex and the court will find me, thanks to all the trial publicity. I'll wind up back in St. Louis. That will be another kind of prison.

So what am I doing to save myself? Spinning my wheels.

Helen had poked around and eliminated Chauncey as the killer—maybe. Jason still seemed a likely suspect, but others were just as good. Helen didn't know what to do next. She was lost.

My life is hopeless, she thought.

To set the seal on her hopelessness, Cassie came back for the third time that week. Her wedding dress had more viewers than an art museum opening. "I've brought my cousin Lila to see my dream dress!!" Cassie's black curls bobbed cheerfully on her shoulders.

Millicent rolled her eyes.

Helen said, "You've already shown it to your mother, your father, both grandmothers, your sister, your aunt, all four bridesmaids, and your best friend."

"Do you think I should go ahead and buy it?" Cassie said.

"No, I think you should bring in the band and the caterer," Helen said. "Everyone else has already seen the dress."

Millicent gasped. Cousin Lila laughed. "Why don't you get the dress before you wear it out, cuz?" Lila said.

Cassie hesitated, then said the three little words they'd been waiting for: "I'll take it."

"Praise the Lord," Millicent said and grabbed Cassie's credit card before she changed her mind.

After Cassie left, Millicent said, "I'm splitting the commission with you, Helen. I waited on her first, but you made the sale."

"I don't deserve it. I could have wrecked everything. I'm losing my patience. These big weddings set women's rights back fifty years."

"Weddings bring out the worst in some women," Millicent said. "We've got Mom trying to recapture her lost youth. She's afraid of growing old. She believes her daughter's wedding is the signal her life is over. The bride is crazy, too. Brides become different people— moody, demanding, given to tears and scenes. Even if they're living with the guy, they're still nuts. It's the commitment. Before, they could pack up and leave if something went wrong. They can't do that if they marry the guy. So they're scared.

"You've got two frightened people, the mother and the daughter, and they can't comfort each other. And don't forget Daddy. He has a midlife crisis and boffs his secretary.

"You know what? There's a reason for all that craziness. It's nature's way of getting the bride out of her parents' house and into her own."

Helen laughed.

Millicent looked out the shop window. "LaTonya and her mother are coming for her final fitting."

"At five fifty?" Helen said. "We close at six. I'm not sure I can take another bride."

"LaTonya isn't another bride," Millicent said.

LaTonya was almost as tall as Helen, with flawless dark skin. Her body was big boned and sculpted. She was a preppie princess in pre-law at Harvard.

Her mother, Dorcas, wore a faded pink flowered housedress and plastic thongs. Millicent saw that the bride's mother had no interest in spending money on herself, but she'd do anything for her darling daughter.

Mom and daughter first went to Millicent's archrival, Haute Bridal. "They wouldn't show us a dress," Dorcas said. "Said my baby girl would be happier here where they had cheaper stuff."

Dorcas spoke without bitterness. Helen would have picketed the place—or burned it down.

"We bought here because Millicent was so nice," Dorcas said. "It was the right place to go."

Dorcas had spent five thousand dollars on LaTonya's dress and veil. Dorcas's sister bought a thousand-dollar dress. Her aunt spent seven hundred bucks. Millicent knew Dorcas owned a string of wing-and-chip shops and raked in a million bucks a year. She was also a gospel singer of local renown.

Helen took the bride upstairs to try on her dress for the final time.

"You look tired," Millicent said to Dorcas. "Sit here in this chair, and we'll have your daughter come down in her dress. I'll put on her veil and everything, so you can see the whole effect."

LaTonya didn't whine about her thighs, hips, or gut.

Helen was grateful for that. She zipped the bride into her dress. Millicent crowned her with a chiffon veil. The white satin dress and brown satin skin were a stunning combination.

Millicent called out, "Here comes the bride."

LaTonya slowly descended the stairs, her head held high. Her white veil floated like a banner.

"Here comes the bride," the mother crooned to the traditional tune.

Then her voice swelled and she sang, "I say, here comes the bride, oh Lord, Lord, Lord." Dorcas turned the tune into a full-throated gospel song.

I say here comes the bride
I am filled with righteous pride.
Thanks be to the Lord, oh yes.

LaTonya gave her mother a dazzling smile.

Millicent had tears in her eyes. "Did you ever see anything so beautiful?" The afternoon's frustrations were borne away on the mother's sweet song.

Dorcas dabbed her eyes with a man's handkerchief. "I've been lost all these weeks, worrying about money and details," she said. "I forgot what this wedding is all about."

The bride, Helen thought. There would be no wedding without the bride.

There would be no murder without the bride, either. Kiki wanted to upstage her mousy daughter at her own wedding. But Desiree was a mouse with the heart of a wildcat. And her mother was dead.

It was Desiree who demanded to see Helen. It was Desiree who fed her the information about Millicent, then sent Helen off on a wild-goose chase that wasted her time.

Desiree knew something—and she didn't want Helen to find out what it was.

The bride was the key to this murder.

Chapter 24

Helen walked home from work in the soft twilight. Fort Lauderdale was preparing for its nightly party. Musicians were setting up in the Las Olas restaurants. Sunburned tourists were ordering pitchers of margaritas. Cruise ship passengers wandered aimlessly through the shops.

Everyone had vacation smiles except Helen. She felt tired and sad. There'd been too many emotional scenes at the bridal shop today. Her eyes suddenly filled with tears. She didn't know why she was crying—and then she did.

She missed Phil. She could see him now, that lean muscular body and those blue denim eyes. She missed his sardonic comments and his sharp intelligence. But most of all, she missed his love. She needed their champagne nights to survive the drudgery of her dead-end job.

With Phil, the Coronado seemed delightfully eccentric. Tonight the place looked seedy. Rust trails dripped from the window air conditioners. The sidewalk was cracked. The purple bougainvillea had dead spots, even after Margery's pruning.

Helen also missed the comfort of her friends. She wanted to sit out by the pool and sip wine with Peggy and Margery, but both their apartments were dark.

But she wouldn't go running to Phil. Not as long as his awful ex, Kendra, the Kentucky Songbird, was living with him. Maybe someday Helen could find the courage to forgive him. But not with Kendra gloating in the background. The woman had seen her naked. It was too much to bear.

Helen saw a light on at Phil's place. Should she peek through his miniblinds?

Why not? She had no pride left after popping up in her black panties.

She crouched down and looked through the slats. Phil's living room was the same welter of Kendra's clothes, cereal bowls, and coffee cups. Helen's stomach turned when she saw a brush bristling with red hair on an open pizza box. A red lace bra sprawled on the sofa.

The woman was shameless.

Phil's bedroom door was shut. Was he locked in there with the braless Kendra? Or had they gone out together?

Helen wanted to knock on Phil's door. She wanted to knock in his head. She didn't do either. She marched home head down and ran into a solid wall of muscle.

It was Detective Bill McIntyre. His crooked-nosed partner, Janet Smith, was standing next to him on Helen's doorstep. Helen's heart started thumping when she saw them.

"Can we talk with you?" McIntyre said.

No! Helen started to shout. But she was afraid to say that. "Come in," she said, hoping she sounded natural.

She unlocked her door. The two detectives followed her. Detective Smith prowled the two-room apartment, picking up knickknacks and putting them down. Helen wanted to tell her to stop, but she didn't. She was starting to sweat.

Detective McIntyre sat on the turquoise couch. His muscular frame dwarfed its spindly fifties design. Thumbs, her traitorous cat, jumped into his lap.

"Can I get you some coffee?" Helen said.

"No thanks," both detectives said.

A bad sign, Helen thought. Cops did not like to drink with suspects. She perched on the edge of the Barcalounger.

"You don't have a phone," Detective McIntyre said. He ran his huge hand through Thumbs's soft fur. The cat purred loudly. Detective Smith was examining a flea-market vase as if it were museum-quality Meissen.

"I hate phones," Helen said.

"No credit cards, either." He scratched Thumbs's ears. The faithless cat rolled over in flagrant feline delight and presented his belly.

"I'm trying to live within my means," Helen said.

"And no bank account."

"I don't trust banks. Is that a crime?" Helen tried to say it boldly, but her voice quavered.

"No. But it is a crime to interfere with a homicide investigation and threaten a potential witness. Jason said you'd threatened him."

"I threatened him? He threatened me. Ask his neighbor. She heard the whole thing."

"He told us what he'd overheard the night of the rehearsal. Jason says you had a fight with the victim."

Helen didn't like Detective McIntyre's tone. "I told you that."

"Only after we heard it from another source."

"I forgot. I was tired." Helen sounded defensive.

"You also forgot to mention that you threatened to kill Kiki. Jason said you shouted, 'Don't you threaten me, lady. If I lose this job, you're a dead woman.'"

"That's a lie." Helen leaped off the Barcalounger, red with rage. "I never said any such thing."

That lying scum. Helen wanted to wring Jason's neck. Then she saw Detectives Smith and McIntyre staring at her. She'd certainly showed her temper. Helen settled back on the Barcalounger and tried to answer more calmly. "You must have noticed I didn't lose my job."

"Kiki didn't have time to complain. She was dead before the shop opened on Saturday," Detective McIntyre said.

"Jason is lying," Helen said. "Are you going to take the word of a drug dealer?"

"I'm not worried about someone who deals a little recreational Ecstasy," McIntyre said. "I have a murder to solve. You've got no business messing in this investigation. I'm making it my business to find out why you're so interested. Good-bye, Ms. Hawthorne."

Detective McIntyre put down her cat and brushed the hair off his trousers, then walked out. Detective Smith followed. This time she was the silent partner.

Helen sank down on the couch, which was still warm from McIntyre's bulky body. Thumbs bumped her hand, hoping for another scratch, but she didn't respond.

Why would Jason go to the police? It was a risky move for a drug dealer. Helen must have hit a nerve, but she didn't know what it was. She couldn't ask him. Not after the police warned her away.

Did Jason panic because she noticed the bandage on his wrist? The police would have seen that, too. Was it something she said—or he said?

Maybe Jason didn't go to the police. Maybe the cops caught him dealing, and he traded lies to avoid an arrest. That made more sense.

Now the two detectives were investigating her. How did they find out her financial information? Did they do a credit check? Was that legal?

Helen didn't know. She did know that the two detectives were smart. They would find out who she really was fast enough. Helen had to act soon or she'd be back in front of that wizened old judge in St. Louis. She could hear her mother, the new Mrs. Lawn Boy Larry, weeping. She could see her greedy ex-husband reaching for her money.

Helen was sick with fear. I need help, she thought. I can't do this alone. The walls in her little apartment seemed to close in on her. She couldn't stay there like a wild thing in a trap.

Phil! He was a private eye. He'd help her. He'd already offered. Why did she throw away his note? This was no time to keep up a silly tiff over black panties and a redheaded tramp. Not when she was headed for prison. Helen would be wearing a prison jumpsuit and Kendra would have years to work her cheap wiles on Phil.

Helen ran to his apartment and pounded on the door, but Phil didn't answer.

"Phil! Are you there?"

Helen heard something that sounded like a cat crying. Then she realized it was a woman's low moan of pleasure.

"You son of a bitch." Helen kicked at his door. The

moans grew more intense. She saw a hefty rock in the garden nearby and thought of throwing it through his window. She decided Phil wasn't worth the effort. She had to save herself.

Margery! Margery would help. Her landlady knew everyone and everything. She'd solve this crisis.

Margery's place was still dark. Maybe she was napping. Helen hammered on the jalousie door until the glass rattled. She wanted Margery to appear in her purple chenille robe, grumpy and sleepy eyed.

"Margery, wake up," Helen called. But her landlady's apartment stayed dark.

Peggy! You'd never guess it to look at her, but the elegant redhead had been in trouble with the police before. Peggy had been led away in handcuffs from the Coronado. She knew what it felt like when the cops were after you. She'd help.

"Peggy! Are you there?" Helen beat on the door. Nothing. She stood on Peggy's doorstep in the desperate silence.

"Peggy, help me," Helen pleaded.

Peggy was gone, too. Even Pete wasn't squawking.

Panic rose up in Helen like a river overflowing its banks. She was drowning in fear. What am I going to do? It's six thirty and I'm all alone. The police are after me. Phil has two-timed me with his slutty ex-wife. My life is falling apart—

Oh, get a grip, she told herself. Millions of women have managed to live without Phil. You can, too. Concentrate on what's important. You're going to be arrested for murder, unless you can figure out who did it.

After all her investigating, what did she know: that Millicent and Chauncey were innocent? That the chauffeur thought he was going to be a millionaire when Kiki died? That Jason was crazed by ambition, disappointment, and drugs? That the bride's lawyer father invited all the suspects to tamper with the crime scene? That the bride's own behavior was also strange?

Then it all fell into place. Helen had an idea so crazy she thought it just might work. She knew who killed Kiki—and how to prove it.

The bride was the key to the murder.

The morning of the wedding, Desiree had wished she could wear her fey cobweb dress. Helen told her it was the bride's prerogative and started to go to the closet to get it. That's when Desiree became hysterical. She would not let Helen open that closet. She insisted on wearing her ugly crystal gown. She used her mother's anger as an excuse, even though Kiki was not there.

After the wedding ceremony, the bride poured coffee all over the hated crystal dress—the dress her mother insisted she wear at the cathedral.

Desiree had been too afraid to open the closet door before the wedding, but not too afraid to destroy a seven-thousand-dollar dress after the ceremony.

Why?

Because Desiree knew her dead mother was in that closet. If Helen opened the door before the wedding, Desiree couldn't marry Luke. The wedding would be canceled because of the murder.

But Desiree could ruin the crystal dress after the wedding. She knew her mother was no longer alive to punish the new Mrs. Luke Praine.

Helen the dupe dutifully opened the door, the body was discovered, and Desiree walked off with thirty million dollars and a new movie-star husband.

Helen's reasoning wouldn't convince the police, but

maybe Desiree's own words would. Helen rummaged in her closet for an old cassette recorder and stuck it in her purse. She would tape the bride's confession.

A phone. She needed a phone next. Helen ran all the way to Las Olas. She stumbled over the uneven sidewalk and pitched face forward on the concrete.

Two women helped her up. "Are you okay?" the older one asked.

Of course she wasn't okay. The police were going to arrest her for murder. Then Helen's head cleared. "I'm fine, thanks. I just scraped my hand."

Both women looked doubtful. Helen hurried to the nearest pay phone. A shaven-headed college student was talking on it. Why didn't he have a cell phone like everyone else his age? Helen glared at the kid until he hung up, then punched the numbers frantically.

A woman answered. "Praine residence," she said. Was she a maid? A housekeeper?

"May I speak to Desiree?" Please be there, Helen thought.

"Who's calling, please?"

Should she say her name? I have no choice, Helen decided. I'm the bait.

"Helen Hawthorne."

"Please hold."

There was a long wait. Helen's hands were so sweaty the phone turned slippery. What if Desiree wouldn't talk to her? What if Desiree didn't remember who she was? Finally, she heard a soft voice.

"This is Desiree."

She could picture the little bride's chinless face and intelligent eyes. She could see her, clinging frantically to her groom while he pried her hands off his arm.

"It's Helen, from Millicent's. I buttoned up your

wedding dress." Great. Next she'd say, I opened the closet door when your mother fell out.

"I remember you, Helen." Desiree gave a little laugh. "We had dinner at Lester's, remember? I told you to call if you found out anything."

Relief flooded through Helen. Desiree just handed her the opening she needed.

"I've been looking into your mother's death, like you asked me to," Helen said. "I think I've found something interesting."

"What?" Desiree said. Her breathy little voice quickened.

"I can't tell you on the phone," Helen said. "Is there any way I can see you?"

"Come over right now. My home is only a few blocks from your apartment. Should I send a car?"

Desiree definitely wanted to hear what Helen had to say.

"I'll walk over. I need the exercise."

This is perfectly safe, Helen thought. I won't be alone in the house. Desiree's housekeeper will be there. I can meet with the killer.

Chapter 25

"Luke is taking the housekeeper home," Desiree said when she opened her front door.

Helen froze. Was she alone here with Desiree? Surely not. A place this big had to be infested with servants. But the mansion was silent as a midnight grave. The bride wore a black dress that could have passed as a nun's habit if it had a cross. Her flat shoes belonged on a woman of sixty. There were no makeup circles under her eyes tonight.

Desiree lived in a 1920s pink stucco palace a few blocks and several light years from the Coronado. It was done in the Early Funeral Parlor style favored by Florida's old money. The gloomy entrance hall was dominated by a vast marble-topped table and a weeping fern in a black urn. The hall opened onto even larger rooms. Helen expected brass signs to announce "Wescott viewing, Parlor A."

"It's a lovely evening. I thought we could have tea in the garden. Unless you'd rather have cocktails." Desiree seemed suddenly concerned about a salesclerk's needs.

At her wedding, the bride wouldn't let Helen have a cup of coffee. Instead, she threw it on her crystal dress.

"I'd like that very much," Helen said fervently. It would be easier to escape if she was outside. "Tea is fine."

Helen didn't plan to drink anything, including the tea. She didn't trust anything Desiree would serve.

She followed Desiree across several acres of carpet and through the French doors. Tea, iced and hot, crustless sandwiches, and tiny cookies waited on a glass-topped table. The garden was a dreary expanse of dark green bushes clipped into fantastic animals and wrought-iron flamingos. Helen guessed the rich didn't buy pink plastic flamingos, but they would have brightened up the yard.

While Desiree busied herself with the tea things, Helen reached into her bag and flicked on the tape recorder.

"How are you feeling?" Helen said.

Desiree's eyes teared. Helen suspected that no one had asked her that question, not even Luke.

"The funeral was a nightmare," Desiree said, handing Helen a nearly transparent cup painted with yellow flowers. "I don't remember most of it. The worst part was finding something for Mother to wear. I had to choose her clothes for all eternity."

Desiree paused at this solemn thought, then put six sugary cookies on her plate. "I finally decided on the pink dress she wore when we shopped for my wedding gown. It had so many memories."

All of them bad. "That day was unforgettable," Helen said truthfully. She wondered if Kiki was buried with or without her underwear.

"I really wanted to bury her in the rose dress," Desiree said. The cookies had disappeared, with only a powder-sugar trail marking their place on the plate. She helped herself to six more. Helen ate nothing, but Desiree didn't seem to notice.

"The dress she died in?" That was creepy.

"She loved it so," Desiree said. "But the police wouldn't release it. They said it was part of the ongoing investigation. Luke said I couldn't do it, anyway. He said you couldn't close the casket on that hoop—if you squash it down, it pops back up."

"He's probably right," Helen said.

"Do you know who killed my mother?" Desiree reached for more cookies.

"I have my suspicions," Helen said, "but I wanted to talk with you first, to clear some things up. I heard your mother also fought with Luke."

"They had a disagreement. It wasn't serious." Desiree studied her teacup. She wouldn't look at Helen.

Helen's next words were cruel, but she had to say them. "Luke said he wouldn't marry you if your mother didn't let him act in that movie."

"He didn't mean it!" Desiree said. "She makes people say terrible things."

Makes. Kiki still lived in her daughter's head.

"Luke loves me. He could have had richer and prettier women, but Luke married me. He's so beautiful. You don't know what it's like to be plain and to love pretty things. I like to look at him. Even his feet are pretty." Desiree's thin lips were trembling. The drab skin underneath folded oddly into her neck.

"Oh, Desiree," Helen said. "He's not a statue."

"But he is a work of art. He's also an artist. And he's mine." Her eyes glittered with greed. Helen knew then that Desiree would kill to possess the man she wanted.

She would murder her mother to make Luke happy. Once Kiki was dead, Luke could have his career.

Desiree started flinging accusations wildly. "I think that chauffeur, Rod Somebody, killed Mother. He thought she'd left him a million dollars, but she didn't. Or it could be Jason. Mother laughed at him when he couldn't, you know . . . perform. You remember the famous Sex on the Beach case, where that guy strangled his girlfriend because she laughed at him when he couldn't do it?"

"That's two suspects," Helen said. "Which one is it— Rod or Jason?"

"I don't know. I don't care. She's dead. Nothing will bring her back."

At least you hope so, Helen thought. She wanted to see how far she could push the bride.

"Desiree, I don't know how to say this, but what if Luke killed her?"

"He didn't!" the bride said. "It had to be the other two. I know Luke didn't do it. I know for a fact!"

Because you did it, Helen thought. But she pushed a little harder. "If anything happens to you, Luke would be a very rich widower."

"I'm not like my mother," Desiree said. "I won't stand in his way. I'll give him everything. What else could he want?"

Helen looked at the chinless little face, the drooping hair, the muddy skin. She thought how Desiree clung to her husband and how he pried her fingers off his arm. She'd killed for that man, but he couldn't stand her touching him.

"His freedom," Helen said. She heard the crunch of gravel and thought Luke might have returned. It was time for her to go.

"I don't like you." The handle of Desiree's teacup snapped in two. "You better watch what you say."

"I'll be very careful," Helen said. "Starting with this statement: I know there's a murderer in this house. I have the evidence. I will ruin the killer."

"I don't believe you. But if you really have the evidence, you can show it to me now," Desiree said. "I'll pay good money for it—more than you'd make in a year."

Triumph leaped through Helen like an electric charge. Gotcha! "You've proved my statement," Helen said. "I think I'd rather show it to the police."

"Say one word, and I'll sue you for slander," Desiree said.

"That's the advantage of being broke," Helen said. "I've got nothing to lose."

Her bluff worked. Desiree was the killer. Helen knew it. Why else would she try to buy Helen's evidence? She patted the cassette recorder. She thought that tape would make the police detectives start asking the right questions.

As she headed home with quick, sure strides, something nagged at her. She couldn't quite get at it. What was it that Desiree had said?

Maybe the little bride was protecting someone besides her husband. Her father, perhaps, driven to the brink of bankruptcy by Kiki's wild spending.

Helen did not believe Kiki's murder was premeditated. She probably said something cruel and her killer exploded in rage, reaching for the wedding dress and pressing it down on her face to shut her up. Then the killer shoved her body in a closet.

Fast, quick, and deadly.

But who did it?

Jason, with his monstrous actor's ego, believed Kiki should help him because she was rich and he was pretty. She'd turned him down and laughed at him. But Desiree wouldn't protect him. Unless he was blackmailing her. Maybe that was the evidence that Desiree wanted to buy.

Her father? He was trying to stick his own daughter with her wedding expenses. Desiree wouldn't pay more money to save him.

No, it didn't make sense. Desiree was the logical candidate for Kiki's killer. She had endured a lifetime of her mother's barbs until she finally cracked. She would convince herself she killed her mother to save her husband's career, but she really did it for her own sanity.

What was it Desiree had said? Helen could feel it flitting through her mind. Desiree had been talking about her mother and Jason. "Mother laughed at him when he couldn't, you know . . . perform. You remember the famous Sex on the Beach case, where that guy strangled his girlfriend because she laughed at him when he couldn't do it?"

Jason and Kiki had been embarrassingly amorous at the church. Kiki had dragged him back there for kinky sex. She'd put on the rose dress and he'd been turned off.

So how did Desiree know her mother had laughed at Jason?

Because she went back to the church after the rehearsal dinner.

Helen stopped dead on the sidewalk, and a man behind her nearly walked up her back. "Hey, lady, put on your brake lights if you're going to stop like that," he said.

Helen ignored him.

Rod. She had to find Rod. The chauffeur would know. Helen was six blocks from the Blue Note. She turned in that direction, long legs eating up the sidewalk.

The Blue Note still looked the same. It would always look the same. A guy was sitting at the bar, drinking away his sorrows. Tonight it wasn't Rod.

Helen put a twenty on the bar. "I need to find the chauffeur Rod. It's important."

The balding bartender took the money and looked at the clock. "If you can wait until nine thirty or so, he may stop by, but I can't guarantee it."

Helen ordered a beer. Twenty minutes later, a yellow stretch Hummer pulled up in front of the Blue Note. A uniformed chauffeur got out. It was Rod, a trimmer, happier Rod. He seemed delighted to see Helen. Rod sat down next to her and ordered a club soda and a burger with no fries and no onions.

"I'm working for a limo rental place," Rod said. "I drive this hummer of a Hummer. Lotta parties. The folks who rent this baby make sure everybody's happy, especially the chauffeur. They tip big-time. I take them to the clubs on South Beach. I usually stop here for a sandwich before work." Rod didn't mention his acting ambitions. He liked the role of South Beach chauffeur.

"Listen, Rod, I have to ask you a question," Helen said. "I saw you right after Kiki's will was read. You weren't feeling too good."

"Are you kidding? I was wasted."

"That, too," Helen said. "You said something I wondered about: 'She's an evil little woman. Looking all sad and talking all soft. Had me thinking about crazy stuff I never would have considered. Almost did it, too.' Were you talking about Kiki?"

"Heck, no," Rod said. "I was talking about Desiree. She's one scary woman. Used to sit in that Rolls when her mother wasn't around and work on me. She'd say, 'Mother is worth thirty million and you're making what?'

"She'd stop and give me time to think about it. Then she'd start up again: 'You're in the will, you know. But not for long. She's trying out new chauffeurs on your day off.'

"She had this soft, sad little voice. It was like having a bad angel whispering in my ear. She looked so pathetic, I felt sorry for her. Desiree got me in such a state I actually thought about killing Kiki, until I came to my senses. You probably think I'm crazy."

"No," Helen said. "I saw Desiree at work. At the bridal shop, Kiki rejected Chauncey's desperate plea for money for his theater. She humiliated him in front of everyone. Desiree slithered in and said the only way he could get his money was to kill her mother."

"She tried to get poor old Chauncey?" Rod said. "He'd never hurt anyone. He just wanted to save his theater."

"She worked on me, too," Helen said. "She had me convinced Millicent killed Kiki. When I finally figured out my boss was innocent, I felt like I'd recovered from a fever."

Rod's burger arrived. The bartender set it on the counter with a napkin and ketchup. Rod ordered another club soda.

"That's it," Rod said. "That's what it was like for me, too. I told you I admired Kiki. I may have been in love with her, or maybe it was just her money. But I never thought of killing her until Desiree started working on me."

"Could she manipulate her mother?" Helen said.

"She could play head games with the devil himself. Kiki was mean, but it was all on the surface. Desiree is sly. She keeps her malice hidden."

"Desiree went back to the church after the rehearsal dinner, didn't she?" Helen said.

"She did. I brought her. Jason was there with Kiki when we arrived. The lights were on in the bride's dressing room. Jason came down the stairs with his fly unzipped and his shirt unbuttoned. One look at his face and you could figure out what happened—or didn't happen.

"Desiree saw it right away. She did a number on Jason, telling him if he was a real man, he'd stand up to her mother. Jason is eye candy. He's not big on brains. He wants a theatrical career, but he doesn't want to work for it. That's why he let Kiki paw him in the first place. I tried to talk Jason into leaving, but he wouldn't listen.

"When Jason wouldn't budge, I tried to get Desiree to go with me. She said she wanted to ride with Jason. I made one last effort to get him out of there. He insisted on staying. He said he wanted to salvage the situation. I knew it was hopeless. I left them both. Kiki was still upstairs.

"I've felt guilty ever since. If I'd persuaded Jason or Desiree to leave with me, would Kiki still be alive?" He paused, waiting for something. Helen realized Rod wanted her to absolve him.

"It's not your fault," she said. "Did you tell the police this?"

"No. I didn't have any proof. Besides, someone else

could have shown up later. The cops may catch whoever smothered Kiki, but they'll never nail the real killer—*Desiree*."

Rod drained his club soda and left some bills on the bar.

"Funny thing," he said. "Desiree is about as sexy as my granny's underwear, but she lives up to her name. She's a real temptress."

Chapter 26

Click click. Click click.

Helen heard the footsteps behind her.

Click click.

She looked over her shoulder and saw a tiny blonde in sky-high heels and a flirty skirt. The streetlights revealed she wasn't as young as she first seemed.

Like Kiki.

The same lights drained the color from the woman's face and painted her with spectral shadows. The wind brought her perfume—hothouse roses.

Helen knew it wasn't Kiki. She was dead and buried in a rose-covered coffin.

"I thought you'd died," a tinkly voice said.

Helen jumped.

"Sorry." That was a deep baritone. "I had trouble parking the car." A big man loped up beside the little blonde.

"Couldn't you just pick it up and drop it in a parking spot?"

The man laughed at her outrageous flattery and the couple walked down the street arm in arm.

What the hell is the matter with me? Helen thought. Of course I saw Kiki. Fort Lauderdale has a hundred Kikis. Palm Beach has a thousand. When one dies, a dozen more take her place.

But how many had daughters like Desiree?

Desiree told Helen she didn't care who killed her mother. Desiree planted murderous thoughts in men's minds. Rod said that, but Helen had seen Desiree do it at the bridal salon with Chauncey. "You could pray for her to die, Chauncey," she'd said, soft and insinuating as Eden's snake. "She's left you a hundred thousand in her will."

Then Helen had an idea so monstrous it stopped her dead. What if Rod was telling the truth, but not the whole truth? Suppose Desiree had whispered her bad-angel advice to Rod in the Rolls—and he took it? Once her mother was dead, Desiree would reward the man who set her free. Did Rod really work for a limo company or did he own that shiny new Hummer? It would be the perfect present for a cooperative chauffeur.

The wind was picking up. A soda bottle clattered down the street. Something ghostly white drifted past Helen's head. She ducked, her heart beating wildly.

It was a plastic grocery bag.

This had to stop. Are you a woman or a wimp? she asked herself.

Helen squared her shoulders and charged down the sidewalk. Strolling couples stepped out of her way. Las Olas's perpetual winter-season revels were in full swing at this hour. Tourists wallowed in the warm night, knowing their less fortunate friends were freezing up north.

A red-faced drunk with brassy blond hair thrust himself in her path. "Hey, baby, wanna meet a real man?"

"Yes, I do. So beat it," Helen said.

"Hey, that's not nice," he whined. But he backed away.

"Whoa, dude, what a ball breaker," said his sidekick, who had a loud shirt and a louder voice.

Yes, I am, Helen thought. And it feels good. It feels better than fainting at the sight of a plastic bag. No one alive or dead is following me. I have nothing to fear. I'm bigger than most muggers.

As she turned off Las Olas, away from its bright lights, Helen saw something move in the dark foliage near the sidewalk.

"Hello?" she said. "Anyone there?"

No sound. The rose of Sharon bush shook, but not from the rising wind. Something was in there. Helen swatted the bush with her purse. A skinny striped cat streaked out and disappeared into the night.

Face your fear and it runs away.

Helen was secretly relieved when she finally saw the Coronado, its white walls glowing like a phantom ship in the darkness. The only light was from Phil's apartment. Once again, she saw Kendra's red lace bra on the couch and heard her passionate moans from his bedroom.

There's your real fear. You're not scared of subtropical spooks and assassins. You're afraid you've lost the man you love. She felt a painful twinge of sadness, then a healing flash of anger.

Helen picked her way up the cracked sidewalk, hoping she wouldn't encounter Phil tonight. She wished the Coronado wasn't so dark. Even the pool lights were off. Peggy and her boyfriend must be having a late-night water frolic. Helen felt a stab of envy. If Phil hadn't fallen for his trampy ex, they could be enjoying the night, too.

I'm such a lousy judge of men, Helen thought. Her eyes filled with tears. Then she saw a subtle shift in the shadows by the pool. Someone was there.

She made her way cautiously across the lawn toward the pool, hoping she wouldn't stumble over the sprinklers. The yard was so dark. If she heard splashing in the pool, she'd back away. She didn't want to catch Peggy and her policeman in flagrante.

But there was no sound. Even the eternally rustling palms were still. Wait! There it was. Someone was definitely by the pool.

"Peggy?" she called. "Is that you?"

No answer.

Helen could make out a lumpy, flour-sack figure with a tight perm, sensible shoes, and a cane. An old woman in a housedress was standing by the pool. Helen almost laughed in relief. She'd been afraid of a harmless old woman. Probably one of Margery's friends, waiting for her to come home.

Helen walked confidently toward the pool. "May I help you, ma'am?"

"What?" a quavery voice said. "I can't hear you."

Helen could see the woman stumping toward her, dragging her right foot, cane in her right hand. Poor old soul.

Helen stopped. Right hand? Shouldn't the cane be in her left hand?

That hesitation saved her life. The old woman moved forward with sudden swiftness. The heavy cane came crashing toward Helen's head, but she ducked before it connected. The cane hit the concrete with a cracking *thwak!*

There was a whistling noise and the cane swung at her again. Helen reached around wildly for a weapon. She nearly fell over the hose coiled on the concrete deck, but she found the long-handled pool net.

She swung it at the old woman's head and heard a much younger voice say, "Ouch. Shit, that hurt."

A gray wig rolled across the concrete and into the pool. That wasn't an old woman. It was a man. She could see his face in the dark.

She heard a *click* sound and the cane swiped at her chest, slicing through her shirt. It left a stinging streak on her upper arm.

What the—?

A sword cane. An actor's prop. What had Donna Sue, the secretary-queen, told her? Actors loved sword canes. She also said swordplay killed people. Helen saw the blood welling up on her arm. He'd cut her. Helen swung at him again, and he ducked.

Her attacker was trained in the art of stage fighting. He used the heavy cane like a sword, thrusting and parrying. Helen tried to block him with the long-handled pool net.

Clang! Bang!

The sword cane connected with the pool net and the shock vibrated up her arms. She felt another stinging slash. A cut opened on her hand. Blood droplets splashed her face—her own blood.

Helen swung wildly. The net's aluminum handle deflected the sword blows, but Helen wasn't sure how long it would last. It was bent in the middle and slippery from her blood.

Helen had one chance to save herself. She swung the net as hard as she could and knocked her attacker off balance. He stumbled over the coiled hose and tumbled into the pool.

Got him! she thought. Then he grabbed the pool net and dragged Helen in with him.

She hit the water with a belly flop and a loud "Oof!" It was cold. The guy grabbed her and tried to pull her under. She kicked his legs. They splashed around wildly. The man was stronger than Helen, but his old-lady shoes and long-sleeved dress weighed him down in the water.

Helen grabbed the attacker's slick, rubbery face and clawed his eye.

He pulled her hair so hard she feared it would come out by the roots.

She pushed him under water. He grabbed her little finger and bent it back. Helen screamed and brought her knee up toward his groin, but she couldn't get much momentum in the water. She had swallowed half the pool and her eyes stung from the chlorine.

She sank her teeth into his hand and he let go of her finger. She tasted his blood this time, a savage salty triumph.

There was a blinding flash. For a moment Helen couldn't see anything. Then her vision cleared. The pool lights were on. She saw three gun barrels pointed at her.

Margery, Peggy, and Phil were standing around the pool, guns drawn. All three looked like they'd dressed in the dark. Phil hadn't had time to put on his shirt.

"What the hell is going on here?" Margery said.

"Don't shoot, it's me!" Helen said.

"Of course it's you," Margery said. "Who else would be sword fighting with my pool net? Who's the other musketeer?"

"He tried to kill me. He slashed me with a sword cane."

Helen could hear sirens screaming nearby. Her attacker made a desperate dive for the ladder on the other side.

"Oh, no, you don't." Helen grabbed his collar and yanked him back toward her. His dress tore down the front. Its long sleeves tangled his arms and held them together like handcuffs.

Helen goggled at his naked chest. Her attacker had huge pendulous breasts with hot-pink nipples. They were foam rubber.

"Holy cow, you can buy a sagging chest," Helen said.

"I got mine free for my birthday," Margery said.

"Helen, you're worse than a man," Peggy said. "Quit looking at tits and tell us who he is."

"You're blocking the light," Helen said. "I think it's Jason, recapping his sword-fight scene from *Richard the Third*."

Helen saw the blood running down her arm. She would need stitches. She'd probably have an ugly scar. She was so angry, she grabbed her assailant by his hair and dunked him once more.

"Helen! Do I have to come in there after you? Who is it?" Margery howled. The sirens howled with her. The cops were almost at the Coronado.

Helen dragged the choking, spluttering man over to the lights for a good look. She stared at his handsome actor's face, then blinked.

"Luke!" she said. "You're the killer."

Chapter 27

"Helen, you're safe."

Phil's voice was a caress. Helen's eyes teared at his tenderness.

Phil knelt down to pull her out of the pool, a semi-naked knight at her service. Helen took his strong hands and remembered how they felt on her bare skin.

Then she thought of them unhooking Kendra's red lace bra.

"You idiot," Helen said as he pulled her up onto the concrete.

"What?" Phil's eyes widened in surprise, and he let go of her. Helen fell back in the pool with a seismic splash, drenching everyone.

"What the hell was that for?" Margery said. Her gray hair hung in wet hanks, but she kept her gun trained on Luke's fake foam chest. He didn't move.

"What are you doing?" a dripping Peggy said. She looked like the winner of a wet T-shirt contest.

Helen could handle a murderer, but a lover was another matter. A woman had only so much courage each day. This time, she climbed out of the pool on her own, using the ladder.

"I'll talk to you later," she said to Phil, who looked stunned.

"I think she's light-headed," Margery said. "Helen, you're bleeding. We'll get you help."

Blood trickled down Helen's arm and dribbled on her feet. Blood smeared her chest. Blood streaked her face like savage paint. Blood was pulsing off the Coronado walls and pool. Helen finally figured out that red was the police lights. The pool seemed to be swimming in red.

Helen started to sway.

"She needs an ambulance," Phil said.

"Then call one and get some clean towels," Margery said. She kept her gun trained on Luke.

Helen felt woozy when she looked at the pulsing bloodred pool. There was something black on the bottom. She looked closer. It was her purse. Inside was the tape recorder. Her conversation with Desiree was drowned in nine feet of water. Helen felt the world go black as she tumbled toward the concrete.

Phil was holding her bandaged hand. If this was a dream, it was a good one. He was so handsome. His eyes were electric blue. His naked chest was lean and lightly tanned. Even his crooked nose was cute.

She felt a draft at her back and knew she was wearing one of those stupid hospital gowns. They belonged in nightmares. This was real.

"Hi, there," Phil said. "You're in the emergency room. They've stitched you up. You're going to be fine."

His chest was smeared with blood.

"Are you okay?" she said. "How did you get hurt?"

"That's your blood. I caught you when you passed out."

Then Helen remembered everything—the conversation with Desiree, the fight with Luke, and Kendra's red bra.

"What's the matter?" he said. "Suddenly you look angry."

Helen had learned one lesson after all her work: Things were not what they seemed. Jason was crazy, but he wasn't a killer. The old woman by the pool was a man.

Helen thought the woman she heard making love in Phil's bed was Kendra. But was the man Phil? Helen assumed it was. But so many of her other assumptions had been wrong.

"I want you to answer me, and I want an honest answer, no matter what the consequences," she said. If Phil had been with Kendra, so be it. Margery had survived Warren. She would get over Phil.

"I promise," Phil said solemnly.

"When I came home tonight, I heard a woman in your bedroom. Was that Kendra?"

"Yes," Phil said.

Helen's heart beat wildly. Now she had to ask the second question: "Was the man you?"

"No," Phil said.

Helen studied his face for signs of lying. Her ex would get shifty eyed and sound extra sincere when he lied. Phil looked her straight in the eye.

"Do you believe me?" he said.

A great stillness descended between them. Helen thought the rest of her life depended on her answer.

"Yes. I do," she said.

"Good," Phil said. She realized he'd been holding his breath as well as her hand.

"Here's what happened," he said. "I came home tonight and found Kendra in my bed with another man. I'd made a deal with her: She couldn't drag any more men back to my apartment. The last one stole my Clapton collection. I didn't care what she did, but not at my place.

"Kendra said this character was a big-time producer who could help her career. Some help. He couldn't even afford a motel room. I told her to pack up."

"She's gone?" Helen said.

Margery barged into the room, a whirl of wet purple. "I heard the whole thing," she said. "At least the scene on the sidewalk. He threw out Kendra along with her rhinestone cowboy. Phil even loaded her suitcases into a cab. She's out of there."

"Oh, Phil." Helen threw herself at Phil and began kissing him wildly. He didn't care that she was covered in bandages. He kissed her right back. His lips were soft and warm. His face was pleasantly scratchy. It felt good to hold him again.

"Oh, I've missed you," she said

"No, I've missed you," Phil said.

Helen could feel exactly how much he missed her.

Margery's hand clamped on her shoulder. "I don't want to be a killjoy, but the cops want to talk to you. Now. They're on their way in. Are you ready for that?"

Helen nodded.

"Good. I'll tell them. And Helen, I'm glad to see you've come to your senses."

Margery winked at her.

*   *   *

The evening after the swimming pool attack, Helen sat on a chaise longue at the Coronado. All traces of the bloody battle were gone. The concrete had been bleached white. The pool was a peaceful oasis. Helen's hand, arms, and chest were plastered with bandages. Her stitches itched, but she didn't care. Phil held her good hand. She floated on clouds of love and painkillers.

Margery and Peggy were drinking white wine out of a new box. Pete the parrot celebrated with a fat cashew. Phil munched more cashews and drank a beer.

"Can I get you anything?" Phil asked her.

"I have everything," Helen said.

Margery rolled her eyes. She looked festive in ruffled shorts and flip-flops trimmed with purple daisies. Except if they were purple, weren't they asters? The question was too difficult for Helen in her current state.

Margery did not want to sit and enjoy the sunset. She had unfinished business. "This morning, I found this on my doorstep."

Margery held a ripped-up paper. It looked like a legal document.

"It's Elsie's dance-lesson contract. She's out two thousand dollars, but that's a stupidity fee. The rest of the contract is canceled."

The party applauded.

"When did that happen?" Helen said.

"I found the door to apartment 2C wide open at six this morning. All those cops running around last night must have scared Warren, and he skipped. He took my bath towels, but the TV and the furniture are OK. I'll rent that apartment quickly during the season. Besides, I still have his toupee." Margery held it up, grinning like a crazed scalper.

"Awwwk!" Pete flapped his wings and paced Peggy's shoulder.

"Put that thing away," Helen said. "Pete hates it as much as I do."

When Pete settled down, Peggy said, "Helen, you have to give us the gory details. You've kept us waiting long enough. You slept all day."

Margery snorted and blew out more smoke than a city bus.

Helen blushed. She'd been in bed, but she hadn't been sleeping. She was amazed what she and Phil could do despite her seventy-six stitches.

"I got some of this from the police," Helen said. "The rest I overheard in the emergency room. It was a circus last night. Luke needed a tetanus shot and stitches for his hand. I bit him pretty hard. I also scratched his eyelid."

"Good," Margery said. The cigarette smoke gave that one word a hellish emphasis.

"The police let Luke call his wife," Helen said. "Desiree called her daddy. Luke tried to explain everything to Desiree. He thought he could throw himself on her mercy."

"I'd rather throw myself on a cactus bed," Margery said.

"Don't the police usually keep suspects separate?" Phil said.

"Luke asked for his lawyer, who was also his father-in-law," Helen said. "Brendan brought Desiree with him as his associate. I don't think the beat cops recognized her. Desiree's been all over the papers, but she gets overlooked."

Peggy and Pete were getting impatient. "Are you going to tell us what happened or not?" Peggy said.

"Awwwk!" Pete said. Phil fed him another cashew.

"Luke told them everything," Helen said. "I heard him. I was in the next ER cubicle. The murder was simple. After the rehearsal dinner, Luke went to the church to talk to Kiki. He had to be in that movie and he had to marry Desiree. He needed her money to finance his career, although he didn't say that to his wife. Luke was sure if he told Kiki how important the movie role was for his career, she would change her mind."

Margery took another drag on her cigarette. "The poor dumb bastard," she said. "Kiki would stop him from taking that role *because* it meant so much to him."

"How did you know?" Helen said.

"I've been around," Margery said. Helen was afraid to ask where.

"When Luke got to the church, Jason and Desiree had already left. Kiki was upstairs. She was wearing the rose dress and she couldn't get out of it. Kiki was about to call her chauffeur to come back, when Luke walked in.

" 'Good, you can help me out of this dress,' she said. Kiki was standing in front of the open closet with the cobweb wedding dress.

" 'Only if you let me be a movie star.' Luke said it as a joke, but he was dead serious.

"So was Kiki. 'Never,' she said. 'I won't have my son-in-law playing a retard. If you want to live on my daughter's money, you have to make some sacrifice. It's hard work being a kept man.' "

"Awwwk!" Pete said.

"This is a sensitive subject. I keep him in cashews," Peggy said, smoothing his ruffled feathers.

"Then Kiki grabbed Luke you-know-where and said, 'Maybe if you try hard enough, I could change my mind.' "

"What a witch," Phil said. "She really propositioned her son-in-law on the eve of his wedding?"

"It gets nastier," Helen said. "Kiki pulled out her daughter's favorite wedding dress. 'I can't believe she wants to wear this thing,' she said. 'She thinks she looks good in it. But then she thinks you love her. And you think you're going to act. Well, start acting now, big boy. If you're good enough, you may fuck your way into the movies. This is your audition.

"'And if you say anything to my daughter, I'll say you came after me.'"

"Luke went crazy," Helen said. "He was going to be a sex slave to the mother-in-law from hell. Kiki would have complete control over him. When she tired of Luke, all she had to do was tell her daughter, and he'd be out on the street. He reacted to preserve his freedom and his career.

"Luke tore the wedding dress from Kiki's hands and threw it over her head. She thrashed and fought in the clingy, cobwebby fabric while he forced her down on the floor. Her hoop skirt tilted up toward her head. Luke pressed down with all his strength and smothered her in yards of white lace and red-black taffeta. It wasn't difficult. Kiki was small and drunk.

"All that fabric protected Luke. Kiki fought hard, but she only left a small scratch on his hand.

"Luke knew about DNA under the nails—he had a small part in some murder mystery. He clipped Kiki's nails with a scissors from the bride's room. He flushed the clippings down the toilet, washed the scissors, and put them away. He bundled the body into the closet and shut the door."

"The perfect murder," Phil said.

"He couldn't have done better if he'd planned it."

Helen stopped, distracted by the sight of Phil. With his silver-white hair in a ponytail, he looked like a blue-eyed brigand.

Margery cleared her throat. Helen started talking before her landlady said something snarly.

"Luke figured that closet wouldn't be opened until after the wedding. He'd heard his bride go on and on about when all the dresses would be worn. Once he married Desiree, Kiki's body had to be found quickly. He wanted his new wife to inherit her fortune.

"The next morning, Luke stuffed everything he'd worn at the rehearsal in a charity pickup box. He still had to explain his scraped hand, but he knew how to do that. He'd seen how the crystal gown had scratched me. Luke made a big deal of scratching his hand during the wedding ceremony. It was captured by all the cameras. His plan was brilliant. He hid the evidence of the murder in plain sight. No wonder Luke held up his new bride's hand like a victorious prizefighter. He'd won."

"So why didn't he get away with murder?" Peggy asked.

"Because he had to find out what I knew. He'd heard that I'd investigated a murder at that bookstore. He talked Desiree into meeting me at Lester's. Luke threw suspicion on Jason, and Desiree blamed Millicent. I got nicely sidetracked.

"Then the whole thing unraveled. When I went to their house, Luke heard part of the conversation with Desiree—the last part. She'd tried to buy my nonexistent evidence. I said someone in the house was a killer and I was going to take the proof to the police. I didn't mention any name. I thought Desiree had smothered her mother. Luke thought I was talking about him. He had to kill me to save his career. Unlike Kiki's murder, my killing was planned."

Helen shivered when she said that. She couldn't help it. Phil put his arm around her, and she was ready to go on.

"Luke used his acting skills. He went to the theater for the disguise. Luke had been there often after hours. He knew where Chauncey kept the spare door key as well as the key to the sword cabinet. The police found his fingerprints all over that padlock. He stole the sword cane, then took the gray wig, dress, and foam-rubber chest from the prop room."

"That wig wound up floating in my pool," Margery said. "I almost shot it. I thought it was a rat."

"Speaking of rats, what happened when Luke confessed to his wife?" Peggy said.

"Desiree dumped him. Luke was stunned."

"I am, too," Peggy said. "Didn't you say she was all over him at Lester's?"

"She was," Helen said. "But then he was a trophy, a rising movie star. Now he's damaged goods. Nothing can save him. She can't be seen with the man who murdered her mother. And she certainly won't pay for his defense. She loves her precious money more than Luke.

"Desiree got all noble sounding and declared, 'I won't use my dear mother's money to defend her killer.'"

"That young man made a serious miscalculation," Margery said.

"Right," Helen said. "He thought he could count on his bride because she hated her mother. He knew his father-in-law fought constantly with his ex-wife. He thought Brendan would be his trial lawyer, but he refused to represent Luke."

"Wow. This is better than a movie. Then what happened?" Peggy said.

"I don't know," Helen said. "The doc came in to stitch me up and I passed out again. I hate needles."

Peggy groaned.

"I know," Margery said. She pulled another Marlboro out of her cigarette case, tapped it, and finally lit it. Peggy drummed her fingers impatiently while Pete patrolled her shoulder.

"I heard this from my lawyer friend, Colby Cox, the big criminal defense lawyer," Margery said. "After his wife abandoned him, Luke still thought he could get a good lawyer cheap, because his case would make the media. But Desiree's father made some calls, including one to Colby. Suddenly none of the top criminal lawyers were interested in defending him.

"Luke got himself a court-appointed public defender. This lawyer was so young Colby says he had Pablum on his tie. But the kid wasn't dumb. Luke thought he was safe because his wife couldn't testify against him. The baby lawyer said Luke was wrong: his wife could—and would—testify.

"That's when Luke took his lawyer's advice to cop a plea," Margery said. "It will be awhile before he's back on the boards. Colby says Desiree's daddy made one more call that night—to a divorce lawyer."

"All that money and how long did that marriage last?" Peggy said.

"Less than a month," Helen said. "I have to thank Margery for saving my life. If she hadn't gone on about the right way to hold a cane when we saw *Richard the Third*, I'd be dead."

"You saved yourself," Margery said through a cloud

of smoke. "It's too bad about Luke, though. He's a good actor."

"His wife is better," Helen said. "I still believe she worked on Luke. I think she slyly prodded him into killing her mother. Desiree was smart. She may have even suggested the closet was a good place to hide the body. She certainly knew her mother was dead in there. That's why she wouldn't let me open the door before the ceremony. That's why she ruined the hated crystal dress afterward. She knew Kiki was dead and could no longer punish her for her coffee-throwing tantrum.

"I wonder if she talked Luke into killing me after I left their house. He only heard part of our conversation. I'll bet you anything Desiree let him think I suspected he was the killer—not her.

"You know the worst part? Desiree will get away with it. That tape I made wound up in the bottom of the pool."

"It probably wouldn't have proved anything anyway," Phil said. "You sure couldn't use it in court."

"Desiree got everything she wanted," Helen said. "Her mother is dead and she has millions."

"But she's lost her handsome husband," Peggy said.

"You can buy a lot of men with thirty million dollars," Margery said.

"I like mine free, but not cheap," Helen said.

"I'm your man," Phil said.

"I knew that," Helen said, and kissed him again.

Epilogue

A Rolls-Royce Silver Cloud pulled up in front of Millicent's Bridal Salon. The vintage Rolls was the color of well-polished family silver. The driver's door opened with an expensive *thunk!* Out stepped a chauffeur in a uniform tailored to show off his broad shoulders and long legs.

Helen watched the hunky chauffeur jog to the rear passenger door. He had the best hired buns Helen had ever seen, except for Rod's.

The chauffeur opened the silver door with a flourish and held out his hand. A candy-pink spike heel emerged first, like a delicate flower seeking the sun. It belonged to a tiny blonde in a Chanel suit. She took the chauffeur's hand, stood up, and pulled him toward her. Then she soul kissed him, running a slender leg along his muscular one.

"It's the ghost of Kiki!" Helen said.

"No, it's her daughter, Desiree," Millicent said.

"Where did she get the chin?" Helen said.

"It's an implant," Millicent said. "Looks like she had other implants, too. She's a C cup at the very least."

"Look at the way she's kissing her chauffeur—right on the street."

"What body part is that?" Millicent said.

Helen laughed. Desiree dismissed the chauffeur with a pat on his shapely rump.

"Battle stations," Millicent said. Helen felt the hair stand up on the back of her neck. Millicent had used the same words for Desiree's mother not so long ago.

Desiree strutted into the store and said, "Millie, darling."

Millicent winced. She hated being called that.

"I need a dress," Desiree said. "But I don't want you to show me anything right now. I want to look around. Leave me." She waved her hand, a bored queen dismissing her lady-in-waiting.

Desiree acted as if Helen were invisible. I mean nothing to her, Helen thought. Yet I helped put on her bridal gown—and put her husband in jail.

Helen gawked as the tiny figure strutted around the salon. Breasts and chins could be implanted, mousy hair could be dyed and styled, but where did Desiree get that air of authority?

It was only two months since her husband had been arrested for Kiki's murder, but Desiree had transformed herself. Helen still wasn't fully recovered from Luke's attack. The wounds on her arm and chest were raw and pink, and she had trouble lifting heavy wedding dresses with her injured hand.

Helen went back to the salon too early. Millicent had sent flowers and called twice a week. One Friday, when Helen was lounging around her apartment in cat-furred shorts, the salon owner showed up at her door.

Millicent's white hair, red nails, and trim black suit gave her extra authority, but she didn't use it. Instead,

Millicent begged. "Please come back," she said. "Business is booming. I've hired new sales staff, but they have the personalities of palm trees. I need you, Helen."

Helen needed the money. But she didn't miss the bridal salon. The surging emotions, the frantic family fights, and sudden tear storms were tiring. The peevish brides depressed her. The happy ones opened old wounds in Helen's heart.

She longed to be away from the bridal business. Each night, she checked the classified ads for another job, but the search seemed hopeless. The ad inviting her to "join the team of service professionals working in a luxury resort" turned out to be for valet car parkers.

Helen was disgusted that the best-paying women's jobs were for "gentlemen's escorts. Earn $1000 a day, no experience required."

I bet, thought Helen and threw the paper across the floor. One page skidded under the coffee table. Thumbs promptly sat on it.

Helen crawled under the table to retrieve it. The cat's paw was on an ad that said: "Pet grooming assistant and sales clerk—must love animals. Apply in person." The Barker Brothers Pampered Pet Boutique was only four blocks from the Coronado.

"Thumbs, I love you," Helen said. She opened a whole can of tuna to reward her big-pawed cat.

She put on her best black suit and walked over to the shop. Helen hit it off with the owner instantly. Helen didn't have to tell Jeff that she loved animals—he spotted the cat hairs on her suit. They talked for almost two hours.

"You're my first choice," Jeff said. "But I have to wait until my partner, Ray, comes home in two weeks to make the final decision."

Every time Helen studied the ads, she wondered: Who placed the awful ad in the *City Times*? If someone wanted to ruin Millicent's business, they'd failed miserably. Yes, brides canceled their orders, and there were some slow weeks right after it ran. But those brides came back and brought more. The new clientele was hipper and richer. They thought the ad was "a total riot," as one said.

Kiki's murder had been good for business. Now even the victim's daughter was returning.

The new Desiree completed her circuit of the shop. She marched back to Millicent and said, "Millie, darling, I've decided to forgive you for that tacky ad."

Millicent blushed but said nothing. Helen stared at her.

"Now let's find me a dress. I want to try on that one. That one. And that." Desiree pointed to about thirty thousand dollars' worth of dresses. They were bold, bosom- and back-baring styles.

"Is this for a special occasion?" Millicent said.

"Yes. My divorce. I want them all in black. Fetch them, please." Desiree flounced back to the largest fitting room.

Helen followed Millicent to the dress racks and hissed, "You placed that ad?"

She didn't wait for an answer. Helen knew Millicent had. She remembered Eric the ad taker saying the woman had long white hair and bloodred nail polish. Eric had also said she was "old. Older than my mom. I'd say she was about fifty-five."

"I am not," Millicent had cried in outrage.

Now her furious denial made sense.

Helen angrily paced the shop, afraid of her growing rage. Millicent pretended to be picking out black dresses. She wouldn't look at Helen. Finally she said, "Helen, I had to put that ad in the paper. It was the only way to save my business. Kiki's family refused to pay."

"I feel like a complete fool," Helen said.

Men had made a fool out of her often enough. But it was worse being betrayed by her own sex. Helen liked and trusted Millicent.

"You used me," Helen said. "I investigated a murder because of that ad. I nearly got myself killed."

"Helen, please, I didn't mean it."

But Helen felt frustrated, powerless, and fed up. The pretty pink salon looked like a poisoned bonbon. The walls were closing in on her. The billowing bridal gowns reached out to smother her. The snake tangle of lace and ribbons threatened to strangle her.

Helen was sick of her species. Even the best people seemed calculating. The worst were impossibly cruel. Animals were better behaved. She craved their warm and accepting company. She didn't know if she'd get the job at the pet groomer, but she had to leave here. She ran to the back room and grabbed her purse.

Millicent was staggering down the hall under her burden of black dresses. "Helen, are you really leaving?" she said.

"Good-bye, Millicent," Helen said. "I admire you, but I can't work for you anymore."

"But where are you going?" Millicent seemed genuinely concerned.

"To the dogs," Helen said.

Read on for a preview
of Elaine Viets's next
Dead-End Job mystery

DOG GONE

Coming from Signet in May 2006

"I want this party to be perfect," Tammie Grimsby said. "But I can't take any stress. No stress at all."

Oh, brother, Helen Hawthorne thought. The only stress in this woman's life was on her spandex.

Tammie's teeny white shorts showed the divide in her peachlike posterior. Her sports bra revealed considerable cleavage. Tammie's stupendous diaphragm development produced a disappointing little-girl voice. The effect was outrageously, ridiculously sexy.

Why do I always get the weird customers? Helen wondered. But she knew the answer to that question. She was working in a weird business.

"This is a birthday party, right?" Helen said. She took the party orders at Jeff and Ray's shop.

"For twenty guests." Tammie sighed and her implants heaved like ships in a storm-tossed sea. "My little boy must be the star."

"What about a birthday cake?" Helen said. "Customers love our peanut butter cakes."

"Peanut butter makes my baby boy sick," Tammie said.

"How about a nice garlic chicken cake with yogurt icing?" Helen said.

"No cake, period," Tammie said. "With twenty guests, there will be fights. Besides, they're all on diets. I don't know why I did this to myself. It's too much stress."

Tammie had invited twenty tiny dogs to her Yorkie's birthday party. Helen guessed they would all be white fluff muffins, except the birthday boy. Malteses, bichons frises and shih tzus, all yipping, yapping, sniffing and shedding. Dust-mop dogs. The whole party wouldn't weigh as much as the well-toned Tammie.

Helen repeated the party line. "The Barker Brothers Pampered Pet Boutique in Fort Lauderdale prides itself on perfect pet parties," she said solemnly. "Your Prince will have the best birthday money can buy." If I can get his airhead owner to concentrate long enough, she thought.

Prince sat regally in the crook of Tammie's arm. The Yorkie had the calculating eyes of a con artist.

"My itty-bitty baby eats only the finest fillet. I have to hand-feed him," Tammie said.

Right, Helen thought. I'd live on fillet, too, if I could get away with it. On her pay, she was lucky she could afford hamburger.

The beady-eyed Yorkie stared at Helen, as if daring her to disagree. She didn't begrudge the dog its soft life. Prince paid a high price for his fillet. Helen saw the intelligence in the dark eyes, and felt oddly sorry for the little Yorkie. Prince could manipulate the addlepated Tammie, but he knew he was stuck with her. Helen was glad Prince was a five-pound dog. If he had two legs, the Yorkie could run a drug ring—or the country.

Tammie picked up the little dog, kissed his nose and baby-talked, "You're a particular puppy, aren't you? Oh, yes, you are."

At twenty, fluffy blond Tammie must have been endearing. At forty, she was annoying. Rather like some of Pampered Pet's pampered pets, Helen thought sadly. Cute didn't always age well.

"Those birthday cakes are ugly. Can't you do something more artistic?" Tammie said.

Helen didn't know how to answer her question. The cakes were bone-shaped, iced in white and decorated with sugar roses. Could you make a sugared bone more artistic?

Helen needed the shop diplomat. She signaled Jeff, one of the owners. Jeffrey Tennyson Barker looked like an elegant pedigreed pet himself, with his long nose, sensitive spaniel eyes and thick brown hair.

The Pampered Pet was his baby. Jeff took a touching delight in his upscale boutique. He fussed endlessly over its racks of dresses and fake furs, jewelry showcases, and the glass cases of bonbons on lace doilies, all for dogs. The store also had a salon for grooming canine hair and nails. Jeff loved pleasing customers, even the impossible ones like Tammie.

"If you don't want a cake, may I suggest our doggie bags?" Jeff said. He pulled out a small bag dotted with black paw prints. "We fill it with treats for your guests. Each treat is beautifully prepared."

They were, too. The display case's pastel bonbons were delicately iced and decorated. They were all canine treats: doggie doughnuts, Barkin-Robbins ice-cream cones, lady paws, and pupcakes—miniature cupcakes with sprinkles. Each doggie delicacy ran between one and three bucks.

Tammie was pawing through the racks of dog clothes. "I need a special outfit for my doggie on his day. Ooooh, this is perfect."

She pulled out a blue sweatshirt embroidered with PRINCE. It had a matching bandanna with a silver crown. Tammie shoved the dog's head and front paws into the shirt. The outfit hung on him.

"Ooh. It's too big." Tammie stuck out her lower lip in a pout. She also stuck out her chest, giving Helen a look at more cleavage.

"It will have to be tailored," Jeff said.

"I can take it to Evie, the seamstress," she said. "The party's this evening, but if I pay extra, she'll fix it. But that's sooo stressful. You'll decorate the doggie bags?"

"Certainly," Jeff said. "We'll put colored ribbons on the bags. Does your party have a theme color, such as red or blue? Or would you prefer a rainbow assortment?"

"No rainbow," Tammie said. "I don't want anyone to think my dog is gay."

"My dog is a diesel dyke," Jeff said sweetly.

"My Princey needs his hair done for the party," Tammie said. "How can I have him groomed if we have to go to the seamstress? I want this party perfect but I can't take the stress. I just can't."

"We have a delivery service," Jeff said. "We can pick up your dog or take him home, or both. Do you want to leave him with us now for grooming? Helen will bring him back to your home for a small fee."

"No, silly, he has a fitting at the seamstress's, remember? It's ten o'clock now. Can your girl pick him up at noon? He has to be back home by four. The party is at six and Prince needs a nap before his big night."

Jeff checked the date book. "No problem. Jonathon can take Prince."

Jeff pronounced the name with awe. Jonathon was the prima donna assoluta of the Lauderdale grooming world. He was famous for his towering rages, which made him suddenly pack up his case of supersharp scissors and move to yet another grooming salon. He'd been at the Barker Brothers for six weeks now, and Jeff gloried in the groomer's full date book.

"Good," Tammie said. "I'll just go back and meet the groomer."

"No!" Panic smothered Jeff's pride. "Jonathon hates visitors." The star's contract guaranteed him no personal contact with salon customers, and he'd quit other grooming shops when it had been violated.

But Tammie the gym rat easily outdistanced the sedentary Jeff. There was a shriek and a yelp from the grooming room, followed by an anguished cry: "I am an artist. I cannot work like this."

His precious Jonathon was in distress. Jeff sped to his rescue. "Coming!" he shouted. Helen followed.

The star was majestic in his outrage—and his outfit. He wore a flaring royal purple satin disco suit.

Jonathon's vintage seventies suit was outshone by his magnificent mane, streaked seven shades of blond. It was the envy of any woman who entered a beauty salon. Helen had never seen a hint of dark roots. She suspected Jonathon did his own hair at home with a complicated system of mirrors. Helen had no idea when Jonathon had the time. His own body rivaled Tammie's for gym-produced perfection. He had a cleft chin, a chiseled Roman nose, and the tiniest feet Helen had ever seen on a six-foot man. That was probably why his purple platform shoes didn't look like concrete blocks.

"Every great artist has a temperament," Jeff soothed. "Everyone at your party will recognize a Jonathon cut."

Tammie craved Jonathon's cachet. Jonathon's complexion lapsed into a light lavender. The crisis was averted.

"Helen will stop by your home at noon to pick up Prince," he said, and deftly directed her out the grooming salon door.

The boutique's bell rang.

"Helen, would you get that customer, please, while I talk to Jonathon?" Jeff said.

Two more birthday cakes and ten pounds of treats later, it was time to pick up Prince. Tammie and her husband, Kent Grimsby, lived about ten minutes from the Pampered Pet. Helen drove the shop's hot pink Cadillac, a florid gas guzzler from the seventies known as the Pupmobile. She didn't like pet pickups. The car was long as a hook-and-ladder truck. Helen was driving with a fake license in another name. She was on the run from her ex and the court in Saint Louis and had to stay out of government computers. Driving with a fake license in a huge hot pink car in the crazed Florida traffic was no way to keep a low profile.

But she couldn't tell Jeff what was wrong. Instead, Helen drove as slowly as a seventy year old. The car felt unnatural at this funereal pace. Outraged SUVs honked and roared around her as she steered the house-sized pink Pupmobile down U.S. 1.

How did I ever get reduced to this? Helen thought.

She pulled the Pupmobile up to the kiosk at the Stately Palms Country Club. The ancient white-haired guard napping inside didn't notice its long, lurid form. Helen tapped lightly on the horn, and the guard waved the Pupmobile through. She wondered why he was there. The old guy wasn't even ornamental.

The Grimsby mansion looked like a convention center constructed on cost overruns. Helen expected a marquee in the yard to say: "Appearing this week—"

She parked the Caddy in the circular drive and rang the doorbell. No one answered. Hmm. Must be out of order.

Helen knocked hard on the dark polished front door. It swung open.

Odd. Usually a maid or housekeeper did door duty in the posh homes. Some even had British butlers.

"Hello?" Helen stepped into the entrance hall. "Anyone home?"

The double living room was decorated like a Palm Beach funeral parlor. Huge gold mirrors reflected tapestries, taupe fabrics, tassels and fringe. The gloomy urns could hold several loved ones.

The house was designed to show off the Grimsby dough. Helen could not imagine the owners really living in the place. She couldn't see Tammie eating popcorn and watching a movie or Kent drinking a beer and barbecuing in the backyard. Did megamillionaires drink beer and watch movies?

"Hello?" Helen said, and tiptoed through the living room. Now she was in a dining room that seated twenty.

The table looked like a mahogany runway. The candelabra could have lit up a castle. Over the sideboard was a painting of Tammie in an evening dress. She looked like a nineteenth-century robber baron's wife. The painting was signed with a flourish—"Rax."

"Hello?" A little louder this time. The last thing Helen wanted was to be arrested for breaking and entering.

The breakfast room was next. Helen was sure she'd seen it in an old *Architectural Digest*. She wondered what you ate for breakfast in a room like this: A soufflé of nightingale tongues? Shirred eggs and lamb kidneys? Oats rolled on the thighs of Scottish virgins?

Helen grew more uneasy as she went through a country kitchen the size of a French province. The video room was bigger than the local multiplex.

"Anyone here?" The silence was unnatural. Did she have the right time?

Helen checked her watch. It was 12:02. Tammie might have acted like an airhead, but that party was important to her. She wouldn't forget Prince's noon hair appointment.

Maybe Tammie was taking a nap, recovering from the stress of party planning. Helen wandered through a labyrinth of halls hung with murky British landscapes until she found the master bedroom. The canopy bed looked like it slept six starlets. The miniature canopy bed next to it could hold one Yorkie. Both were empty. So was the master bath. The white terry robe on the door belonged in a hotel.

"Tammie? Prince?" she called. No one answered.

Now Helen was seriously worried. She eyed the bedroom phone. Maybe she should call Jeff. Maybe she should call 911. No, she couldn't bring in the police. They'd ask awkward questions.

Helen kept searching for signs of life.

The French doors in the master bedroom opened onto the pool, which was slightly smaller than Lake Okeechobee. Gaily striped awnings—no, wait, Tammie would never have anything gay—sheltered umbrella tables and teak lounges. Under a vast umbrella, Helen saw two tanned legs on a teak lounge, spread wide and unmoving. The toenails were bloodred.

The hair went up on the back of Helen's neck. "Tammie?" she said.

Her heart slammed against her ribs. Helen felt dizzy. She'd stumbled on a dead body before. She never wanted to see one again. Please, she prayed. Please let Tammie be OK. What if the woman had had a stroke or a heart attack? It happened to perfectly healthy granola chompers.

Helen looked at the splayed legs and winced. What if something worse had happened?

It wasn't natural for a woman to be so still. A fly crawled up one brown leg toward the knee. No manicured hand reached out to shoo it away.

Helen had to see the rest of the body, but she was too afraid to move.

"Tammie, please say you're OK," she begged.

No answer.

Helen unfroze one leg, then the other. She moved carefully around the umbrella table, alert for blood spatters or signs of a struggle. No furniture was broken or overturned, but the waxed legs on the lounge had a lifeless, rubbery look. The two tall glasses by the chaise were unbroken.

Then Helen saw the rest of the body and gave a little shriek.

"Oh, don't be such a prude," Tammie Grimsby said. "Haven't you ever seen a naked woman before?"